MATRICIDE

MATRICIDE

A VALERIUS MYSTERY

JENNIFER BURKE

First published by Level Best Books/Historia 2025

This novel is entirely a work of fiction. The names, characters and incidents portrayed in it are the work of the author's imagination. Any resemblance to actual persons, living or dead, events or localities is entirely coincidental.

Jennifer Burke asserts the moral right to be identified as the author of this work.

Author Photo Credit: Donna Larcom, Northern Exposure Photography

First edition

ISBN: 979-8-89820-097-8

Cover art by Level Best Designs

This book was professionally typeset on Reedsy.
Find out more at reedsy.com

To Jill and Sylvia, for being awesome.

— A MAP OF BAIAE, AD 59 —

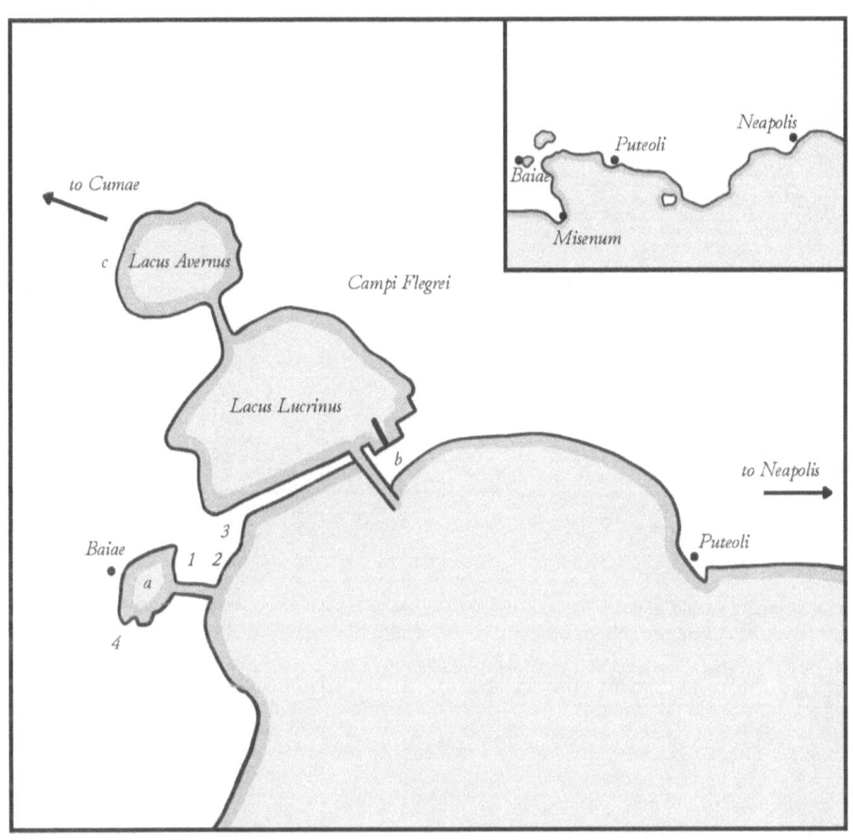

— LEGEND —

BUILDINGS

1. Valerius's villa
2. Piso's villa
3. Nero's villa
4. The Baths of Mercury

PLACES

a. Lacus Baianus
b. Portus Julianus
c. Grotta di Cocceio

NB: The Baths of Mercury are referred to as the Temple of Mercury in modern sources, because the domed ceiling is reminiscent of the Pantheon. It's unknown what it was called in its own time, so I've chosen to call it The Baths of Mercury in this novel.

i

Dramatis Personae

<u>The Family Aemilius</u>
Q. Aemilius Valerius: our hero
Fulvia Drusa: his wife
Octavia Junilla: his sister
Julia Drusilla: his stepdaughter
A. Caldus Ruso aka Mouse: his stepson
G. Aemilius Lucullus Maro: a mad relation
Marcia Laeta: a mad relation by marriage

<u>Slaves, assorted</u>
Juba: too smart to be a bodyguard, again
Stilo: a competent caretaker
Vulso: a competent door porter
Hursa: an incompetent door porter
Zethos: a fish guy
Dio: a helpful bathhouse slave
Felix: an unfortunate gladiator
Lira: a nervous maid

<u>Miscellaneous Items</u>
L. Junius Atreus: a vigile with a responsibility
Lucilla: the responsibility
T. Decimus Rufio: a Praetorian
Celer: another Praetorian
The Sibyl of Cumae: a scam
Mino: an acolyte, or his cousin

Mino: a fisherman, or his cousin

Aemilia Cassia: a freedwoman

<u>Ladies of Baiae, assorted</u>

Tertia Calpurnia: Piso's little sister

Plautia Balbina: Tertia's best friend

Caecilia Didia: an enthusiast of all things Greek

Livilla Faustina: boring, by all accounts

Galeria Alba: awkward and out of her depth

<u>Historical figures (more or less)</u>

Nero: the Emperor of Rome

Agrippina: his mummy dearest

Anicetus: as mysterious as always

Petronius Arbiter: an author and playwright

Lucan: a poet

Calpurnius Piso: a very wealthy man

Atria Galla: his very wealthy wife

Lucius Agermus: a freedman

Chapter One

I had promised Junius Atreus a holiday at my villa, but this wasn't exactly what I'd had in mind. I'd thought we would be escaping the oppressive heat of a Roman summer for the cool ocean breezes of Baiae, but instead the spring nights were still chill with the memory of winter when Atreus and I packed our respective families and journeyed the hundred and fifty miles from Rome to Baiae, the resort town nestled in the curve of the bay between Puteoli and Misenum. His family was much simpler to move than mine, being just a small girl and a single slave. My family was a lot larger. On a logistical scale, taking them all on holiday was an experience that ranked somewhere between Crassus chasing Spartacus back and forth across Samnium and Caesar dividing and conquering Gaul. Fulvia, my wife, and Octavia, my sister, were practical, level-headed women, but unfortunately, we were also joined by Uncle Maro, who was mad, and Aunt Marcia, who was just as mad, and neither of them knew how to travel lightly. Plus, both of Fulvia's children were joining us, one of whom was in that awkward and unhappy phase between boy and man, and the other of whom was celebrating her second month of marriage alone because her husband's uncle had sent him to Ariminium on some sort of family business. There were a lot of us heading down the coast, of varying degrees of contentment and cooperation. Was it any wonder I'd come up with a military comparison when our convoy of carrucae rivalled any cohort of legionaries on manoeuvres?

When we finally rolled into Baiae, we were tired, dispirited, and not even the view of the glittering bay could raise a smile in any of us. Except in little Lucilla, Atreus's niece, who could be forgiven for her perversely sunny attitude since she was five. She was beaming the moment she clambered out of the carruca onto the street.

"Uncle Lucius!" she exclaimed, pointing at the view. "Look!"

The view was indeed a beautiful one. My family's villa was located on the outer edge of the land surrounding the enclosed port, right beside the channel that fed into the Baian Gulf. It wasn't *quite* the most enviable location in Baiae—that honour went to our nearest neighbour, Piso, whose villa claimed most of the land on the seaward side of the port—but it certainly held its own with our other close neighbour, Nero. Of course, the last time I'd been in Baiae, that particular villa had still belonged to Claudius. Now that Nero had inherited, he was no doubt in the process of expanding it so that it was at least as grand as Piso's villa. Nero loved to build things.

Back on the port side of the neighbourhood, the street that ran alongside the front of my villa was a busy one, always full of noise and bustle. It was lined with shops, many of which paid rent to me because they were built into the street-facing wall of the villa. It was a mutually advantageous arrangement; they got to present their wares to a constant stream of wealthy tourists, and I, in the finest traditions of all landlords, got to collect money for nothing.

"Look!" Lucilla exclaimed again. She took Atreus by the hand and tugged him towards the port. The water sparkled, and the boats bobbed. The air was fresh and tasted of salt. For a child whose only other experience with any significant amount of water was the muddy, stinking Tiber, no wonder she was so enthralled.

Atreus threw an apologetic look over his shoulder as she dragged him across the street.

I stretched to unkink my knotted spine, watching as my family emerged in dribs and drabs from their various carrucae like cautious turtles peering out from their shells. The sun beat down on my back, warming me, and a slow sense of satisfaction settled over me. We'd somehow made it this far without killing each other, and that was an accomplishment indeed.

The entrance to the villa was via a portico set between shopfronts. As I approached it, the doors opened, and a small, balding man with an eager smile came bustling towards me.

"Aemilius Valerius, sir," he said, bobbing his head like a particularly frantic bird. "It is an honour to welcome you back to Baiae. I am Stilo, the caretaker."

If I had met Stilo before, I didn't remember it, but I knew from my accountant that the man was doing a good job as caretaker. Stilo was a freedman of my father's, and he kept the shopkeepers paying rent, the fishponds stocked, and the villa clean and tidy.

"Stilo, of course," I said, without committing myself to confirming we'd met in the past by saying it was good to see him again (in case this was the first time) or telling him it was a pleasure to meet him (in case I already had). It wasn't as though he could be offended either way, but there was no use getting off on the wrong foot with the man who knew where the best wine was stashed. "How is the place doing?"

"Very well, sir," he said happily. "I should be happy to give you a detailed account, but you may wish to eat first, and rest? The cook has prepared fresh oysters for your arrival."

Oh yes, Stilo and I were going to be best friends.

"Excellent," I said. "That sounds wonderful."

A group of slaves came out to take care of our luggage, and I looked across the street to where Atreus was leading Lucilla back towards us. Then, curious to see if the villa had changed at all in the years since I'd been here, I led my family and my various hangers-on up to the portico and inside.

The door porter stood at attention beside his broom while we traipsed past him. Down the short corridor, the space opened up into the sunlit atrium. It was bigger than the house in Rome; the neighbours didn't sit quite so closely here in Baiae. The main house was on the right-hand side of the villa complex, with the dining rooms and other public rooms built around the central atrium. Behind the atrium were the sleeping quarters, again, much larger than the house in Rome. I don't know that anyone in my family had ever sired an entire century's worth of children, but if they had, they could certainly have fit them all in here.

To the left of the main house, there was an expansive garden filled with shady trees, statuary, and a fountain that bubbled into a pond. On the other side of the garden, through the colonnades, was a bathhouse and a steam room that were fed by the hot springs that were so plentiful in this area. We were within a stone's throw of the Phlegraean Fields.

Lunch was served in the informal triclinium. The slaves who served us were clean and polite, and none of them cringed. That was a sign that Stilo was a good master to them in my stead. Atreus watched them as he ate, his expression thoughtful, and I figured he was making the same assessment.

After lunch, the women went to bathe, and Atreus, Uncle Maro, and I wandered the gardens. It was nice to be able to walk around after spending the last week travelling. However comfortable you first found a carruca to be, it wore off after an hour or two rattling down the road. There was only so much that cushions could do. My tailbone held the memory of every bump, pothole, and wheel rut between here and Rome.

When Uncle Maro pottered off to inspect the fishponds, Atreus and I stopped in the shade of a laurel tree. I tugged a leaf from the tree and crushed it between my fingers. Its aroma teased my appetite back into life despite my full stomach.

"You own all of this," Atreus said flatly.

It wasn't a question, so I didn't bother dodging it with some bullshit about how I was a single link in a chain made up of all my ancestors and descendants, and merely the temporary custodian of my future heir's wealth. "Yes."

His expression did something complicated. "It's a *palace*!"

"It's Baiae," I said. "That's the whole point of Baiae. Besides, you'll take that back when you see Piso's villa. It has three private jetties. And, not that I've seen it, but would you believe Nero's is smaller than Piso's?"

The corner of his mouth twitched. "His villa?"

"Of course, his villa." I raised my eyebrows. "What else would I be talking about?"

He snorted, but the look he gave me was so fondly exasperated that I knew he wasn't too annoyed.

I knocked my shoulder against his. "In case you weren't aware, when I said I'd take you on a holiday to my villa, this isn't what I meant."

He dipped his head in a nod. "I know." He let out a long breath. "I know that you can't refuse an invitation from the emperor."

"Well, neither can you," I said. "And he did invite both of us."

"You think he'd even notice if I didn't turn up?"

"He's an emperor," I said, considering. "He might notice the insult of your absence. Besides, *I'd* notice if you weren't here, and I'd miss you, and then I'd sulk the whole time and make myself and my entire family miserable. So thank you for coming with me."

The quirk at the corner of his mouth turned into an actual smile. "Well, I'm mostly here for the oysters."

Liar.

Junius Atreus and I were still finding our balance. I was a rich idiot without a care in the world, and he was a plebeian vigile who worked for a living. On a scale of Dionysus to Apollo, we were at very different ends. Still, we were meeting in the middle more and more as I worked away at his iron spine and encouraged it to bend a little. A few months ago, I'd gifted him a slave girl, Iris, so that he had someone to watch Lucilla when he had to work, and the world hadn't ended yet. Atreus sometimes looked at me as though he was suspicious it might, and it would definitely be my fault if it did, but for the most part, he was slowly learning to accept help when it was offered, just as I was slowly learning not to push him too hard.

The womenfolk—Fulvia, Octavia, Julia, and Aunt Marcia—crossed the garden on their way back to the main house. They were too far away to be sure, but I could only presume they were pink and clean and refreshed.

Juba, my bodyguard, appeared suddenly beside Atreus and me in a way that should have been physically impossible for a man his size. He ought to have been visible from miles away, like the Colossus of Rhodes. But somehow Juba always managed to move as subtly as a wisp of smoke curling off a brazier.

"Sir," he said. "Your uncle has decided to go and look at the shops before he bathes."

"Jupiter, yes," I said. "Go with him. He'll probably get mugged in seconds without you. Either that or initiated into whatever strange cult everyone's decided to join this year. Plus, he could die under a rockslide of his purchases without you there to carry them for him."

Juba inclined his head in a nod. "Yes, sir. That's what I thought."

I took my purse off my belt and upended it into my palm. I picked out a few silver sestertii and held them out to him, because I suspected that Juba had mentioned something about the shops to Maro, and my mad uncle was highly suggestible when it came to home renovation and decoration. He'd elbow an elderly matron to the ground and trample right over her if she were trying to get between him and the chance to buy some Samian dinnerware. When Maro was on a mission, nothing would stop him, which meant that Atreus and I, if we sent the attendant slave away, had the bathhouse to ourselves for at least the next hour.

"Good job, Juba," I said, tipping the coins into his palm. I nodded towards the bathhouse. "Shall we, Atreus?"

And so we did.

* * *

We were afforded one uninterrupted evening before the invitations started to roll in. Obviously I couldn't ignore any from Nero, but I was able to be choosy about some of the others. My family had always been wealthy enough that doors had never been closed to me, but now that I was known as one of Nero's friends, the once constant trickle of dinner invitations had turned into a flood. In Rome, I was at least somewhat protected by Hursa's inability to deliver a message. Here in Baiae, unfortunately, the door slave was annoyingly competent, and the morning after our arrival, I breezed into the informal triclinium to be met with not only an oyster and fish omelette big enough to use as a shield, but also a neat list of all the invitations I'd received since word had got out I was in town. There was nothing yet from Nero, who had invited me here to celebrate the Quinquatria, the festival of Minerva, so I was free to make my choice from the others. I chose Calpurnius Piso because he was my closest neighbour, and also because I hadn't been joking about his villa: if Atreus thought that mine was a palace, he'd be picking his jaw up off the marble tiles after stepping inside Piso's.

Not that he was in any fit condition to go to a dinner party at Piso's villa. Atreus only had one decent tunic, and that was because I'd given him one of mine. And since he was taller than I was, it was obvious it hadn't been made for him, which was fine when he was wrapped in a toga (also borrowed), but immediately obvious in slightly less formal gatherings. That iron spine of Atreus's was going to have to practice how to bend again today.

For once in my life I'd been early to breakfast, so I had the pleasure of chatting with Uncle Maro and Aunt Marcia before everyone else arrived. Maro was particularly keen to show off the bronze lampstand he'd bought yesterday, and even more keen to chase up the maker and order a dozen more for his latest home renovation project. The lamp stand, which was currently in pride of place at the head of the dining table, was designed to look like a tree with the branches lopped off. Silver leaves wreathed the top of it. I pretended to be duly impressed, which pleased Maro. He was a man of expensive tastes, yet simple pleasures. He must have spent a fortune ten times over in his never-ending quest to complete his home renovations, yet he was freshly delighted every day by some new piece of furniture, pattern of fabric, or idea for a fresco.

He was lucky Aunt Marcia was as mad as he was, or she would have divorced him years ago.

I dug into my omelette while the rest of the family appeared in dribs and drabs. Mouse, my stepson, was first, followed by Atreus and Lucilla. Lucilla planted herself beside Mouse, and he rolled his eyes because he was at the age where he was supposed to be annoyed by children younger than him, but he secretly liked having Lucilla's stubborn worship. Mouse had been a shy, timid boy when I'd met him, hence the nickname, but I was confident he'd find his way out of his shell in time to be an obnoxious adolescent, just as nature and the gods intended.

Atreus took a seat at the other end of the table to me.

"Good morning, Atreus," I said.

"Good morning, sir."

The slaves brought in more omelettes, as well as bread and oil, and nuts and fruit, because in Baiae it was probably against the law to start the day with a modest meal.

Fulvia and Octavia were the last to join us. Fulvia kissed me on the cheek and then took the seat next to mine.

"Do you have any plans for the day?" I asked her.

"Octavia and I thought we'd go to the beach," she said.

"And Julia?" I asked.

"We'll ask her once she wakes up," Fulvia said wryly.

My stepdaughter and I had been getting along well lately, since she'd done some growing up. And, if I was honest, since I'd done the same. But some things, like her tardiness, never changed. Not that I could lecture her on that. My beating everyone else to breakfast was unprecedented.

"And what about you?" Fulvia asked, reaching out to help herself to a spear of asparagus that I'd been saving for last. "What are your plans? You're welcome to join us at the beach, of course."

"Atreus and I are going shopping for a new tunic for him," I said, because he'd be less likely to argue with me in front of my family.

"Sir, that's not necessary," he said.

Less likely, but it apparently wasn't completely outside the realms of possibility.

"Of course it is," Fulvia said, before I could answer. "Atreus, we have been invited to spend time with the emperor. One must dress accordingly. You must allow Quintus to guide you in this matter."

"It's not often Quintus is right," Octavia agreed, "but, in this case, he is."

"While you're patting me on the back, be careful to avoid the knife you left there," I said.

Octavia flashed me a cheeky smile.

"Octavia and I would be happy to take Lucilla with us to the beach," Fulvia continued. "I think she would have more fun playing in the sand than looking at fabrics, don't you?"

Well, wouldn't we all when it came to it? But Atreus nodded, his expression tightly uncomfortable. It always was when I, or my family, tried to do nice things for him. "Thank you," he said at last, and it almost sounded genuine.

"I'm sure Lucilla will enjoy that."

"And I'm going to go looking for the fellow who made the lamp stands," Maro said happily, although nobody had asked him. "The shopkeeper says he lives over in Puteoli." He blinked at Marcia. "Oh! Shall we take a pilentum or hire a boat, dearest? It does look like a beautiful day to be a sailor!" He laughed. "Well, I shall be the sailor. You shall be the bewitching nereid."

If I'd been a man of less hardy constitution, my omelette would have made a reappearance at Uncle Maro's idea of sweet talk. But Aunt Marcia blushed and giggled, so I supposed Maro knew his audience.

After breakfast, Atreus and I set out into the street. It was a beautiful day. The boats bobbed in the circular lake of the port, and the sun was warm and the breeze cool. I sucked in a lungful of salt air as we wandered past the first few shopfronts.

"The place that sells fabric is just along here," I said. "Throw a few extra sestertii, and they'll have their seamstress make them on the spot."

"You don't have your own slave for that?" Atreus asked, and I couldn't tell if he was joking or not.

"At home, yes," I said. "Here, no. At least, I don't think so. I haven't had a proper look at the household ledgers yet. Poor Stilo handed them over last night like a boy presenting his wax tablet to his tutor, as though he's holding his breath for me to either commend him for his excellent work or beat him with a cane. I should probably do that before he suffocates. Commend him, I mean."

Atreus didn't look amused. "It's too much."

He wasn't talking about the ledgers.

"It's not," I said. "Fulvia's right. You'll be dining with the emperor. You can't do that in the same tunic you wear when you smack heads together down in the Aventine. How you look and how you act also reflects on me. So let me buy you a decent tunic, Atreus. It's how patronage works."

His expression was serious, his green gaze troubled. "But you aren't my patron, Valerius, and I'm not your client."

"No," I agreed, "but we're at least friends, aren't we?"

"More than friends," he conceded.

"Then let me buy you a fucking tunic, Atreus," I said. "As your more-than-friend."

A gaggle of matrons shielded by parasols forced us into silence as we stopped to let them pass. They were as bright and loud as parrots. They were also possibly drunk, even though it was barely past breakfast time. The cluster of slaves holding the parasols wore stoic expressions. Whether they'd be loaded up like pack mules in an hour, or fishing their drunken mistresses out of the water by lunchtime, their expressions said they knew they were in for a long day.

That was Baiae all over. As long as it had been a popular resort town, it had been a popular target for moralists. Was it Varro who said that Baiae was the place where married women were common property, old men came to act like boys, and boys came to act like girls? More recently, even Seneca had spoken out about Baiae's licentiousness, complaining that the town itself demanded vice, but of course that had done nothing to destroy Baiae's popularity. It had increased it, probably. I wondered if there was a collegium of savvy Baian businessmen who'd commissioned the essay.

The ladies bustled into the jeweller's shop, and Atreus and I continued on our way.

Across the street, sailors and port workers shouted to each other as they worked. Water slapped against the harbour wall and the hulls of the boats. Ropes snapped. An oxen and a cart were backed carefully down a slope to where a boat waited to be unloaded.

There were no huge ships here like those one saw at Ostia. These weren't the ships that came direct from across the sea. The boats that came to Baiae's port were smaller. They were the ones that followed the coastline, dipping in and out of harbours and ports along the way. They might have carried cargo from exotic and faraway provinces, but that cargo had been unloaded off larger ships first.

The port at Baiae was for smaller boats and pleasure craft. Further across the bay was Portus Julius, the massive port built by Augustus's right-hand-man, Agrippa, as a naval base, complete with tunnels cut through the nearby hills to allow quick access to Cumae. These days, the fleet wasn't kept at

Portus Julius, but further west at Misenum, where it was commanded by Anicetus, a former slave, friend of Nero, and imperial spymaster. Anicetus wore a lot of hats. I'd always found him a nondescript fellow. That probably suited him.

The ox bellowed, the cart lurched alarmingly, and the men surrounding it all shouted at each other about whose fault everything was.

"Can oxen swim?" I asked.

"Probably not with a cart attached," Atreus said, eyebrows raised.

"Well, I'm sure they know what they're doing," I said, although I wasn't, and Atreus, judging by those eyebrows, was also unconvinced.

We moved on.

Across the enclosed port, the rest of Baiae rose up sharply from the water. The sunlight shone brightly on the red tile roofs of the buildings stacked along the terraces of the town. Trees and gardens fringed the terraces, and hills rose up behind them. Despite the disapproval of the moralists, Baiae was truly beautiful.

The fabric shop was located beside a perfumery, and a cloud of rose, cinnamon, and jasmine tickled my nostrils as we passed.

"It's the next one, I think," I told Atreus. It had been years since I'd been in Baiae. I'd been about Mouse's age the last time, and I certainly hadn't paid much attention to the shopfronts. But my memory proved correct, and a tile on the wall told us that we were in the right place.

It was dark inside after the bright sunlight, and it took a moment for my eyes to adjust. And then my vision was assaulted by acres of different fabrics, from linen to silk, to something that was so see-through it could have been woven from a spider's thread. Lamps burned in bronze holders that hung from chains, and there were several seats and couches set amongst the displays. The scents here were almost as distinct as those from the perfumery, though fortunately not as strong. Notes of madder, oak galls, and saffron permeated the air.

A girl with her hair pulled neatly back into a braid approached us. "Good morning, sirs."

"Good morning," I said. "Is your mistress in? I am Aemilius Valerius."

The girl's eyes widened. "Just a moment, sir. I'll get her."

She darted out into the back rooms, and a moment later, a whirlwind of a woman swept out to take her place. She was small and bright-eyed, though those eyes had more lines around them than I remembered.

"*Quintus!*" she exclaimed, and then clapped a hand over her mouth. "Aemilius Valerius, I mean, sir."

"Well, I've done some growing up," I said. "Not too much, though. How have you been, Cassia?"

Aemilia Cassia was a freedwoman of my father's. Unlike most of his slaves, she'd been freed long before his death. When it had happened, I'd wondered why, since she had clearly been his favourite. She'd been my favourite too. My father had bought her after the death of my mother, to be Octavia's wet nurse, and for much of my childhood, she'd been a fixture of the household. Then, when I was about six, my father had granted Cassia her freedom and set her up with this shop in Baiae.

"I am very well," she said, and squeezed my hands. "Is Octavia here too?"

"She is," I said. "And you must go and visit her. I know she'll be glad to see you. And how is Caelio?"

"He is well," she said. "He has a girlfriend now."

"No!" I exclaimed. "Isn't he *twelve*?"

"Sixteen," she said. "Did Philosthones's lessons with the abacus not stick?"

When I was a child, I hadn't understood why my father had freed Cassia when none of us wanted her to leave. But actually, Philosthones's lessons *had* stuck, and I'd eventually done the calculations. My father had loved Cassia enough that he hadn't wanted their son to live a slave's life. Caelio had been born a citizen, and my father had regularly visited Baiae. I sometimes wondered why he hadn't set Cassia up in Rome, but I'd never asked him before his death. We hadn't been close, which I regretted now.

Atreus was watching our exchange with interest. This was not how a landlord and a tenant usually interacted, and vice versa.

"Atreus," I said, eventually taking pity on him. "This is Aemilia Cassia, a freedwoman of my household. If someone must take the blame for how I was raised, it ought to be her."

Cassia's eyes sparkled. "If it had been up to me, you would have been beaten a lot more."

"Yes," I agreed. "That might have done the trick. Anyway, Atreus and I are here in Baiae at the emperor's invitation, and Atreus needs a few new tunics. Can you do anything to help him?"

"Of course!" Cassia exclaimed.

"A *few*?" Atreus asked suspiciously.

We both ignored him.

Cassia called for the girl with the braid, and she took Atreus out the back to the seamstress so that she could measure him. Then Cassia led me over to one of the couches, and we sat.

"Maro's in town as well," I told her. "He's still endlessly renovating and redecorating. He'd love some of these silks."

"You must send him my way then," Cassia said. "Maro was always…" She paused, as though choosing her words carefully, and then said, "Kind."

I didn't like that pause, and my expression must have shown my worry.

Cassia put her hand over mine and smiled. "I mean it, I promise. But slaves will often say someone is kind to them, when what they mean is they are able to go about their duties unnoticed, so it seemed the wrong word to use because Maro was genuinely kind. He would ask everyone from your father to the boy who swept the floors their opinion of tile samples, and treat each answer as though it were equal."

"He is genuinely mad," I said fondly.

"Oh, yes," Cassia agreed with a smile. "But in the best way."

She was right about that.

We talked for a while longer. It was strange talking with Cassia again. She was familiar to me, and yet so many years had passed that everything had changed. I was no longer a child who ran to her with skinned knees. I was the master of the household now, and she was no longer a part of it. I was her patron, I supposed, although I was a distant one. Cassia had never needed my support to manage her business, although I did know that she paid less rent, by a mile, than the other tenants. That arrangement had been in place since she'd moved here, and I hadn't changed it after my father's death. It was clearly what he'd wanted. Talking to her now, it was as though the years had slipped away. I wouldn't have been surprised to see her carrying Octavia on her hip, holding out her hand to me so that I wasn't left behind. I wouldn't have been surprised to see my father walk into the room. It was a strange sensation, both comforting and unsettling at the same time.

It didn't take long for Atreus to reappear with a folded tunic hanging over his arm, and a promise that another two would be delivered to the villa as promptly as possible. Atreus stood there awkwardly while I paid Cassia and shook off my father's ghost.

"Don't give me that look," I said as we stepped back outside into the sunlight. "We're both moving in imperial circles nowadays. This isn't charity. It's an investment, in my career as much as yours."

It was such a familiar pattern—my insistence on improving his life, and his insistence that he didn't need my help—that we could have had the argument in our sleep.

We had just stepped out of the shade of the awning when another familiar pattern, one I didn't enjoy anywhere near as much, pushed the first one aside.

Abruptly, one of the brightly-clad matrons we'd seen earlier burst out of the perfumery, almost colliding with us. I caught her by the arms as she stumbled, my heart racing at the sight of her stricken, tear-stained face. And before I could open my mouth to ask her what was wrong, she drew a shuddering breath and then, at a volume I could hardly credit, given the state of her, she screamed, "She's dead! Oh, Jupiter! She's *dead!*"

And, for a moment, even the screeching gulls fell silent.

* * *

Usually, when Fortuna saw fit to drop a corpse in front of Atreus and me, we didn't know the identity of the murderer. This time, perhaps out of respect for the fact we were on a holiday, that most capricious of goddesses had decided to make things much easier for us.

The perfumer was a woman. She was older, with threads of grey in her thick, dark curls. She was plump and dressed in a fine yellow tunic overlaid with an expensive blue stola. She wore gold rings and bangles and pearl earrings. She had collapsed in the front room of the shop, which, like Cassia's, was furnished with expensive couches and decorations, in order to make her rich clientele feel properly respected before they dropped a small fortune on some exotic fragrance. She had fallen in front of one of the couches, and a pool of blood had spread out from underneath the stab wound in her belly. The coppery scent of blood wove in with the overly sweet floral notes that permeated the air.

She had been trying to reach a couch: a trail of blood, some spots, some smears where she had stepped in it, led from her body into the back rooms of the shop. The knife that had stabbed her was still in her belly. I leaned over her and pulled it out. The familiar sensation of a corpse gripping a blade reminded me of my military days.

Now armed, I straightened up, and Atreus and I moved towards the back room.

Outside, the matron who had been screaming had subsided into sobs and was being tended to by her friends and their small army of slaves.

We met other slaves in the room beyond the shopfront, white-faced, their trembling hands covering their mouths. They didn't speak, but one of them pointed shakily towards a curtain-covered door. The blood on the curtain, at the height a hand would have gripped it to pull it aside, would have been a signpost we could have followed even without the slave's assistance.

Atreus wrenched the curtain all the way aside, and it rattled on its rod.

The man sitting slumped on the stool in front of the workbench was dishevelled and distraught. He stared at us with wild eyes. His face was wet, and his jaw slack. His fingers twitched in his lap as though he had lost all control of them.

The trail of blood began on the floor in front of him. This, then, was where the argument had started. And ended too, I supposed.

"I killed her," he told us, his voice wavering. "I killed my m-mother. I-I-I didn't mean to!"

His protestation seemed irrelevant given the outcome, but I kept that thought to myself, just in case he had another knife tucked away in his tunic.

The killer's frantic gaze shifted back and forth between us before it landed on Atreus.

"I didn't mean to!" he said again, a tone of something almost like belligerence creeping in, as though he was aggrieved that we hadn't immediately agreed with him. "She wouldn't *listen*!"

I exchanged a look with Atreus, then handed him the knife and backed out of the room.

"Send for the magistrate," I told one of the wide-eyed slaves. "Immediately!"

I went back inside the room.

There was no magistrate in Baiae, as it happened—the closest was Cumae—but there were certainly a lot of interested bystanders, many of whom had pushed their way into the shop and seemed in the mood for some good old fashioned mob violence. Leaving Atreus with a murderer while I tried to talk down a small but determined crowd of port workers wasn't an experience that filled me with delight, and I was pleased when a small group of soldiers turned up.

Praetorians, to my surprise. And, to my further surprise, I recognised one of them, and he recognised me.

"Aemilius Valerius," he said, a wry smile tugging at the corner of his mouth as his companions began to push the spectators away. He winked. "Fancy seeing you here."

"Rufio," I said. "It's good to see you."

We clasped hands in greeting.

Rufio was tall, handsome, and had a winning smile. He might have even been my type, except I had someone tall and handsome of my own. Atreus was slightly taller, in fact, which was probably to compensate for the fact that he didn't have a winning smile. Well, he did, but he didn't throw it around in public like Rufio.

Rufio was a Praetorian tribune, and the fact that he'd been wandering along the waterfront could only mean one thing.

"Nero has arrived?" I asked him.

"Last night," Rufio said, his brows tugging together as he looked down at the body of the perfumer. "Juno's tits. Who did this?"

"Her son," I said. "Hence the growing mob. He's in the back with Atreus. I've sent a slave to fetch the magistrate."

"From Cumae?" Rufio raised his eyebrows. "Oh, good luck getting him here unless you're inviting him for dinner." He nodded at his men, who were now blocking the door. "We'll take charge of the guilty man and get him to the magistrate. Her *son*, did you say?"

"Yes."

Rufio's expression darkened.

All crimes were against the law, of course, by their very definition, but some were against the gods themselves. Matricide was one of them. According to the punishment prescribed by the law, the man would be sewn into a sack with a dog and a few snakes, and then tossed into the Tiber. Well, into the nearest body of water deep enough to do the trick, which here in Baiae would be the ocean. A horrific death to match an unthinkably horrific crime.

I was glad that Rufio was willing to take charge of matters from here. There was no mystery itching at the back of my skull, and the perfumer and her son were not patricians, or senators, or friends of the emperor. There was nothing here that was any of my business to investigate. For once, I could be nothing more than a bystander, and leave the actual work to Rufio and his men, and to the magistrate in Cumae.

I went to tell Atreus the good news.

As we were leaving, the son, now insistently telling one of Rufio's men that his mother just didn't listen, Rufio said, "Are you coming to Piso's party tonight?"

"Yes," I said. "And you?"

"I go where the emperor goes," he told us with a grin. And then he added, in a tone too casual to actually be casual, "And will Octavia Junilla be accompanying you?"

Well, there was an added complication to my holiday, I supposed, but certainly one more pleasant than a bloody corpse. Since her divorce, Octavia had refused to entertain any advances. In theory, as her paterfamilias, I could force her to marry whoever I wanted. In practice, I wasn't that much of an idiot. But a few months ago at Nero's Juvenalia, I'd seen the appraising looks she and Rufio had exchanged, and I'd wondered. So had Rufio, apparently.

I said, to test him, "Octavia Junilla does as she pleases."

And when his smile grew, I knew that I liked him, and I suspected I'd see a lot more of him in my future.

Starting with tonight.

Chapter Two

Calpurnius Piso's dinner party was held on a boat, because why not? It was Baiae. When we arrived at his villa, we were escorted to one of Piso's three private jetties, where we boarded the boat. It was a liburna, with a row of oarsmen down each side who were partitioned from the deck by wooden walls. It was the sort of boat the navy used for fast raids and quick landings, but instead of the deck being crowded with soldiers, a long, low dining table took up most of the area—the mast with its bright green sail jutted right through the centre of it. There were no couches, but there were plenty of cushions. At the prow, near the large swan's figurehead, musicians were already playing. And at the rear, in the deckhouse just behind the steering paddle, slaves waited with food and wine.

Fulvia's grip tightened on my arm as we stepped aboard, but her smile didn't falter.

Piso was a handsome man of average height. He wore a green tunic that matched the sail, a toga, and a coronet of dark curls. He knew who I was thanks to the slave whose job it was to whisper in his ear and remind him, but his greeting was warm and genuine, as though he was welcoming family.

"Valerius!" He clasped my hand and then released it so he could clap me on the shoulder. "How good to see you! It's been so long since you were in Baiae!"

"Not since I was a boy," I agreed. "Thank you for inviting us to dinner."

Piso smiled. "Any friend of Nero's is a friend of mine." Then he looked past me. "Maro! Are you still remodelling your house in the city?"

A slave beckoned us forward to the table.

Atreus and Maro and I were placed at one end, with all the women at the other. There were a few familiar faces already seated, men I knew from Rome: Petronius the writer, and Lucan the poet.

"Here he is," Petronius said, and raised a cup of wine in my direction. "I was just telling Piso we couldn't leave the jetty until the guest of honour arrived!"

I looked pointedly at the gap at the end of the table as I settled myself down on the cushions. "I don't think it's me we're waiting for, Petro."

Petronius only laughed.

It was good to be in their company again. Nero had surrounded himself with poets and artists, and their constant battles of one-upmanship and backstabbing had annoyed me at first, but now amused me. Some of the poets took it very seriously, and I assumed that Nero saw straight through them, since only the two of them who truly didn't care where they ranked in Nero's favour were here tonight. Lucan was far too decent to dream of sabotaging another poet, and Petronius just enjoyed creating drama both off and on the page. To call Lucan and Petronius friends of Nero wasn't just a euphemism for them having the emperor's ear—they were, genuinely, his friends.

Atreus and I passed a little while catching up with Petronius and Lucan. Well, I did the catching up while Atreus nodded at appropriate moments and tried not to look too uncomfortable in the presence of men who could easily buy him a hundred times over. He was better with Petronius and Lucan than he was with most other patricians, but that wasn't saying much. He still approached every conversation like he was facing a torturer's interrogation.

The sun was just setting when Nero and his Praetorians approached, the guards marching on either side of the emperor's litter. At the jetty, the Praetorians fell back, which surprised me. The rest of us had left our bodyguards on the shore, but the rest of us weren't Nero. It said a lot about Nero's friendship with Piso that he trusted him enough to board the boat without his soldiers. The only soldier he brought with him was Rufio, and Rufio was in a toga, and not his armour.

There was another Praetorian tribune, dressed in his armour, who glowered jealously as Rufio followed the emperor aboard the boat. He had a round, reddish face that, when it was twisted up with bitterness, reminded me of a smashed crab. I was very glad Nero had chosen to bring Rufio aboard instead.

As soon as Nero was seated at the head of the table, with Piso on one side and Rufio on the other, we left the jetty.

The last rays of sunlight glittered on the water of the bay, and the cool salt breeze ruffled my hair and tugged at the edges of my toga. As soon as the rowers found their rhythm, the boat darted forward at speed, leaving the coastline behind.

The musicians played, and the slaves served wine with the first course—fish stew and bread—and those of us around the table laughed and talked as we ate. Baiae retreated into the hazy distance as we cut across the surface of the dark sea. As the night drew in, pinpoints of light appeared along the coastline, and the field of stars brightened above us. The moon kept pace with us, bobbing through the scant clouds.

The waves lapped against the hull, gentle as a whisper, but I could feel the weight behind them—the pull of darker currents beneath. Lanterns cast amber halos, and laughter flickered across the deck like flame. A teenage girl down the other end of the table was helped to her feet by a slave, and it caught Piso's attention.

"Do we need to go back, Tertia?" he called, and then said to us, "My sister. She sometimes gets seasick."

But the girl only smiled and waved. "I am well, thank you!"

I saw that she was only swapping positions with another woman, so that she and Julia might sit together. They were both of an age, I supposed, and had a lot of comparing of jewellery and hairstyles and whatever else it was we men told ourselves that young women cared about. If we convinced ourselves they only cared about silly fripperies, we could pretend they weren't honing their skills at character assassination. Teenage girls were brutal.

"Come, Valerius," Petronius said, lounging with his usual careless elegance. "The whole town is talking of the perfumer's murder. Rufio is singing your praises."

For my skill in helping to detain the killer, or because I was Octavia's brother? But I didn't say that aloud. Petronius didn't need to get that gossip from me.

I glanced at Rufio, who was seated between Nero and Piso, and he snorted. "I don't sing praises, Petronius. I report facts."

Petronius leaned forward and said across the table in a whisper that would have carried through a theatre, "If you or I repeat a story, Valerius, we're gossiping old hens, but our honoured Praetorian friend here is only reporting facts."

Rufio's mouth twitched, and Nero laughed.

Lucan leaned forward. "Rufio says the son confessed?"

I took a sip of wine to wet my throat. It had a little too much salt, perhaps to encourage us to drink more quickly. "He didn't have much choice." I nodded at Atreus. "We followed the trail of blood right to him."

"It's shocking," Piso said, shaking his head. "Atria, my wife, spoke well of the perfumer. She was very respected throughout the town. And Baiae is a small town, really. Despite its reputation for licentiousness, it's safer here than in Rome."

That was like saying the sea was wetter than the desert. Even going out for dinner in Rome was placing your life into the hands of the gods. There was a reason I travelled everywhere in the city with a bodyguard and, most times, a vigile. But Rome was the beating heart of the empire; you put up with a little blood.

"You are always in the middle of things, Valerius," Petronis said, lifting his glass in my direction. His tone was customarily sardonic because Petronius made fun of the world and everyone in it at any opportunity, but his gaze was warm. "I'm jealous. Some of us have to manufacture dramas fit for the stage, and yet you stumble right into them!"

"Clearly you're not spending enough time with me then," I said, "or you could stumble into them alongside me and save the Muses from doing all the work for you."

Petro laughed and toasted the sky. "To the Muses."

A breeze curled in from the sea, pushing at the sail. Somewhere down the other end of the deck, a flute began a jaunty tune. Slaves moved among us, bearing dishes of oysters, and the scent of honey and spices floated on the salt air.

Then Nero said, abruptly, "Mothers and sons. Always a tragedy waiting to happen."

An awkward silence fell, noticeable enough to catch the attention of the women at the lower end of the table. I caught Fulvia's curious gaze.

"Or a comedy," Petronius said, his laughter breaking the silence. "What's the difference, really?"

Nero laughed too, and the strange and sudden tension broke as balance was restored.

It was a night filled with food, wine, and good company, made magical by the setting. The wind was calm enough that our ride was smooth, and after a while, I barely even felt the movement of the boat across the ocean. Although that might have been the wine—after only a few cups it was difficult to tell the difference between the waves underneath the boat and those inside my stomach.

Hours later, when we finally bumped up against the jetty at Piso's house, I wobbled back onto dry land on very unsteady legs.

Nero laughed and clapped me on the shoulder. "You shall feel the curse of the finest wine collection in Baiae tomorrow, Valerius! Piso's Gauranum comes from his own vineyard, and it has teeth!"

I laughed too.

Nero slung his arm around my shoulders as we stepped off the dock onto one of the marble terraces that led up to the vast network of buildings that made up Piso's villa. On one of the broad terraces, the litter bearers, bodyguards, and Praetorians all waited to claim their respective dinner guests.

"Your friend isn't happy that he didn't get an invitation aboard," I said to Rufio, nodding at the Praetorian tribune who was still glowering all these hours later. Or perhaps he'd spent the length of our boat ride in quiet contemplation and only rediscovered his glower when we'd come back onto land. I doubted it, though. His glower gave the sense that it could endure.

"Celer?" Rufio snorted. "Not my friend."

"Your brother in arms, then," I suggested.

Rufio didn't correct me, but his expression implied that if they were brothers, he had an opinion as to which one of them should have been left on a mountainside at birth.

My family and I said our farewells—Rufio slipped by me to exchange some quiet words with Octavia that left them both smiling—and set off for home.

Atreus and I walked behind the litters, with Juba beside us. It was only a short distance to my villa, and the night was cool and pleasant. Also, mindful of Nero's words, I thought it would be a good idea to at least try to sober up a little before bed.

"That was a good night," I said.

"Mmm." Even Atreus had to admit it, though I'm sure it hurt his pride to do so.

"What about you, Juba? I hope your evening wasn't too boring."

"I played knucklebones with some of the litter bearers," he said. "Won a few coins from it. And Piso's slaves brought us bread and olives."

I always liked to ask Juba how he was treated in another man's house; it helped me to form an opinion of my host. Of course, overlooking the visiting slaves who sat around for hours while their masters socialised was no true moral failing, but I'd found that the man who allowed his slaves to extend hospitality to others usually made a decent friend, and lately, with my fledgling career almost ready to take wing, I was in the business of cultivating friends. Piso would be a useful friend to have, and, hopefully, a decent one as well.

The slave walking in front of our litters had a torch, but the moonlight was so bright that we didn't need it. The air tasted of salt, and the breeze tugged at my hair. Baiae rose up before us, its streets carved into the steep hills that encircled the bay. Torchlight and lamplight gleamed faintly from distant porticos, outshone by the brilliant stars above.

When we reached the villa, Vulso, the door slave greeted us with soft house slippers and helped us to unwrap ourselves from our togas without tying us in knots, which I was unused to. Was this what a competent door slave was like? Hursa had lowered my expectations so successfully that I was just delighted whenever I arrived home in Rome, to find, against all odds, that my house was still standing.

"I think the night was a success," Fulvia said, showing me a pleased smile. "No scandals, no arguments, and no murders."

"You say that like it happens every time I leave the house for dinner."

"Well, not *every* time," she allowed, "but it has happened enough that I wonder what animals I should be sacrificing to what gods in order to put a stop to it."

"A modest elephant ought to do it," I suggested.

Fulvia laughed and kissed me on the cheek. "Goodnight, Quintus."

"Goodnight."

The womenfolk wandered off towards bed. Maro dithered for a while, deciding he needed a snack first, so he joined Atreus and me in the informal triclinium. I sent a slave to fetch a latrunculi board. Atreus and I played, and Maro browsed over a plate of nuts and olives.

"It's all very well to have dinner on a boat," Maro said, "but a man can't eat as much as he would like when his stomach is subject to the whims of the ocean." He selected an olive and popped it in his mouth. "Still, the fish stew was excellent. You know what this means, of course, Quintus?"

"Do I know what the fish stew means?" I moved a piece on the board, hoping Atreus wouldn't spot the opening I'd left him.

"Not the stew, idiot," Maro said fondly. "The entire evening."

"What does it mean?"

"It means you'll have to reciprocate," Maro said. "You must invite Piso and his family to dinner here—Nero too, of course, though when did an emperor need an invitation to open a door? And it must be extravagant. Since we don't have a boat, I suppose the entertainment will have to be more traditional."

"Music and poetry," I said. "Nero loves those, and even the most excruciating pastoral wouldn't upset your stomach."

Maro's bushy eyebrows tugged together. "I said traditional, my boy, not forgettable. You must *impress*!"

Atreus's mouth twitched as he made his next move in the game. Of course, it was to exploit my previous move and to capture one of my pieces.

"What do you suggest then?" I asked, knowing that Maro had an opinion. He always did. He might have been mad when it came to his home renovations, but underneath all that, the old man was canny and shrewd. He was old enough to have seen it all in the world of politics and smart enough to want nothing to do with it. That didn't mean he wouldn't push me in the right direction, of course.

"Gladiators," he said smugly.

I raised my eyebrows. "Gladiators?"

Maro's eyes were bright. "We are close to Cumae, are we not? Isn't this where Aeneas himself journeyed to the underworld with the guidance of the Cumaean Sibyl and received a prophecy from his dead father about the destiny of Rome?"

"Yes," I said. "Although I'm still not sure where the gladiators come into the story."

"They come into the story because a poetry recital is nothing extraordinary." Maro's eyes lit up, and he beamed. "But a recreation is! We could dine in the garden, while all around us the events of The Aeneid are played out, including the fights. You shall be the talk of Baiae, and of Rome, too!"

"I thought this was about repaying Piso's hospitality."

Maro tapped the side of his nose. "Every man is the artisan of his own fortune, my boy. Nero's approval has already cemented the foundations of your reputation in Rome, and now your name must remain on the tongues of the senators as well. You are known as a friend of Nero, but what you want is every patrician who wears the purple stripe to be fighting each other to be known as *your* friend."

"Maro, that sounds like a nightmare."

"No," he corrected me sternly. "It sounds like a political career, which is both a privilege and a burden that you, as your father's only son, have inherited. You come from generations of illustrious Aemilii, Quintus. Don't be the one to fuck it up."

Well, that was Roman public life in a nutshell, wasn't it? I rolled my eyes at Maro, but he was entirely correct. It was my duty to my family, and to Rome, to uphold the Aemilii name, and, where possible, to advance it.

I let out a long breath. "I'll ask Stilo, I suppose. He runs the villa. He must have some idea where to hire entertainers and gladiators."

"Nonsense," Maro said. "I'll organise everything myself. I have friends here in Baiae." He tapped the side of his nose again, as though he was letting me in on a secret. "Also, thanks to your little foray into the world of the theatre recently, I've learned a lot about how to stage a play."

This time, my long breath was a groan. Of course Maro wanted to be in charge. Since he wasn't in Rome, he was deprived of his favourite things in the world: renovating and decorating. What better outlet was there for his madness than an extravagant dinner that also doubled as a play and a gladiatorial display? I bet he'd been plotting this from the moment he'd seen Piso's boat and decided we needed to do something just as impressive. "Just keep me out of it then, please."

His eyes sparkled. "So I have your full authority on this matter?"

"Within reason, Maro. I'd prefer all the walls stay in their original positions."

He laughed, as though it was a joke, and clapped me on the shoulder. Then he rose to his feet, calling for a slave with a torch, and took the dish of olives with him.

"I think he's gone to inspect the garden," I said to Atreus, and looked down at the board. "Shit."

"Another round then," Atreus said, too proud to gloat about his victory, and reset the board.

We played for a while longer. Around us, the house was silent and dark. A few slaves passed back and forth, and one of them, a teenaged boy, stood silently in the corner and watched our game of latrunculi through sleepy eyes. He had brought a fresh dish of olives after Maro left, and wine, but neither Atreus nor I was particularly hungry after Piso's nautical feast.

"Go to bed, boy," I said. "We can find the kitchen if we need to."

The boy nodded and padded away silently on his bare feet.

And then Atreus and I were alone, but we remained seated across from one another. The villa was mine, but I didn't know it well, and I had no idea how many other slaves might pass by the doorway as they tended their duties. Was there a different door slave at night? If so, would his replacement be wandering past? Which men had Stilo instructed to patrol for burglars, and would they come into the main part of the house? What time did the kitchen slaves begin their day's work? Atreus was seated across from me, and there was nobody else with us, but we were less free here than we were in Rome. In Rome, we at least had his place in the Aventine. Not always, of course, because he shared it with Lucilla and Iris, but Juba—whatever my father had paid for him, he was worth a hundred times more—often volunteered to accompany them shopping, leaving us the apartment.

Juba had done the same for us yesterday, in the bathhouse, but it was a risk Atreus and I had both agreed we couldn't take again. If I'd told that teenaged slave to join me in my bed and the world found out, nobody would even blink. But Atreus was a Roman citizen, and his reputation would be ruined if he was thought to have unmanned himself by being a patrician's boy. The truth was even more damning because those were not our roles. If Atreus was lucky, he might survive the ensuing scandal, but I certainly wouldn't. And my family's reputation would also be destroyed.

"You come from generations of illustrious Aemilii, Quintus. Don't be the one to fuck it up."

We played another game of latrunculi, our fingers lingering when they touched, but we remained on separate couches. I studied his handsome, serious face, my gaze mapping the line of his jaw and the planes of his cheeks and mouth, the way the lamplight caught in his green-flecked eyes, and told myself that it was enough, for now. And when we finally rose and went our separate ways, I told myself that his softly spoken "good night" was enough, too.

* * *

During the night, clouds swept in from the sea, and the day dawned overcast.

The lamps were lit in the informal triclinium for breakfast, and Maro pronounced that we might see a storm by the end of the day. My womenfolk discussed whether or not to put off their shopping trip, but decided to forge ahead since everything was so close.

"And I want to visit Cassia, of course," Octavia said. "If we're caught in the rain, I'm sure we'll survive it."

Mouse and Lucilla, who had been hoping for a visit to the nearby beach to play in the sand and the shallows, were disappointed to be told they would have to wait for sunnier weather.

Maro was brimming with enthusiasm for his gladiatorial feast, or reenactment of The Aeneid, or whatever final, mad form our dinner would take, and already making out the guest list. He had apparently decided overnight that it wasn't enough to invite just Piso and his family, and Nero, but what seemed like half of Baiae.

"Well, of course, everything must be extravagant yet modest," he said. "And fashionable yet traditional."

"Old but new," Octavia suggested mischievously.

Maro jabbed his stylus in her direction. "Exactly so! Exactly so!"

Julia tittered and then hid her smile behind her hand, and a wave of warm affection rolled over me for my entire extended family, as maddening as some of them were. Maro, mostly, although they all had their moments.

Stilo approached during breakfast. "Excuse me, sir."

I swallowed a mouthful of puls. "What is it?"

"You have an invitation," he said, a frown creasing his forehead. "Well, a request…? I'm not sure I know how to interpret it, but there's a man at the door who says his master, Anicetus, would like to see you."

Anicetus.

I couldn't help but catch Octavia's eye. Officially, Anicetus was the head of the fleet at Misenum. Unofficially, he was Nero's spymaster. Octavia's ex-husband had been working for Anicetus in an attempt to bring legionary corruption and treason to light when he'd been murdered.

Her expression, so bright a moment ago when she was making fun of Maro, was suddenly grave.

"Well," I said, trying to keep my tone light, "be sure to tell him that I shall certainly make the time to visit Anicetus in Misenum."

Stilo made an unhappy sound. "Sir, he says he has a cisium ready to take you *now*." His slight emphasis said that he was willing to be outraged if I was, and certainly in most circumstances it would be presumptuous of a freedman to make demands of a patrician's valuable time. But Anicetus was no ordinary freedman, and I wasn't proud enough, or stupid enough, to ignore a summons from him.

"Well, let's not keep him waiting then." I exchanged a look with Atreus, and we both rose from the table.

The slave who had brought the message was also the cisiarii, and he grumbled when he realised he had two passengers instead of one, and that we'd all be wedged together like stacked amphorae for the duration of the journey. Fortunately, it was only a short hop from Baiae to Misenum.

The day was cloudy, and the sea was grey. There was a bite to the cool breeze, especially once we left the streets of Baiae and the cisiarii let the horses set a blistering pace. Despite the jaw-dropping views of the hills that rose on one side of us and the cliffs that dropped to the ocean on the other, I kept my mouth shut to avoid swallowing any bugs. I had no idea what in Tartarus Anicetus wanted with me, but I was more curious than cautious. I was loyal to Nero and to Rome, and Anicetus knew it.

As we skirted the edge of the Phlegraean Fields, I thought back to what Maro had said last night about Aeneas and his descent into the underworld. The land here was black and fertile, but pools of mud bubbled, and sulphur fumes rose like steam from vents in the earth. The entrance to the underworld was beside Lake Avernus, and it was said that any bird that flew over the lake would die. And yet, it was so beautiful here, and the soil was so rich, that wealthy patricians built their villas beside the waters of Lake Avernus, and vineyards encroached on the Phlegraean Fields.

The town of Misenum was built on the narrow cape that jutted out into the ocean and reached towards the islands of Procida and Ischia. The end of the cape towered above the water, its dramatic cliff tops offering a view of the bay it protected, and of the wide sea beyond. Anicetus's villa was in the main town, before the cape rose dramatically. From the outside, there was nothing to distinguish it, which was just like the man himself. As we pulled up outside on the street, a man in the red cloak of a military officer left the house, our only indication that behind these nondescript walls, miles away from Rome, the imperial machine was in motion.

The door slave peered after the officer, and then caught sight of Atreus and me climbing down from the cisium. He was only a young man, but he had a shrewd and sharp-eyed gaze.

"Aemilius Valerius," he said, ducking his head respectfully. Then he lifted his chin and blinked at Atreus. "And Junius Atreus."

Atreus and I exchanged a glance. Since Atreus hadn't been included in the summons to Misenum, the fact the door slave surmised his name was an unsettling reminder of how much Anicetus—and, by extension, this slave—knew about my life. We'd only been in Baiae two days, yet Anicetus already knew Atreus had come with me.

"Please," said the slave. "Follow me."

He led us through into the sunlit atrium, where we skirted the impluvium and continued on through the tablinum and then out through the colonnades and into the garden. A row of neatly trimmed cypresses flanked the path that led to the fountain.

Anicetus was seated on a stone bench by the fountain, perusing a scroll. He rose when he saw us, setting the scroll aside. "Ah, Valerius and Atreus. Thank you for coming."

As though we'd had any choice.

"Walk with me," he said, and I guessed we didn't have a choice about that either.

Still, the gardens were pleasant even if I was ambivalent about the company, so we fell into step with Anicetus and took a stroll. The statue of Neptune, standing on a plinth in the square pond of the fountain, regarded us haughtily as he wrestled a dolphin. At least, I hoped he was wrestling it, but there was no way to be sure. Whatever it was, though, he had no right to look so smug about it.

"Octavia Junilla remains in my prayers," Anicetus said, and I hoped it was meant as reassurance that he remembered the debt that he owed her, and also the loyalty of my family to the emperor. Nero was a friend, but Anicetus? Anicetus moved in such murky waters that I could never get the measure of him. I was quite sure he intended that. "Is she well?"

"She is," I replied.

"I am very glad to hear that." He paused and looked up at the cloudy sky. "It's been an interesting few months. Well, you will understand this, Valerius. Sometimes, even in victory, nothing is certain."

I inclined my head in agreement, wondering what he was getting at.

He tugged a green sprig off a cypress tree and crushed it between his thumb and forefinger before bringing it to his nose and inhaling the scent, and then he said, "Agrippina is coming to Baiae."

"What?" My blood ran cold.

"She seeks to reconcile with her son," Anicetus said, as benignly as though he was commenting on the weather.

"And will she?" I asked.

"Publicly, perhaps," he said. "Privately, I think not. That business with the Third Gallica—well, of course, she frames it as doing everything to ensure Nero his position as emperor, and such a defence could still be made if only she hadn't threatened to support Britannicus in a fit of temper. That whole business drove something of a rift between them, and Nero has not forgotten it. Agrippina is, clearly, Nero's strongest ally whenever it suits her own ambitions." His mouth twitched. "It's when she feels their ambitions do not align that she is dangerous."

I grimaced. She was always dangerous, as far as I was concerned.

Our short walk brought us back towards the fountain. From this approach, I could see what looked like a tiny boat sunk and resting on the tiles at the bottom of the fountain. I thought it must be a child's toy, although the detail seemed too intricate for something you'd pick up at a market stall. I hadn't known Anicetus had children, but then what I didn't know about Anicetus could fill the Circus Maximus.

"Agrippina does not approve of Poppaea Sabina," the man said mildly, pulling my attention back to him.

We all made sacrifices for Rome. Otho, Nero's close companion, had sacrificed his wife. Otho was still married to Poppaea Sabina, but all of Rome knew whose bed she slept in. She was a very clever woman. When I'd met her, I'd thought she and her husband were well matched in matters of taste and ambition. It turned out she'd decided she could do better. I didn't know what went on behind closed doors in their marriage, but I could only imagine they'd had some awkward conversations recently.

"What does Agrippina's approval matter to Nero?" I asked. "How much power does she still have?"

"There are plenty of men who made the mistake of underestimating her who are now ashes," Anicetus said. "I don't know what she's planning. I wish that I did. But I wanted to warn you that she's coming, and that just because the streets of Baiae appear safer than those of Rome, you need to watch your back."

"And Octavia?" I asked.

Anicetus gave me a regretful smile. "Yes," he said at last. "I'm afraid Octavia Junilla also needs to watch hers, too."

* * *

When we arrived back in Baiae, the rest of the family was out. For a moment, cold fear stirred in my gut, and I took a breath and reminded myself that Agrippina wasn't here yet, and that there was no greater danger to Octavia in the Baian streets than overpaying for souvenirs. Still, I was glad I'd left Juba to go shopping with the womenfolk instead of bringing him to Misenum with us. Although how he would have fitted in the cisium with me, Atreus, and the cisiarii was a mystery. Sheer stubbornness, probably.

Atreus and I headed out along the street to find them. The perfumer's shop was closed, but that hadn't stopped a modest crowd of gossips from gathering there to see what they could see. Which was nothing except the shuttered door. They were making the most of it, though, sharing their opinions loudly while they bought stuffed vine leaves from the boy who'd been clever enough to turn up and sell them.

Atreus and I strode past quickly, and we weren't recognised.

Cassia's shop was open, and the same girl who'd greeted us yesterday waved shyly as we passed.

We followed the curve of the harbour toward the main part of the town, keeping an eye out for my family as more clouds drew in and the day darkened. Let the omen be absent, as the saying went. We had just reached one of the smaller temples by the waterfront when we met my family coming back the other way.

Lucilla wriggled out of Juba's hold when she saw us, her sandals slapping across the stones as she hurried to fling herself into Atreus's arms. He picked her up and swung her onto his hip as I went and greeted Fulvia, Octavia, and Julia. A pair of household slaves from the villa were carrying the shopping baskets. Mouse was dawdling behind them, clearly disinterested in the expedition, although he grinned when he saw me.

"The rain's coming," I said. "Let's get home."

"How was your visit to Misenum?" Fulvia asked me.

"Let's get home," I repeated, and Fulvia exchanged a look with Octavia.

There were certain conversations it was better to have behind closed doors and in the safety of one's own villa. The fact that the emperor's mother, who hated me and probably not only wished me dead but also had the track record to show she could make it happen, was coming to Baiae was probably foremost among those conversations that were best held in private. The fact that Agrippina considered me an enemy was unsettling enough, but it was Octavia I feared for even more. I could handle myself in a fair fight— although the chances of Agrippina arranging one of those instead of a knife in the dark were slim—but Octavia, for all her sharp wit and cleverness, had no training with a weapon.

When we got back to the villa, we sent Lucilla and Mouse to the kitchen for food, and the rest of us gathered in the triclinium. I closed the sliding doors that made the room a thoroughfare during the day, and then leaned against the desk and tried to gather my thoughts. Atreus and Juba stood by the door that led into the atrium, while my womenfolk gathered closer to me, worry in their gazes.

"What's going on?" Fulvia asked. "Tell us, Quintus."

"We went to visit Anicetus," I said, nodding at Atreus, "and he told us that Agrippina is on her way to Baiae, and he doesn't know her intentions. He was also careful to remind me not to underestimate her."

"But why would she want to kill you?" Julia asked, her eyes large. "You're not that important!"

My mouth twitched at her words. Julia and I hadn't always gotten on, and there was a time when words like that wouldn't have come wrapped in a sentiment of concern. I didn't miss those days—or their attendant headaches—but it amused me nonetheless to be reminded of them. Fulvia liked to say that Julia had grown up, but that was only because she was too kind to say we both had.

"I agree," I said, "but Atreus and I were both involved in cutting her off from a fairly significant source of income and influence. And so was Octavia, indirectly. Whether she holds a grudge for that, or whether it is enough to earn her revenge simply because we have prospered by exposing her treason to the palace, I don't know. If it was up to me, I'd keep my distance from her for the rest of both our days, but will she do the same? If Anicetus can't be certain, then I sure as shit have no idea."

Julia nodded worriedly and reached out and gripped Fulvia's hand.

"What ought we do?" Octavia asked.

I shook my head. "I don't know what we can do, except be mindful of our safety. I admit I would be happier if you all stayed inside instead of venturing out to the shops or the beach. Jupiter, I'd send you all back to Rome tomorrow if I could."

"Where we would be in exactly the same danger," Fulvia, as sensible as ever, pointed out.

I pinched the bridge of my nose. "We are not such big fish in Rome as we are here. Baiae is a very little pond."

"Exactly," Octavia said, lifting her chin. "If Agrippina was in Rome at the same time we were, you wouldn't even notice, because it's where you might expect her to be. Well, she has a villa here, doesn't she, on Lake Lucrinus, so why shouldn't she visit it? It doesn't have to be a conspiracy that she's here at the same time we are, when it could easily be a coincidence."

There was probably a handy philosophical axiom that cautioned against making elephants out of flies, but I couldn't shake my unease. If Anicetus had thought to warn us of Agrippina's imminent arrival, then obviously it had occurred to him that we might be in danger from her. And if he thought that, then I wasn't enough of a fool to disregard his concern.

"You may be right," I said, "and I hope you are, but there's no such thing as undue caution when it comes to Agrippina. If you go out, please take some of the male slaves with you; I'll ask Stilo who would be best suited to protect you if there's any trouble. And take Juba."

I looked across at Juba, and he nodded to show his understanding.

"If we take Juba," Fulvia asked, "then who shall protect you?"

"Well, I hope that Atreus and I can protect ourselves," I said with a faint smile.

Fulvia didn't smile in return, because we both knew that Juba had saved my life on more than one occasion. But she did me the courtesy of not arguing, because, when it came down to making a choice between my own safety and the safety of my wife, my sister, and my stepdaughter, then what sort of man would I be if I chose myself?

The news of Agrippina's arrival and the possibility that my family might be in danger kept me on edge for the rest of the day. I tried to read, but found no escape in it. I lurked in the now-open tablinum, where I could see across the atrium to the passageway that led to the street, and glanced up from the scroll every time one of the slaves flitted across the edge of my vision.

Vulso answered the door once to Cassia, who was delivering Atreus's new tunics, and he showed her to one of the side rooms. Moments later, Octavia joined her, and the low murmur of their voices, although I could not make out the words, was soothing. I didn't interrupt them.

Lucilla came and sat with me at one point, and played with a handful of colourful glass beads.

"Those are pretty," I told her.

She gave me a solemn stare as she laid the beads out on the couch. "My bracelet broke."

"Ah," I said. The seven or eight beads she was carrying around did not make up the length of a bracelet, even for a wrist as tiny as hers. "Do you know where the other beads are?"

"A fish ate them," she told me confidently, and I made a mental note to warn the cook to carefully check any of the fish he prepared from the villa's fish ponds.

Moments later, Iris appeared. "There you are!" The scar on her cheek shifted when she gave me a cautious smile. "Sir."

She held out her hand to Lucilla, who slid off the couch. Before she allowed Iris to escort her away, she presented me with one of the beads. "That's for you, Valerius."

"Thank you," I said, and rolled the bead between my thumb and forefinger.

Perhaps she had salvaged most of the other beads after all, and was now on a mission to parcel them out as gifts to everyone she found.

The rest of the afternoon passed slowly.

A man with an amphora of oil turned up. Cassia left. Maro and Marcia arrived back home. The storm that had been threatening all day finally broke, with rain pounding into the impluvium and thunder rumbling throughout the town. Lightning flashed overhead.

We ate in the informal triclinium, and the rain was so loud on the tiles of the roof that we could hardly hear ourselves speak. Julia jolted when one particularly brilliant bolt of lightning lit up the doorway, followed by a crash of thunder, and one of the slaves dropped an empty platter.

"At least we're not out on Piso's boat tonight," Maro said jovially.

He was right about that. The storm was wild.

"No," I agreed. "This is the perfect night to stay indoors and go to bed early."

And then, just as we were digging into pear patina and honey fritters for dessert, Vulso, the door slave, came rushing into the room. He must have cut close to the impluvium to get to us and got his sandals wet; he skidded on the tiles like a racehorse failing to make a bend at the circus, and caught himself on the apologetic slave who'd just picked up the platter.

"Master!" he exclaimed. "There is a slave from next door here! Calpurnius Piso's sister, Calpurnia Tertia, is missing, and they are asking if we can send men to help in the search!"

Well then. So much for an early night.

Chapter Three

The rain was blinding. It had made the road slippery and churned the dirt into mud. I pulled my cloak around me tightly and my hood forward, but it did little to keep me dry. In moments, the fabric was stuck to me like a second skin. Along with Atreus, Juba, and about a dozen of the male slaves from the villa, I struck out into the storm, following Piso's frantic messenger towards the massive villa next door that only last night had been the scene of a much happier occasion. Thunder crashed, and the black ocean boiled, and the slaves struggled to keep the lanterns alight in the storm.

As we approached Piso's villa, a pair of men on horses galloped out of one of the gates in the wall. If we'd been any closer, they would have scattered us like knucklebones. I squinted after them, but they were lost to the rain and the darkness already. I wondered where they were going at such breakneck speed. Did Piso think he knew where his missing sister might be? Or was he sending out for more reinforcements for the search party? Whatever the case, I hoped Calpurnia Tertia was found soon. It was an awful night to be out in the weather.

Piso looked as though he'd been out in it for hours. He was drenched, his hair plastered to his skull, and his woollen cloak pulled almost to his heels by the weight of the water it held. When we found him on the road outside the entrance to his villa, he was gesturing to a similarly sodden slave who was holding a covered lantern that barely cast any light at all in the storm.

"Valerius!" Piso shouted when he saw me. "Thank you for coming! I've sent men for Nero's villa and to some friends in town, but you're my closest neighbour."

The men on horses were those messengers, I guessed.

"When and where did you last see Calpurnia Tertia?" I asked him, raising a hand to wipe rain from my eyes.

"She didn't come to dinner." Piso's voice was hoarse, and I wondered how long he'd been shouting for her around the villa.

"And her slaves, sir?" Atreus asked, sounding as put-together as always despite the pouring rain that battered us.

Piso shook his head. Even the darkness couldn't hide his expression of distress. "One of the girls said she saw her about an hour before dinner. She asked the girl to fetch her cloak. The girl thought she wanted it for a visit tomorrow, but she thinks now that Tertia was going out on her own."

On her own.

That was a dangerous thing in the evening in Rome. It was dangerous everywhere, probably, but I couldn't help but consider Baiae's reputation. Was it only last night that Piso had pointed out that Baiae, despite its reputation, was safe? It didn't feel safe now, thinking of a young girl out in the darkness, in the rain, alone. Maybe she had a reason to go out on her own, to meet an unsuitable lover. Of course, all lovers were unsuitable for patrician sisters and daughters and wives, but in Baiae, famously, the usual rules did not apply.

"Is there anyone in particular she would want to visit?" I asked.

"Well, she has her friends, of course." Piso wiped rain from his face. "She has a circle of friends here in Baiae. Her closest would be Plautia Balbina. Plautia is a widow; she has a place up near the Baths of Mercury. I've already sent someone there to ask, but I can't think why Tertia would go alone, without telling anyone."

Atreus and I exchanged a look.

"Does she have a boyfriend, sir?" Atreus asked.

Piso looked shocked. "No! No, I am certain of it!"

And wasn't that the refrain of every paterfamilias? None of us really knew what our womenfolk were up to, even though we liked to tell ourselves we did. I wondered if Tertia had caught someone's eye, and vice versa, and Piso had remained totally oblivious.

"Where have you searched so far, sir?" Atreus asked.

"All of the villa," Piso said.

"The grounds too?"

"Yes." He shook his head. "I just can't think of why she would leave in weather like this."

Or why she would leave at all, given the luxury behind the walls of the villa, unless there was some man she was sneaking out to visit. That had to be it. Calpurnia Tertia was probably tucked away in some man's warm, dry bed while her brother and his unfortunate neighbours were running around searching for her in the storm.

Still, that was what had to be done, and if it reminded me of my worst days in the military, slogging through mud (or at least standing there watching the legionaries do it), then at least when we were done I could sink straight into a hot bath and recover. That was more than you could say for the army. The restorative drinks after a muddy march were much nicer now that I was no longer a junior tribune, too.

"Use my slaves as you see fit," I told Piso. "I want to speak with your door slave."

Piso called the dripping man over. His testimony was useless. Of course, he had been at his post, although he had left, briefly, to visit the slaves' latrine. Had Tertia been waiting for the front door to be unattended, she easily could have slipped out at that time. The poor slave was distraught, but I doubted Piso could blame the man for needing to take a piss.

"Did Calpurnia Tertia leave the house today?" Atreus asked. He drew his battered wax tablet out of his belt and flipped it open. Rain splattered on the surface of the wax.

The poor slave was confused. "Well, perhaps now? We have been searching and cannot find her."

"No, I mean earlier today," Atreus clarified.

"Oh!" The slave tugged at the neckline of his wet tunic, pulling it off his skin. The moment he let it go, it stuck again. Drops of water hung from his eyelashes and chased down his nose. "Um, yes. This morning she went shopping with the mistress, and this afternoon she made a visit to a friend. I think it was Plautia Balbina, sir? The litter bearers will know. But she was back in time for dinner, though the master says she didn't go. I—I didn't see her leave again! I didn't think anyone would, with this rain."

"You're sure that she was back in time for dinner?" Atreus asked.

"Yes, sir," the slave said. He looked to Piso. "Stichus was sweeping the atrium when she got back, master. He saw her, too."

Piso furrowed his brow and nodded.

Atreus tapped his stylus on his tablet. "And what messages has Calpurnia Tertia received in the past few days?"

The door slave blinked, taking a moment to think. "Nothing unusual at all, sir. An invitation to go shopping with Plautia Balbina and Caecilia Didia." His gaze darted again to his master.

"Both ladies of impeccable virtue," Piso said.

The slave nodded, a rivulet of water pouring from his chin. "And she has been seeking to buy a dog. A man came this morning and said he knew of a fine litter in Puteoli, and that he would bring them by tomorrow for her to look at them if she was interested."

"Did she speak to this man?" I asked him.

The slave shook his head. "I relayed the message to her, and she said to tell him to come tomorrow with the pups." His lower lip wobbled. "Sir, I swear, there has been nothing out of the ordinary!"

The slave's distress was obvious. Whether it spoke to his honesty or not, I couldn't be certain, but I was inclined to believe him.

Hobnails rang on the stones of the street, signalling the arrival of more reinforcements: Rufio and a group of his Praetorians.

"What's the plan?" Rufio asked us, in the no-nonsense tone of a man who knew there was a job to be done, and was prepared to stick it out until it was completed, however hard it was.

"There are only two ways to town from here," I said. "Back past my villa, or back past the emperor's. We ought to split into two groups, and meet again when the road does."

His fellow tribune, the one with the glower and the face like a smashed crab, was with him. He looked as though he wanted to complain about my plan, but the strategy was a sound one.

We were on a narrow cape, one of two arms that circled the port but didn't quite meet, allowing ships a passage through the channel into the port. The road hugged both sides of the cape all the way back to where it joined the main part of the land again. If Tertia had gone into the main part of town, it was impossible to say which route she would have chosen.

I still thought it most likely she was safe and well in some boyfriend's custody, but better to search now and do everything we could than to do nothing if she truly was missing and in need of help.

Rufio nodded, squinting through the rain back in the direction he'd come. "It's a good plan," he agreed. "When we get into the town proper, we'll divide her friends' addresses between us and check them all."

"It's just so unlike her," Piso said, as though he was trying to help us understand he wasn't overreacting, or perhaps even trying to convince himself. He wore the uncomfortable expression of a man who wanted all this fuss to be for nothing, even though he was afraid it might not be.

We broke apart. Piso and Rufio, along with Piso's slaves and Rufio's Praetorians, headed back on the seaward side of the harbour's outer curve, which would take them past Nero's villa. Atreus, Juba, and I led my villa's household slaves back the way we came, towards the channel and the route that hugged the port all the way back to the town's natural shoreline.

"Spread out," Atreus instructed our men, "and keep your eyes open."

Lightning flashed overhead.

"She's probably tucked up nice and dry somewhere," I said, trying to lift the mood a little.

Atreus threw me a look. "I doubt it."

Juba hummed in agreement.

"Why? Do you agree with Piso that she doesn't have a secret boyfriend?"

"No." Atreus wiped hair out of his eyes. "I think that if she had a secret boyfriend, she'd have some pretext to visit him without anyone noticing she was missing. Who would sneak out, knowing they'd be missed sooner or later and the alarm would be raised, when they could make arrangements to visit a friend, and visit the boyfriend instead?"

"Maybe she doesn't trust the slaves enough to lie for her," I suggested.

"You wouldn't need them to lie, sir," Juba said. "It's the friend who has to lie in that scenario, not the slaves. The slaves accompany you to your friend's house, and then are sent to the kitchens to eat because your friend is so generous to them. Who's to say who you'll meet in a private room once your slaves are busy stuffing themselves on snacks?"

Juba had a point. He usually did. Calpurnia Tertia didn't need to sneak out at night to visit an unsuitable lover as long as she had a close friend to facilitate their meetings.

"Maybe she's run off and married him then," I said, "and they're currently on their way to the provinces to escape Piso's wrath."

"In this weather, sir?" Juba asked. "And only taking a cloak?"

Juba had more good points than a porcupine tonight, apparently.

We were within shouting distance of my villa's walls when one of the slaves gave a fearful cry. "Master! Over here!"

I turned to look, and lightning lit up the road.

There, underneath a straggly young carob tree, was a flash of green. Had we been told what colour Tertia's cloak was? It didn't matter. Even sodden and muddy, the cloak was too bright and fine to have been dropped by some labourer from the port.

Juba reached her first, rolling her over onto her back, and then called for a lantern.

She was dead. Her jaw was slack, her muddy hair stuck to one cheek, and her skin was pale as marble. As cold too, probably, I thought as Juba's fingertips trailed down her cheek.

Another flash of lightning lit the sky briefly.

"She was strangled," Juba said.

"How do you know that?" I asked. He hadn't even touched her neck.

"The blood vessels in her eyes have burst," he said matter-of-factly. He slid his fingers down under her jaw, to her throat. "I can feel where the cord has dug in, but it's not here now."

All those hours he'd spent with Leander, the vigiles' physician, hadn't gone to waste. Juba was one of the cleverest men I knew, with a quick and greedy mind. I used to joke to him that he was wasted as my bodyguard. I no longer joked about it, not because it wasn't the truth, but because it was. And it was an uncomfortable one.

I took a moment to close my eyes and say a silent prayer for Calpurnia Tertia. Whatever had brought her out tonight, I hoped that the rest of her journey was more peaceful.

I drew a breath and opened my eyes again. I pointed at one of the slaves whose torch was still withstanding the rain. "Go and fetch Piso. As fast as you can."

The man set off at a run through the rain while the rest of us waited, silently, with the dead girl.

* * *

To witness another man's grief, and to think of that grief as a drop in a pond, ripples spreading out as more and more people heard the news, was a sobering experience. Piso's grief, fresh and raw, had not been solemn and dignified. He'd fallen to his knees beside his sister's body and wept.

The Stoics didn't have an answer to that chilling moment of horror and disbelief, did they?

Tonight, there would be weeping all throughout Piso's villa, from the family, and the slaves, and the day that dawned tomorrow would be a bleak one for them, whatever the weather.

When we arrived back at the villa, I broke the news to my family, and then Atreus and I went straight to the baths. We dismissed the attendant and then moved quickly from the tepidarium into the caldarium. The sudden heat jolted my rain-deadened brain into working order again, and then numbed it again at a slow boil.

We took turns with the strigil to scrape oil off one another's backs, and let the steam soothe us. I paid particular attention to the wet hair at the nape of Atreus's neck, running my thumb across it to tease the strands apart, and basking in the way he leaned back into my touch. But if I thought I was distracting him from the grim scenes we'd just witnessed. I was mistaken.

"Where the fuck was she going on her own, after dark, with a storm about to break?" he muttered.

"I have no idea." I leaned forward and pressed a quick kiss to the top of his spine. "I'm the unimaginative idiot who thought it must be a boyfriend, before you and Juba pointed out just how easily any man's wife, sisters, and daughters could have an entire legion of them and he'd never know."

"People always find a way to fuck," Atreus said with a snort. "Even maidens and matrons."

"The great days of the moral republic truly are behind us," I said lazily, and didn't really care, because of course Atreus was right, and I was sure that people had been no more virtuous in those golden years that Cato the Younger had famously banged on about than now. As always, it didn't matter what anyone did—it only mattered if they got caught. I bet that every man who vehemently decried another's moral decrepitude in the senate was secretly pissing himself in relief that his own hadn't come to light.

Atreus and I didn't take as long in the baths as either of us would have wanted. We got out and dressed, then went to the informal triclinium where we had abandoned our dinner, which felt like a week ago instead of a little more than an hour before.

"What happened, Quintus?" Octavia asked, and I supposed at least the family had given me the courtesy to let me soak the mud off before they hit me with a barrage of questions.

"She was strangled, Juba says." I looked around for confirmation, and Juba, like the silent ghost he was, slipped into the room as though summoned, and nodded gravely at my words. "That's all we know for now. Piso has taken her body back to his house; I expect her funeral will be in a few days."

I hoped the rain had cleared by then. I hated to think how long it would take her Tertia to burn in a downpour like tonight's, and what a miserable experience it would be to stand by and watch it.

Julia leaned against Fulvia's side. "But she was so *nice.*"

I remembered that Julia had been seated next to Tertia at the dinner party on the boat.

"Did she say anything to you last night that might have given you some indication of where she was going tonight?"

Julia blinked at me. "Well, I only just met her. We weren't exactly exchanging all our secrets." There was a hint of the old, snarky Julia in her response, and she must have heard it too, because she looked a little shamefaced. "I mean, she was kind and welcoming, and we were the same age, so she said she was going to invite me to spend some time with her and her friends, so that I wouldn't have to sit at home with nothing to do."

"Do you think she meant something outside the home?" I asked her.

"I don't know." Julia blinked. "I know she meant outside *my* home, but that could have been just going next door for honey cakes and gossip for all I know."

That was reasonable.

"Poor Piso," murmured Fulvia, and put an arm around Julia.

Mad Uncle Maro popped an olive in his mouth, tilting his head thoughtfully. He tugged at some of the strange hair that grew out of his ears. "Piso must know your reputation."

Here it came.

"You ought to volunteer your services," Maro declared.

"I don't offer any services," I said.

"Well, of course you do," Maro said. He nodded at Atreus. "You and Atreus both. Everyone knows that Seneca came to you to find out who attacked Lucan that time, and you did it, didn't you?"

"Eventually," I said. "And in a very roundabout way."

"Well then," Maro said, "when he asks you for help to find his sister's murderer, and he will, then you must agree."

"This is Baiae, not Rome," I said. "I'm not a magistrate's assistant here."

Maro barked out a laugh. "No, you're something even more important, you fool. You're Nero's friend."

I let out a long breath. "If he asks, then of course Atreus and I will poke around. But there's no guarantee he will ask."

Maro gave me a look he'd been giving me since I was old enough to remember. The one that said he thought I was an idiot, and he was probably right.

To punish him for it, I reached over and stole his dish of olives, and wondered what the morning would bring.

* * *

The day dawned shockingly bright after last night's storm, with barely a cloud in the sky. There were still puddles in the garden from the storm, and Zethos, the keeper of the fish ponds, was worried about the amount of freshwater that had got into the ponds and what it would do to the fish. On the other hand, Stilo was pleased the cistern under the impluvium was full, and the rain had washed the dust off the roof tiles, making them seem brighter in the sunlight.

My womenfolk had left the house before I even turned up to breakfast, and I was informed they'd gone to Piso's house to offer their condolences to Atria Galla, Piso's wife. Juba, as per my instructions, had gone with them. I was glad. The shadow of Agrippina hanging over us all was bad enough, but combined with last night's unthinkable violence against Calpurnia Tertia, I needed to be reassured my family was as safe as possible. And Juba had proved his loyalty and his strength, every time it had counted.

I ate breakfast with Atreus and Maro. We had boiled eggs with roasted pine nuts and garum, served on a bed of lettuce leaves and blanched asparagus.

"You ought to eat another egg," Maro commented. "You'll need your strength today. Piso will no doubt be calling on you later."

"This might be Baiae, Maro, but you're not the Cumaean Sibyl."

My mad relation tapped the side of his nose. "No, but I'm old enough to know how these things go. Mark my words, Quintus."

"I don't want to mark your words," I said. "I want you to be wrong."

He wasn't.

Calpurnius Piso arrived while we were still eating. He was dressed in a brown tunic and a dark toga pulla to indicate he was in mourning. His clothing was pristine, but the man wrapped inside it was haggard, as though not only had he not slept last night, but he hadn't for the last decade of his life. It was astonishing how quickly grief carved out hollows under a man's eyes and made him old.

I met him in the tablinum. The doors were open on either side, allowing the light from the atrium and the peristyle to illuminate the room. Piso sank heavily into a chair and dragged a hand through his hair.

Outside, in the distance, I could hear Mouse and Lucilla laughing as they played. The sound was incongruous, almost jarring, but Piso didn't seem to hear it. A slave brought wine, and he left it untouched.

"Lucan tells me that if I want to find out what happened, then you are the man I should speak to," he said at last. "He says that Seneca himself has previously called upon you."

"I was able to help in that matter, yes," I said, sounding far more dignified, I hoped, than the actual circumstances warranted. What had happened when Seneca had approached me was that Atreus, Juba, and I had run around the city like headless chickens until we'd finally stumbled over enough rocks that we'd dislodged the one that turned out to be hiding the killer. "And I would gladly see what I can find out about Calpurnia Tertia's death, in the hope that it might give you the answers you seek. But I can make no guarantees."

Piso met my gaze. "I'm not fool enough to expect guarantees, Valerius. I just want someone to do their best."

"I promise I can do that."

Roman society was built on a system of favours and gratitude, and not just between a patrician and his clients, but between men of equal rank as well. Piso wasn't just offering friendship with his request—it would mean that he would be obligated to me, and at some hazy point in the future it would be my turn to call in a favour, and he wouldn't be able to refuse it without breaching the social contract and suffering a loss to his reputation. I might ask him for a loan, or to vote a particular way in the senate, or to marry one of his family members; to ask for a favour was an act of trust, because there was no telling what I'd want in return. Even I didn't know. For now, it was enough to garner the support of powerful friends, because I might one day need to leverage it in my political career. My political career was still very much non-existent, since I wasn't old enough to be elected as a quaestor, but there was no harm in laying the foundations of it now. Also, I'd looked at Tertia's face last night, and Piso's now, and even if he'd been a sandal maker instead of a senator, I told myself I'd want to help him just as much.

I hoped it wasn't a lie.

I sent for Atreus, and he entered the tablinum and stood in the corner with his wax tablet open and his stylus ready. We might have all dined as friends only two nights ago on Piso's boat, but today we fell back into the roles of magistrate's patrician assistant and lowly plebeian vigile because Piso didn't want friends today. He wanted answers. If there were usual questions to ask in circumstances like these, Atreus and I asked them: Who were Tertia's personal slaves, and could we speak with them? Was there anyone else who might have seen when she left the villa? When could we speak with the other family members in case there was something they could tell us about Tertia's mood lately? Who were her friends, and where in Baiae did they live?

Piso answered every question openly and, in my possibly skewed judgement, honestly. If he had wanted his sister dead, for reasons I could not even begin to imagine, then not only was he an incredible actor, but his plan had also been ridiculously convoluted. She lived with him. He presumably could have slipped poison into her wine at any moment and blamed the whole thing on a sudden, tragic illness. For the same reason, I was disinclined to believe anyone under his roof, either family member or slave, was responsible for Tertia's death. Which wasn't to say we would discount the possibility entirely, just that our questioning that direction was probably unlikely to lead anywhere. And Atreus and I were experts at following trails that led nowhere.

Piso rambled a little as he spoke; he was still in shock. He talked about how Atria Galla and the female slaves had washed and dressed Tertia's body, as was the custom, and had laid her first on the ground—just as she had been at birth—and then on a couch in the atrium where she would remain until burial. The libitinarii from Cumae had been sent for, and would apply cosmetics to her face to disguise the pallor of death. Still, the cremation would have to be held before her sisters, Calpurnia Prima and Calpurnia

Secunda, had time to arrive from Rome. The sisters might have been named by some old traditionalist, labelled in order of delivery like amphorae stacked in a storeroom, but the way Piso spoke of Tertia, it was clear she had been loved and adored. A few times, he spoke of things she'd done while growing up, things that almost made him smile before reality caught up with him and he was jolted back into shock and disbelief.

"She had—" He shook his head. "When she was little, whenever we came to Baiae, she used to collect shells and paint faces on them. She would turn them into strange, grinning creatures and line them up in her room. I thought she'd grown out of it, but last week a new one found its way onto my desk."

"And she had no boyfriend that you know of, sir?" Atreus asked gently. "Or no interest in that direction?"

Piso shook his head, his eyes damp. "No. Well, there has been interest back in Rome, of course. She is a Calpurnii. But nothing too serious yet. There are—there *were*—no negotiations in place. As for boyfriends?" He wiped a hand over his eyes and shook his head. "No, none that I am aware of."

He seemed less sure than last night, but hours staring bleakly at his sister's corpse must have challenged most of his beliefs.

"I asked my wife," he said. "They were close. Atria says she also doesn't think so, but they had different friend groups. Tertia had more friends here than Atria does."

"Why is that, sir?" Atreus asked.

"Oh," Piso said. "Don't you know? Atria is plebeian. We have been married for a decade, and she is no longer frozen out in Rome for her low birth, or at least there are enough people there that we have lost old friends over it and been able to make no shortage of new ones, but here in Baiae some of the women can be vicious about such things." His mouth gave a wry, bitter twist. "Not vicious enough to turn down invitations to dinner, of course."

A plebeian wife. Why hadn't I heard of that scandalous bit of gossip before? Probably because I would have been a teenager when Piso had married, and couldn't have given less of a shit about anything or anyone apart from myself. And, since then, Piso had become one of Nero's closest friends, and presumably everyone in Rome was smart enough to see which way the wind blew for him and shut their mouth about his wife's lowborn origins.

"Of course," I agreed. "So here in Baiae, Tertia ran in different social circles than your wife?"

Piso nodded and then gestured at Atreus and his wax tablet. "Yes. Her friends might know more than Atria and me." His face grew haunted again. "We ought not have come here. If we had only stayed in Rome. But she was so happy here. We all were."

I reached out and clasped his arm. "I'm sorry for your loss, Piso. Atreus and I will do everything we can to find the man responsible."

The rest went unsaid, but I knew we both heard it: *For what good it will do.*

Finding Tertia's killer wouldn't heal the injury he had done to Piso and his family, and of course to Tertia herself. But in an imperfect world—and what world was more flawed than one in which young women were strangled in the street?—it was the only consolation I could offer.

Piso nodded. "Thank you."

He drank a sip of his wine at last, and then pushed himself to his feet and left.

His absence did not lighten my mood. His grief, so freely shared, now fell heavily on my shoulders too. I finished the wine Piso hadn't, and stared out into the atrium. I thought of Calpurnia Tertia, lying on a couch in Piso's atrium next door, her eyes closed, her hair braided, herbs and flowers tucked in around her to hide the smell of death over the coming days.

"More wine," I called out, knowing there would be a slave lurking nearby.

Atreus set his tablet and stylus down on the table. "No. We're going for a walk."

"That doesn't sound like a practical way to indulge in some well-earned misery," I pointed out.

"It's not," he agreed. "Iris! Lucilla! Aulus!"

It was a short walk to the shorefront; we were surrounded by it, but Atreus had done his research, because partway along the narrow band of land that curved back towards town, there was a path down to a small, rocky beach. Lucilla and Mouse were delighted to get out of the villa and get their feet wet. So was Iris, who stood in the shallows with a parasol in her hand and a shy smile on her scarred face.

Atreus and I sat on the beach and ate bread and cheese and olives, and the sunlight beat down on my shoulders and warmed me through. The wine we drank was very watered down, and not at all as strong as the sort I'd been intending to guzzle.

An approaching boat was at first a distant smudge on the horizon, but it grew larger and larger as it approached the harbour.

The breeze was brisk and tasted like salt on my lips.

"This was a better idea than getting drunk," I admitted at last, and Atreus just threw me one of those looks. The ones that said *You're an idiot, but I like you anyway*. "She was Julia's age. Still a girl."

Atreus nodded.

"It's stupid. I didn't even know her."

"Uncle Lucius!" Lucilla came splashing out of the shallows, bearing an interesting rock. She beamed as Atreus looked suitably impressed, and then dashed back towards the water.

"It's not a moral weakness to care for others," Atreus said mildly. "Even if you don't know them."

"Atreus, I appreciate the sentiment, but I've seen you kicking heads in."

His mouth quirked. "It's true that I do tend to care less for men who want to punch me in the face when they meet me, and I have been known to respond in kind. But do you know what Piso wanted today?"

I raised my eyebrows. "To find the man who killed his sister."

"Of course. But he also wanted someone to listen." Atreus handed me another piece of bread. "And you are very good at that."

"So are you," I said.

He smiled. "I can't be that friend to men of Piso's rank, but you can. It's why we work so well together."

"When we're not running around in the dark like a pair of fools."

He hummed. "Yes, apart from that bit."

Mouse and Lucilla splashed away in the water, and Iris laughed.

"She's not really my niece," he said at last.

"Lucilla?"

"I had a friend, growing up," Atreus said. "A best friend. Do you remember about half a decade ago when a sickness swept the Aventine?"

I shook my head, my mouth suddenly dry. "No."

Before meeting Atreus, I hadn't paid any attention to what happened in the Aventine. Why would I? I was a spoiled patrician brat who only went into neighbourhoods like the Aventine so I could feel a thrill at slumming it. I'd paid no real attention to the people who lived there. Their lives were so distant to mine we might have been living on opposite edges of the empire, instead of in the same city.

"Our families were close," Atreus said. "We'd even joined the vigiles together. We used to joke that my mother should marry his father, then we'd really be brothers. Never mind that, as far as anyone knows, my father's still kicking around out there somewhere." He snorted, and I suspected there was a lifetime of hurt and anger hidden behind the derisive sound that he would never admit. "Anyway, the sickness came, and when it was gone again, it was only me and Lucilla left. My friend had named her for me."

"How old was she?" I asked softly.

"Less than a year," he said. "She slept in a box beside my cot in the barracks for a month, before I found the apartment. And we've been there ever since. There was a distant cousin she could have gone to, some woman and her husband at Ostia, and plenty of people who told me she should have."

"That's ridiculous," I protested, even though I knew it wasn't. But even though it might have been the practical solution, it wasn't the right one. Not for Atreus, or Lucilla, and especially for the dead man who'd named his daughter after his best friend.

"Maybe," he said. "I was too proud and angry to admit it, if it was. There were plenty of times it felt like I was wrong, when I hadn't slept in days between work and looking after her. But here we are."

I watched the children playing in the water. "There are worse places to be."

He knocked his shoulder against mine. "Very true."

I didn't quite understand why he'd shared the story with me, or how it related to my feeling bad that Tertia was dead—or my immediate instinct to get drunk because of it. But perhaps it didn't. Perhaps I'd unintentionally bared my soul a little with my reaction to Piso's grief, and Atreus had simply bared his in return. Or maybe the point of Atreus's story was that we all loved and we all grieved, whether we were born on the Palatine Hill, the gutters of the Transtiberina, or anywhere and everywhere in between.

I ate a chunk of cheese and let the warmth of the sun soak through me.

Atreus would make a philosopher out of me yet.

* * *

We met the womenfolk on our return to the villa. They were quiet and dignified. We were barefoot, damp, and sweaty. Mouse and Lucilla were keen to show off their collection of shells and rocks, and Fulvia caught my gaze and smiled.

"How was it?" I asked, holding out my elbow.

She linked her arm through mine. "That poor family, Quintus. But thank you for taking Aulus out. It looks as though you all had a good time."

"It was mostly a distraction from my bad mood," I said. "Piso wants me to find out who killed Tertia."

She nodded, her brow creasing. "Be careful. Be *safe.*"

"I'll do my best."

She squeezed my arm. "You'd better."

I was looking forward to a peaceful lunch and a quiet afternoon when we got back to the villa, so that Atreus and I could plan some sort of strategy when it came to looking into Tertia's murder. Unfortunately, I hadn't taken Mad Uncle Maro into account. When we arrived home, it was to shouting and yelling. Thinking the worst, because we were usually right on that score, Atreus and I dashed toward the source of the noise, only to discover a half-grown yellow dog trying to eat an entire scroll, while two of the indoor slaves tried to prevent it. There was a man with his arm in a sling pressed up against the wall, eyes wide with fear as he watched. And, perched on the desk, Uncle Maro was quaffing a cup of wine, looking as though he quite enjoyed all the chaos.

"Ah, Quintus!" he exclaimed when he saw me. "Good news, my boy, good news. It's a stroke of luck, I tell you, but some fellow knocked on the door selling dogs, can you believe it? Apparently, they didn't want any next door, so he tried here. Anyway, I bought one!"

"You bought a dog?" I asked, as the creature released the scroll, sending the two indoor slaves tumbling onto their backsides. The dog beamed at them, skinny tail lashing, and the man with his arm in a sling pressed even further back against the wall, as though he was fervently hoping the wall, and not the dog, would swallow him.

"Oh, don't be silly, Felix!" Maro exclaimed, laughing heartily. "Look at him! He's perfectly friendly!" He swigged another mouthful of wine and then said, offhandedly, "Oh, and I also bought this gladiator."

He bought a what, now?

* * *

There was nothing like some familiar domestic chaos to settle the nerves. After first exciting them, of course. We all convened for lunch, and Maro fed the dog pieces of pork and cheese. Mouse and Lucilla were delighted to have a dog. I was already wondering how delighted they'd be when they found out it was staying in Baiae because there was no way it would be joining us for the long journey home. My untrained family was bad enough—an untrained dog would be a nightmare.

"Well, we went to pay our respects to Piso first thing, of course," Maro said, and Aunt Marcia nodded, "and then we went over to Puteoli. There's a gladiator school there, and we need trained fighters for our battle scenes."

I wasn't sure we needed battle scenes to begin with, but once Maro was on a roll, there was no stopping him, so I only nodded.

"Well, the lanista said we could watch one of the practice fights," Maro said, "and so we did. And it was Felix, and some other fellow who was big as an ox. They were clearly outmatched, weren't they, Marcia?"

Aunt Marcia nodded. "The other fellow was a secutor, and Felix is a retiarius."

I'd always personally felt the retiarius had the disadvantage in the area, armed with only a net and a trident, both of which were difficult to wield in close combat. If he missed his first shot and the other man was on him, he was in serious trouble. He also wore the least armour of any of the gladiators.

"A *new* retiarius," Maro said, and clicked his tongue disapprovingly. "And, I'll be honest, I don't see much potential there at all."

"No," Marcia agreed. "The poor thing couldn't even throw his net out properly."

"Yes, and he lost badly!" Maro exclaimed.

I let out a breath. "Maro, please tell me you didn't buy a gladiator because he got hurt and you felt sorry for him."

"What? Don't be ridiculous!" Maro said. "He wasn't hurt at all! It was a practice fight. What sort of idiot lanista hurts his gladiators in training? Do you know how much they cost, Quintus?"

"No," I said, "but you do, since you bought one."

He huffed out a breath. "Well, we'd seen fishermen casting their nets on the way there, so I thought I'd go and offer the fellow some tips."

"On account of your experience of having noticed a fisherman?"

Octavia hid a snort behind her hand.

"Oh, you can laugh all you want, both of you," Maro said grandly, "but the poor boy needed all the help he could get, trust me!"

"Go on, then." I chewed a crust of bread, exasperated at Maro's ridiculousness, but also happily distracted from my earlier misery, and warm with affection for the crazy old man.

"It went rather well, I think," Maro said. "Anyway, just before it came time to leave, the lanista was giving us a tour of the barracks, and that was when I fell down the stairs and landed on Felix. Poor fellow broke my fall, and I'm afraid I broke his arm. Of course, he's worthless to his master when he can't fight, and he was already terrible to begin with, so I offered to buy him. Seemed like the least I could do, really."

I was almost afraid to ask, but I did. "And how much did he cost you?"

"Twenty thousand denarii," Maro said.

I couldn't look at Atreus, because I was sure he was choking on his lunch right now. Felix's previous master had certainly seen Maro coming. "And what are you going to do with him? You're not thinking of starting your own gladiatorial school, are you?"

"Oh, Jupiter, no." Maro waved his hand. "I'll think of something, I expect. It might turn out he has a wealth of talents, but I suppose we won't know until his Latin improves. Can barely speak a word of it, can he, Marcia?"

"Barely a word," my aunt agreed.

"You bought a gladiator who can't fight, can't speak Latin, and, going on what I saw in the tablinum earlier, is also scared of dogs? For twenty thousand denarii?"

"Yes," Maro said, "but I have a good feeling about him, Quintus!"

I didn't. I'd owned a racehorse called Felix once, whose greatest sporting triumph was the number of charioteers he had injured or maimed. Sadly, apart from those times he was smearing charioteers along the ground of the Circus Maximus, he hadn't liked to break a sweat. So my experience with the name Felix was not a good one, and from what Maro had told me, I wasn't optimistic that was about to change. But I could allow that I felt at least a little twinge of sympathy for Felix the gladiator. He'd just been minding his own business when a crazy old man had approached him, speaking gibberish, pretending to be a fisherman, and then falling down the steps on top of him.

"And then, when we were on our way home, we ran into the fellow selling the dog," Maro said, feeding it another piece of cheese. "Aren't you a clever boy?"

Well, he'd certainly chewed through Cicero faster than I ever had.

I caught Atreus's gaze and discovered he was hiding a smile.

Yes, my family was oftentimes infuriating, and certainly a good portion of it was mad, but it was whole. And today of all days, that seemed like a thought worth holding onto.

Chapter Four

The following day, Atreus and I set about trying to speak to as many of Tertia's friends as we could. We started with her closest, Plautia Balbina. Plautia lived in a modestly extravagant house on one of the terraces of the town, close to the Baths of Mercury, where her gardens overlooked the port and the bay. The view was stunning.

She met us in her garden, an incongruous figure clad in a dark stola while all around her everything else was bright and verdant. Her mourning clothes didn't suit her any more than they suited anyone who ever had to wear them. In Plautia's case, as she was not a member of the family, she wasn't obligated to wear dark colours between now and the funeral, but it was clear that she had loved Tertia as though they shared blood.

"She was like a little sister to me," she said, her hand shaking as she lifted a cup of wine to take a delicate sip.

Plautia was hardly more than a girl herself; she could only have been in her early twenties at most. She had wide grey eyes and golden hair so skilfully tended that I couldn't tell if it was dyed or not. She wore it loose, instead of pinned up in intricate loops and curls—another sign of mourning. She was beautiful, in a soft, delicate way, like the sweet-scented lilies that bloomed in the garden.

"Had you known her long?" I asked.

Plautia nodded. "She was one of my first friends when I married and moved here. She would have lived here all year round had she been able, like me, but of course, that wasn't possible. Piso wished for her to be in Rome for most of the year, and so she was. But whenever she came here for the summer, we spent most of our time together."

"Your paterfamilias doesn't insist you should be in Rome too?" I asked.

Plautia lowered her gaze for a moment. "I am a widow, Valerius. My husband passed away last year, and he had no other living family."

Plautia was, I supposed, in an enviable position. A woman without either a husband or another male relative to act as paterfamilias was a rare thing. And she was obviously wealthy, too. She could have picked up a suitable replacement for her husband in Rome in the space of a heartbeat, but perhaps she was clever enough to realise what a gamble that could be. As it was, she was alone, but she was also free.

I was Fulvia's third husband. Her first had been awful—still was, but they were no longer married. At least, I thought he was awful, but Fulvia seemed to handle him well enough. I'd often wondered if the reason they got divorced was that he got tired of losing every argument. Her second husband, from what she had said, had been a much better man, but had unfortunately been surrounded by awful relatives. Fulvia, having no desire to subject herself to the authority of her dead husband's paterfamilias, had jumped at the chance to try her luck with me. And she must have liked the result, because she was sticking with me so far. And I was sticking with her as long as she'd have me.

"My apologies," I said, "and also my condolences."

She lowered her eyes demurely. "Thank you, Aemilius Valerius."

"Can you tell us more about Tertia?" Atrus asked. "What kind of person was she? Did she have any friends other than those her brother knew about?"

Plautia's gaze lifted again, and this time there was a stubborn tilt to her chin. "She was a sweet and virtuous girl. Are you asking me if she had a lover?"

Atreus didn't even blink. "Yes, that's what I'm asking."

Plautia's gaze widened, and she drew in a shocked breath. And then she let it out again, and deflated like an empty wineskin. "I'm sorry. I expect you have to ask these awful things. But no, she had no lovers."

"Are you sure of that?" I asked.

Plautia's mouth pressed into a line that was harder than the rest of her for a moment, and then she said, "I'm sure. There were no secrets between us."

I nodded, but Atreus creased his handsome brow in thought and said, "Did she have any secrets from her brother?"

"From Piso?" Plautia blinked rapidly for a moment, lashes fluttering like the wings of a fragile butterfly. "Well, I don't know. She didn't confide in me every conversation they had. All I can say for certain is that if she was keeping secrets from him, they were of no consequence." She spread her delicate palms. "There was nothing in her heart that anyone would have a need to hide."

Atreus nodded, but I knew he wasn't convinced. Neither was I. Plautia might have been naive, but Atreus and I were more cynical. Was there such a thing as a person alive who wasn't hiding at least a few secrets? Mine was sitting right beside me, nodding as though he agreed with Plautia. But then Tertia had been a teenager, and presumably kept away from the sort of vices that might cause her family any embarrassment, so perhaps she had led a truly faultless life. A fish kept in a marble pond would never know about all the vices of the wider ocean.

"Tertia came to visit you, the day she died," Atreus said. "Is that right?"

Plautia lifted her chin. "Yes. We saw one another most days, either here or at her house."

"Did she seem troubled? Nervous?" Atreus asked.

Plautia made a fist in her stola, tugging at the fabric roughly. Then, as if startled by her own response, she straightened her hand out and smoothed the wrinkles away. "No. I'm sorry. Had I known it was the last time we would speak…" She shook her head, the breeze catching the ends of her hair. "It all seems so unreal. She was no different than on any other day. I don't understand any of this."

A slave brought bread and oil and olives, and laid the dishes out in front of us.

Plautia drew a breath and regained her composure. "The oil is from my latifundium in Baetica."

I took a piece of bread and dipped the corner in the oil. The taste was rich and smooth. "You have a latifundium in Baetica?"

Plautia dipped her chin. "My husband left me very comfortable."

Given that we were seated in the garden of her Baian villa and she'd just mentioned an entire agricultural estate in Baetica, "comfortable" might have been underselling it. But then Plautia didn't seem like the sort of woman who would crassly mention her wealth, even if she could have bought and sold Baetica ten times over. She was too modest and shy for that.

I thought of Tertia, and wondered if perhaps she had held some secrets—something worth running into the night into an upcoming storm for—and had simply never confided them to Plautia because Plautia just wouldn't have understood. Or encouraged. When you wanted to get laid, you didn't go looking for a sympathetic ear or an accomplice in a Vestal Virgin.

"You were Tertia's best friend," I said, "but she had other friends too, yes?"

Plautia nodded.

"Were there any she was also close with?"

Atreus knew what I was getting at. He added, "A friend you didn't approve of, maybe?"

Plautia's eyes widened. "Oh. Well, I suppose…" She bit her lower lip. "Caecilia Didia is a lovely woman."

"But?" I prompted.

Plautia flushed. "Well, she can be loud, sometimes, and immodest."

Caecilia Didia was one of the friends Piso had mentioned to us, so if she was truly so immodest, she must have kept it well under wraps. And coming from Plautia, it was hard to tell if immodest meant Caecilia had fucked an entire barracks of legionaries or she had once accidentally farted at lunch. But I nodded seriously and said, "And you are not fond of Caecilia?"

Plautia looked guilty about admitting it, and she shook her head quickly and looked away. "I am not."

"I'm sure a woman like yourself has many other friends," I prompted. "Both you and Tertia."

They were young, pretty, and rich. What wasn't to like about that, especially in a place as glittering and shallow as Baiae?

"Not really," Plautia said. "Well, Tertia went to a lot of dinners and parties, of course, because her family are the Calpurnii. But I'm afraid my family is not patrician. My husband was not even an equite."

There was a lot of money in Baiae, both old and new, and the two did not always mix.

"Ah," I said. "Well, it is a new world with Nero as emperor, people say."

Plautia gazed at her lap and said, "Perhaps in Rome, but what people say and what people do in Baiae are often very different things."

It was an unexpectedly sharp remark from such a sweet and delicate young woman, and it snagged my interest immediately. "Did Piso not approve of his patrician sister being friends with you?"

"No!" she said, her head snapping up. "Piso has been nothing but kind!" Colour rose in her cheeks, and she looked down again. She cleared her throat. "He has always been very good to me and never makes me feel unwelcome, but some other people are not as nice."

The way she flushed and leapt to Piso's defence made me wonder if she had a little crush on the man. And why not? He was rich, good-looking, and, from what I could tell, had none of the attendant personality flaws that usually came hand in hand with those traits—he wasn't an arrogant arschole. He was a rare specimen indeed.

There wasn't a lot more we could get out of Plautia. She only had positive things to say about Tertia, and when we rose to leave, she reiterated them all again: how sweet she was, how kind she was, and how they were like sisters. She implored us tearfully to find her friend's killer, and I solemnly promised to do everything I could. Which, in practical terms, was a very empty promise indeed, but Plautia gave me a shaky smile as though she believed the killer was as good as caught, and Atreus and I took our leave.

"Thoughts?" I asked as we walked along the road, the brisk breeze from the ocean lifting the dust at our heels.

Atreus hummed. "None that stand out as yet."

"And there I was hoping you'd solved the murder on the strength of one vague conversation."

Atreus smiled and then stopped to look out over the bay. From here, up a few terraced roads from the shore, the bay was laid out in front of us beautifully. The sunlight sparkled like shards of glass on the blue ocean.

Boats bobbed in the sheltered harbour. Others were barely specks close to the horizon. I could see my villa from here, and Piso's—next door and probably ten times as large—and the imperial villa on the other side of Piso's. It had once belonged to Claudius, but was Nero's now.

I glanced at Atreus.

His brow was furrowed, and his gaze was fixed on the villas and, I guessed, on the tiny smudge of green that was the tree under which we'd found Tertia in the storm. He might not have had any particular thoughts when we were talking to Plautia, but I knew him well enough to see the signs that one was forming now.

A cat with half an ear missing strutted down the street like a conqueror and stopped so I could give it a scratch. I obliged, and it moved on again, tail upright.

Atreus finally pulled his attention away from the view, and we began to walk again.

Plautia's door slave had given us directions to Caecilia Didia's house, and we found our way easily enough. The house was on a narrowish plot a few streets up from Plautia's home—not a villa with expansive gardens, but more like the houses one saw at home on the Caelian Hill. It was more narrowly spaced together with its neighbours than Plautia's had been, with shared walls between their porticos. The houses in this part of town were newer and built when space was already at a premium in Baiae. Still, despite the fact it sat shoulder-to-shoulder with its neighbours, there was nothing modest about the house at all. As soon as the door slave ushered us into the atrium, we were greeted with potted palm trees, bright mosaics and frescoes, and enough statues to fill every seat in the Theatre of Pompey.

The door slave settled us in the tablinum, where we were stabbed in the back with the fronds from an aggressive fern, and a slave boy in a very short chiton and bare feet brought us wine and a tray of honey cakes that were still warm from the oven.

I dug into a honey cake and studied the fresco on the wall. It appeared to be Leda and the swan, and the swan was getting very inappropriate.

Caecilia Didia, the mistress of the house, made her dramatic entrance moments later, accompanied by the ringing of cymbals. It was so theatrical that I wouldn't have been surprised to see her lowered from the ceiling by some sort of stage mechanism. As it was, she leaned in the doorway, then the cymbals clashed again, and the sound propelled her into the tablinum.

She was not wearing a tunic and a stola. She was wearing an orange Greek peplos, pinned at both bare shoulders, with a gold belt, thin sandals with gold fastenings, and enough gold bracelets and rings that she must have had difficulty raising her arms. She rattled when she moved. The orange of her peplos was exactly the wrong shade, and it clashed with her copper curls.

"Aemilius Valerius?" she asked me, settling into a wicker chair with a clatter of jewellery.

"Yes," I said, "and Junius Atreus, who is assisting me in this matter. Thank you for seeing me."

"Well, of course!" Caecilia exclaimed, looking at me as though I was mad, and not her. "If I may be of any help at all, then of course! What do you need to know?"

"You were a friend of Tertia, is that right?"

"Yes," she said, and her expression grew distant for a moment before she blinked and shook her head. "It's just terrible. Baiae has a reputation, as we all know, but it's far safer than Rome!"

She was right about that. Baiae, unlike Rome, was only supposed to murder reputations.

"Do you spend a lot of time here?" Atreus asked.

"Oh, yes!" Caecilia exclaimed. The sunlight from the atrium glinted off her coppery hair. "My husband only comes for the summers because he has important business in Rome—the senate, you know—but I adore it here. I'm here all year round nowadays. It's where I feel closest to the divine."

I exchanged a look with Atreus. "The divine?"

"Yes," she said earnestly, and clutched her hands together. Her bangles clanked and rattled. "Where else can one be so close to the spiritual world but here in Baiae?"

Most people didn't come to Baiae looking for the gods, but Caecilia Didia didn't seem like most people.

"I hadn't considered that," I said. "And do you find Baiae to be a spiritual place?"

"Well, of course!" Her eyes brightened. "Why, this is where Aeneus entered the underworld and met with the Cumaean Sibyl! Rome herself would not have been founded if not for the sibyl!"

The sibyl had told Aeneus how to reach the underworld and speak to his dead father and, crucially, how to get back again. And then he'd gone on to found Rome, but that wasn't the last anyone ever heard of the sibyl. Centuries later, in the reign of the last king, Tarquinius Superbus, the Cumaean Sibyl had turned up in Rome with nine books of prophecies to sell. The king had refused, so she'd burned three. He'd refused again, so the next three went up in flames. The augurs begged him to buy the last three, which he did, and the old woman had vanished from the face of the earth. The Sibylline Books had then been kept in the Temple of Jupiter and consulted by the Senate during days of great uncertainty for the Republic. One wondered if they foresaw the temple burning down. These days, after scholars and priests had spent decades reassembling the prophecies from the fragments scattered throughout the world in different collections, the prophecies were kept in the Temple of Apollo Palatinus. Hopefully, it was more fireproof.

"What sort of person was Tertia?" I asked, thinking of the girl who painted faces on seashells.

Caecilia tilted her head and hummed. "Oh, she was a very kind girl. I can't think of anyone who would want to hurt her."

"She had no enemies you knew of?" I asked.

"Oh, Valerius!" Caecilia exclaimed. She shifted, and the neckline of her peplos gaped to reveal her cleavage. If it was an attempt at seduction, she'd entirely missed her mark. "She hardly knew a soul outside of her household. She was a dear, sweet girl, but very sheltered. No wonder she and Plautia were so close. I don't think she had many friends here in Baiae at all, apart from us ladies in the cult!"

"The cult?" I asked.

"The cult of the Cumaean Sibyl," Caecilia said brightly.

"The cult of the Cumaean Sibyl," I repeated.

Caecilia nodded, her earrings jangling. "Yes, we honour and worship the sibyl, and ask for her guidance in all things."

It wasn't the strangest thing I'd heard. The Cumaean Sibyl might not have had a place in the state pantheon, but the cult at least sounded Roman enough, by which I meant we'd stolen it from the Greeks. And Caecilia's devotion explained her choice of wardrobe and home decorations. I'd been in a cult myself once—everyone in the military had worshipped Mithras alongside our Roman gods—and as long as their aims were generally aligned with those of Rome, nobody cared. Of course, there were cults that were against Rome, and these were dangerous, but a group of women believing they could communicate with a long-dead soothsayer seemed benign enough.

"Did Piso know that Tertia was part of the cult?" I asked curiously.

"Of course!" Caecilia said. She pressed a hand to her exposed cleavage. "Tertia never would have done anything to disappoint Piso. She loved him dearly."

"So, there's nothing that happens at this cult that would anger a paterfamilias?"

Caecilia surprised me with a laugh. "Jupiter, no! We're not a bunch of wild Baccanites, running around tearing our clothes off and leaping on the first dick we find!"

I was so startled that I laughed too. Caecilia Didia was weird, but I was fast warming to her. Even Atreus allowed himself a smile.

I took another honey cake. "So what happens in this cult of yours?"

"Well, it's very personal," she said. "We descend into the underworld, where we provide offerings to the sibyl, and then she provides us with her knowledge of things that are yet to pass. It's a truly spiritual experience, and the sibyl is just so beautiful."

"Wait," I said. "You've *seen* the sibyl?"

Caecilia laughed again. "Well, of course, Valerius! The Cumaean Sibyl is as real as you or I!" And then she drew a short, excited breath, as though the thought had just occurred to her and she couldn't wait to share it. "Oh! You should ask her who killed Tertia! I'd bet that she could tell you!"

I almost choked on my honey cake.

* * *

After speaking with Caecilia Didia, Atreus and I found a shady bench outside a nearby temple and sat.

"It's a scam," Atreus said.

He was very probably right. Because, as Caecilia had happily explained things to us, the reappearance of the Cumaean Sibyl seemed less like a miracle and more like blatant bullshit. At least, it was certainly easier to consider it bullshit than to believe that the mystical soothsayer had somehow regained her youth and reappeared in the world after five hundred years. The cynic in me wouldn't allow it.

"If my recollection of Virgil is right, Aeneas had to perform certain sacrifices to Apollo and find a golden bough to present to Proserpina," I said, "and not pay a couple of aurei just to be permitted into the sibyl's presence."

We hadn't been able to pin Caecilia Didia down to an exact amount—possibly she was so wealthy she didn't care, but possibly she was unwilling to tell us in case we stomped all over the idea of her cult. Which we were currently doing, it was true, but at least we were polite enough to do it after we'd left.

"Religion is always about paying," I said. "You pay the gods with a sacrifice, and you might slip the priests a little extra to jump the queue, or make sure that the smoke from your burnt offering reaches the highest, or just so they might petition the gods a little harder on your behalf once you've toddled off home again. But someone's getting very rich off the ladies of Baiae indeed."

Atreus hummed. "Caecilia Didia was right about one thing, though. We should definitely ask the sibyl who killed Tertia."

"Agreed." I stretched, and my back made an unpleasant cracking sound. "But before we go searching in grottos for a five-hundred-year-old soothsayer, is it time for lunch yet?"

"A soothsayer who can tell the future, but apparently didn't tell Tertia she was in danger," Atreus reminded me.

"Well, soothsayers are an unreliable bunch. They're known for it."

He smiled. "True."

I stood. "So, lunch?"

Atreus fell into step beside me.

The early days of an investigation were always like this. We walked around until our feet were sore, and spoke to different people who told us different things, and hoped to eventually discern who was lying and about what. It was a slow and frustrating process, but much easier now that Atreus and I worked well together. In his case, that meant trusting me to ask the right questions in rich houses where he wasn't allowed the same latitude, and in my case, it meant buying a lot of meals from street vendors and greasy thermopolia.

We found a likely thermopolium closer down to the shorefront. It was busy, which was always a good sign, and appeared to be frequented equally by port labourers, local shopkeepers, and tourists. We eventually got a seat at the counter, in front of one of the steaming dolia, and I was delighted to find the fish stew was almost as delicious as the one we'd had the night of Piso's boat party. I was sure it was a lot cheaper.

"It's not the same without Juba here," I said, digging out something that looked like a tentacle and eating it.

Atreus nodded. "He's a good man to have at our backs."

The best, and I hated it. I hated it because I owed him my life, more than once, and it was obvious what I had to do to repay him. Except I was dragging my feet, because Jupiter knew I'd never find another bodyguard like him. And because there was no one I trusted more with my family's safety.

I grunted and changed the subject, even though I was the one who'd brought him up in the first place. "I'm thinking of bringing Vulso back to Rome with us when we leave."

Atreus snorted.

"What? The man is a genius."

"He really isn't," Atreus said. "He's competent. He only seems like a genius because you're comparing him to Hursa."

"That may be true." It was definitely true. "Do you think I should bring him to Rome?"

"And do what with Hursa? Nobody who knows him would buy him, and besides, you secretly like a touch of chaos in your life."

"I do not." I did, but I pretended not to. "Though you're right. Nobody would buy him, and it's not as though I could move him to any other job in the house. He'd be a disaster in the kitchen, and can you imagine the damage he'd cause if I armed him with a broom or a shovel?" I narrowed my eyes thoughtfully. "Do you need a door slave, Atreus?"

He narrowed his eyes right back. "Don't you dare."

I laughed, enjoying the fact that I could openly tease him in public. Nobody here knew us. Nobody knew that I was a patrician magistrate's assistant, and he was a lowly vigile. And certainly nobody knew that we were more than that, so much more, behind closed doors. In this moment, we were no different from any pair of friends who sat down to eat lunch together at the counter of the thermopolium. It was the sort of freedom we rarely got to enjoy.

I nudged Atreus with my shoulder. "Who else is on our list?"

He nudged his bowl along the counter to make room for his wax tablet. "Livilla Faustina and Galeria Alba."

"And do they both live here in town, or will my feet be feeling this for days to come?"

"According to Vulso, they both live here in town," Atreus said.

"You see? Vulso is a genius!"

"Only when compared with Hursa," Atreus replied, and it made me smile to find ourselves back at such a silly, familiar argument. We'd had plenty of arguments in the past, but it felt refreshing to have one that had been created as a joke and meant nothing.

"Well, that's not fair. A rock is a genius when compared with Hursa."

"Well, a rock would get less wrong," Atreus allowed.

We finished our lunch and, replenished, walked back up the slope of the street. We had a vague idea where we were going—Baiae had plenty of temples and bathhouses and other public buildings that acted as landmarks— and it was a pleasant enough day that I didn't mind the walk. We were making it because of terrible circumstances, it was true, but a part of me was pleased to have a reason to spend the day alone with Atreus. I could wrestle with my conscience about that in the middle of the night, but in the meantime, I was fulfilling my promise to Piso, and my duty to the law, and I was doing it with Atreus at my side. I'd had worse days.

Livilla Faustina's door slave advised us that she was not in. His tone was frosty, but his gaze was curious, so I offered him a sestertius to loosen his tongue. He was happy to chat after that.

"The mistress visits her friends often," he told us, eying my purse as though he was wondering what he'd have to say to get it to open again. "They're all proper ladies, and the mistress would never do anything scandalous." He shrugged his narrow shoulders and then looked back into the atrium to make sure he wasn't being overheard. "Listen, she's getting older now, and she's about as dull as dishwater, so if you're looking for gossip, you won't find anything interesting here. She weaves, she reads, and she complains to the gardener if the rows of lilies aren't planted straight."

"Is she religious?" Atreus asked.

The door slave crinkled his brow and then scratched his nose. "She prays to the household lares every night, if that's what you mean, and goes to the temples when she's supposed to."

"Hmm." I tapped my fingers on my purse thoughtfully, and his gaze was drawn to the movement. "Have she mentioned the Cumaean Sibyl?"

"No." His nose wrinkled again. "Though I did hear the master saying she needed to stop spending money on silly prophecies. Is that what you mean?"

For a man who'd told us we'd find no gossip here, he was certainly proving himself a liar.

"That's exactly what I mean," I confirmed, and deposited another sestertius into his greedy little paw. "Was the master very unhappy?"

The slave paused to consider his answer, and then he shrugged again. "I don't think so. It wasn't a fight or anything, and she brushed it right off, and then they started talking about what they wanted for lunch."

People after my own heart, clearly.

The door slave, to his disappointment and ours, didn't have any other information worth paying for, but he pointed out the way to Galeria Alba's house for us.

Galeria Alba was home, and she received us in one of the rooms off her atrium, where she was seated with several slaves. Galeria was a round-faced woman aged in her late twenties. She had mousy brown hair, dark eyes, and she was quite heavily pregnant. As soon as we asked her about the Cult of the Cumaean Sibyl, she waved the slaves away. Only one of them, an older woman with a disapproving scowl aimed in our direction, stayed.

"I'm not from here," Galeria said in a hesitant tone. "When I arrived, I didn't know anyone. But my husband imports olive oil, and was good friends with Plautia Balbina's husband, and so Plautia welcomed me into her social group." She paused and picked at the hem of her sleeve. "They are all very nice."

"Are they?" I asked, not trusting her hesitant tone.

"Yes." Her eyes widened. "There are! But I'm not a very bold person. I—I trip over my tongue more than not, and they are all so clever and well-read. When Plautia's husband passed away, I felt as though I didn't have much of a reason to be in the group anymore, and when I got pregnant, I'm afraid I used it as an excuse to stay home." She leaned forward as though divulging a great secret. "I said I was ill, even though I wasn't."

"Did you like Tertia?" I asked her.

"Yes, she was lovely," Galeria said, her lower lip trembling. "She was only a girl! I can't believe that anyone would want to hurt her."

I nodded and gave her a moment to grapple with her disbelief.

"It must have been a stranger," she said, a questioning tone to her voice as though she was hoping I would agree with her. When I didn't, she dropped her gaze for a moment before looking up again. "Nobody who knew her could have wanted to do such a thing."

"When you say Plautia welcomed you into her social group, do you mean the cult?" I asked her.

"Yes." Galeria twisted her fingers together in her lap and glanced towards her slave for reassurance. "Though the group meets more often than that, for lunch and things. I only went to see the sibyl once, and it was frightening. I had to walk down this narrow passageway in the cave, and it grew hotter and hotter, and the air smelled bad, and I was afraid I wouldn't be able to find my way out again."

"And you saw the sibyl?" I asked her, intrigued.

Galeria nodded. "Yes. She's not old like the stories say. She's young and quite pretty. But it's very disorienting. You cross the water, and it's so dark down there, so steep and narrow, and then the sibyl's cave is full of smoke—my head is swimming just thinking about it! And the priest takes your offering and asks you questions—my head was so full of the smoke that I don't even remember what I said—and then the sibyl gives you your prophecy."

"What did you give the priest as an offering?" I asked.

Galeria flushed. "Four aurei."

Four.

It was a fortune.

Her flush grew in our stunned silence. "I felt awful. I had to explain to my husband where the money had gone. He didn't punish me for it, but I almost wish he had. He was just so *disappointed*." She blinked rapidly, and I hoped for her sake that the rift between them was healed.

"And what prophecy did you get in return for that?" I asked her gently.

Galeria rubbed a hand over her pregnant belly. "She told me that in a year I would be a mother." She blinked again, and tears filled her eyes. "And that's part of what made it so frightening, don't you see? It's *real*."

* * *

"It's not real," I said when we'd left Galeria's house and were standing in the shade of an olive tree in a public garden. Our route had brought us almost back to where we'd started, near the Baths of Mercury.

"It's a scam," Atreus agreed. He tucked his thumbs into his belt and rocked back on his heels for a moment. "It doesn't take a prophetess to guess that a newly wedded woman might be pregnant within the year. Whoever the sibyl and her priests are, they're taking these women for a fortune."

"Do you think it relates to Tertia's murder?"

Atreus shook his head. "I don't know. It's too early to say anything for certain. At the moment, this sibyl business is a thread I'd like to pull on, just to see what unravels."

"Any other threads sticking out?" I asked him.

He gazed down at the harbour thoughtfully. "Not yet."

I knew from his expression that there was one starting to come loose, even if it wasn't long enough to grab hold of yet. I followed the direction of his gaze. He appeared to be looking at Piso's house, or maybe the imperial villa to the east of it, or my much more modest one to the west. Maybe he was looking at the tree we'd found Tertia under, or the row of shopfronts outside my villa, and thinking of the perfumer's son, and wondering what possessed anyone to summon the rage to try to kill another person, and to sometimes succeed.

I wasn't a stranger to killing. No man who'd served in the army was. But the men I'd killed there had been that fate had dropped in front of me. They had been enemies who would have killed me unless I'd killed them first. The same could be said for the men I'd fought at Atreus's side while hunting down killers. I couldn't imagine having the hatred inside me that the perfumer's son did, or whoever had put a cord around Tertia's neck and twisted it until she was dead. One was a crime attempted in the angry heat of the moment, and the other a crime that must have been planned beforehand in a cold and contained rage, but both seemed equally impossible to comprehend.

A flock of birds wheeled across the sky, and I wondered what an auger would make of them.

"If I remember correctly, the sibyl's grotto is on the shore of Lake Avernus," I said. "We can go there tomorrow and poke around."

Atreus nodded and then said, "Do you believe that stuff about prophecies?"

I considered it for a moment. "I believe in the Sibylline Books. But I don't believe the Cumaean Sibyl is still here."

"Wasn't she granted immortality by Apollo?"

"And wasn't there a story that she was so old and wizened towards the end that she was small enough to keep in a jar?" I asked. "If she's still around five hundred years after she sold the books to Tarquinus Superbus, she must be as tiny as a mote of dust by now, and certainly not sitting in a grotto dispensing prophecies to Baian matrons."

Atreus's mouth quirked.

"I believe that augurs can read omens," I said. "And maybe I've dropped a few coins into the hands of a street fortune teller once or twice. But I don't know. Maybe reading omens or even palms is no different than reading the winds and the tides, and we don't call fishermen fortune tellers."

"True." Atreus gave a thoughtful hum. "Why did Tertia walk towards your villa when it would have been faster to get into town by going down the road between Piso's villa and Nero's?"

I gazed down at the port. Atreus was right. Coming past my villa would have added extra time to her walk. "Because she wasn't going to town."

"It was night," Atreus said. "The port was closed. The shops were closed."

"Shit." My heart beat faster as the realisation dawned. "She was coming to see *me*."

Atreus's expression was grave. "Everyone we've spoken to so far has said that Calpurnia Tertia didn't have any secrets. But she must have had at least one she felt she needed to share with the man who is developing a reputation for finding killers."

"And someone murdered her for it," I finished for him.

We stood there for a long while in silence, and I contemplated how close Tertia had come to making it to my villa. Had she known someone was watching her? Following her? Had she sensed she was in danger when she'd set out into the awful weather?

And then Atreus's gaze sharpened, and he lifted a hand to point down at the bay. "Look."

Down in the ocean, a large bireme with a crimson sail skirted close to the entrance to the port. It was moving fast; the rowers must have been pulling in the same direction as the wind. People gathered at the shore to watch it pass, and my stomach clenched, because I knew long before it made the turn towards Port Julius who it could be.

And suddenly the murder of Tertia Calpurnia and the reappearance of the Cumaean Sibyl seemed like the least of my problems, because Agrippina, Nero's mother, had just arrived in Baiae.

Chapter Five

I would have liked to spend the afternoon digging more into Calpurnia Tertia's life, but Nero had other plans. Those plans arrived in the form of a young slave wearing a bright crimson tunic and bearing an invitation for Atreus and me to attend a commissatio at Nero's villa tonight. I wasn't necessarily in the mood for a drinking party, but an invitation from the emperor wasn't optional, and perhaps spending some time not thinking about Tertia would allow my thoughts to gather unimpeded in a sheltered corner of my mind while the rest of it was distracted with wine and song. Not that I had many thoughts as yet: I agreed with Atreus that we needed to track down the woman who was calling herself the Cumaean Sibyl, and I agreed that it was likely Tertia had been hiding a secret that she'd decided to share with me the night she was killed.

An invitation to a commissatio—an imperial commissatio, no less—meant a bath, a shave, and fresh clothes. Atreus looked good in one of the new tunics Cassia had delivered for him, and a borrowed toga. I liked to think I scrubbed up well, too, especially once I'd been appropriately shaved and buffed and plucked by one of the slaves who claimed it was his responsibility. He was another household slave who, like Vulso, I was considering taking with us when we went back to Rome. He was wasted here in Baiae, considering we rarely visited—although that might change now that I was friends with Nero. Still, it was ridiculous to keep him here in Baiae when I would get much more use out of him in Rome, though it would mean no more visits to my barber in Fish Alley, and I did enjoy those. Not so much for the shave, but for the show. Fish Alley was better than the theatre.

Atreus and I left the villa as the late afternoon shadows were beginning to lengthen. It was only a short walk to Nero's villa, so we decided to forgo the use of litters. It was a pleasant stroll, even wrapped in togas, and we stopped for a moment beside the tree where we'd found Tertia's body. In the daylight, the spot looked idyllic, the sort of place some old Greek philosopher might sit with his students and ponder the mysteries of the universe while the sea rose and fell gently behind them. It was difficult now to imagine it had been the scene of such horror.

We walked on.

"Do you think Piso will be there tonight?" Atreus asked me.

"I don't know." I considered it. "I wonder if he was even asked. Usually, you wouldn't invite a man who is still in mourning out anywhere, and they haven't even had the funeral yet, so it's expected that the family is still in seclusion. But Piso is Nero's friend. If I thought my friend could use a drink, I'd invite him. But I also wouldn't be offended if he didn't turn up, given the circumstances."

Atreus nodded, a small crease digging into his forehead just above his nose.

We passed the entrance to Piso's villa, and then crossed the tree-lined road between his villa and Nero's. As we approached, we could see several litters coming the other way from the main part of town. It confirmed to me what Atreus had said earlier—this route, and not the one past my villa, was shorter. If Tertia had been intending to meet someone in the town, she would have come this way.

As we approached the expansive walls of the imperial villa, we were greeted by smiling slaves who were set up along the way. Some were playing the flute or banging on drums. One of them tickled the strings of a lyre. Some were dancing. All of them were dressed as nymphs. When we finally reached the entrance to the villa, a man washed our feet, another man dried them, and a third provided us with soft slippers in place of our sandals. And then a girl in a yellow chiton stepped forward to welcome us and showed us into the villa.

It was immense.

Unlike Piso's villa and mine, which sat entirely on the flat land that had been reclaimed to build the port, the imperial villa was built on the terraces that began on the promontory and cascaded down towards the ocean. I was pleased to find that tonight's commissatio was to be held in the nymphaeum, a triclinium famously designed to mimic the sea cave of the cyclops without, of course, any of the usual sea cave features like dirt, seaweed, and slime. The nymphaeum was a massive rectangular room. The apse at one end was dominated by a statue of Polyphemus the cyclops, with Ulysses kneeling at his feet. On each wall leading to the apse, there were niches in which other statues stood. Some of them were fountains, with water trickling out of them that made music to compete with that of the slaves.

But the most wondrous feature of the nymphaeum was the channel of water that looped through the room in front of the marble dining couches, the current steady enough so that food could be placed on wooden platters and sailed past every diner. A man didn't just eat in the nymphaeum; he went fishing for his dinner.

Rufio met us at the entrance to the nymphaeum and clasped both our hands in greeting. "Valerius. Atreus. It's good to see you."

He led us through the marble hall to where Nero was waiting, reclining on a pile of cushions on the marble platform in front of the statues of Ulysses and Polyphemus. Nero rose when we approached, a smile warming his features.

"Valerius! Atreus! Come, you are by me."

Nero's marble platform was large enough for half a dozen men. Petronius and Lucan were already reclining on one side of him, so I took the honoured position on the emperor's other side, and Atreus lowered himself warily down on my other side. If being in the place of honour beside the emperor felt heady to me, poor Atreus must have thought he was trapped in a fever dream.

Slaves darted forward with cushions and pillows, making sure that we were comfortable.

A tray of olives floated past in the channel in front of us.

"It's awful, what happened to Calpurnia Tertia," Nero said, his brow creasing. "I asked Piso if he wanted to join us, but he declined."

"Still in the worst of it," Petronius said. "Poor bastard."

Lucan nodded, his gaze catching mine. He'd recently suffered a sudden loss, also, although one didn't publicly mourn a slave the way one mourned a sister. That didn't mean he didn't know what grief felt like, though. And Petro? Well, Petronius, I suspected, would refuse to weep for anything, just to spite the universe. Then he'd write a poem or a story so sharp, so scathing, that it would tear shreds off anyone who read it and cause them to weep instead. I liked Petro and hoped never to find myself facing the pointy end of his stylus.

"We will allow ourselves one lament," Nero said, and a nearby slave darted away upon hearing the words.

Moments later, he was back, a lyre slung across his back, holding the hand of a young woman. Both slaves wore flimsy chitons—the boy's was an exomis, fastened at his left shoulder, leaving half his chest bare. It was very short. The young woman's was only slightly more substantial. The pair waited at the edge of the room until the last of tonight's guests were settled, and then they moved forward. To my surprise, the boy stepped straight into the channel of flowing water that looped past all the marble couches, drawing in a sharp intake of breath as the cold water tickled his thighs. Then, smiling, he made a stirrup out of his hands. The young woman stepped daintily into his hands and across the water to the island in the middle of the room. Then the boy pulled himself out of the water, the hem of his chiton riding up so that it barely covered his arse, and joined her. He lifted the lyre off his back and began to play.

When she sang, the young woman had the voice of a nightingale, haunting and beautiful. No wonder Nero had said we would allow ourselves just the one lament, because the girl's song pulled on my heartstrings as deftly as the boy pulled on the strings of the lyre. Her voice led me gently towards melancholy and then back again.

There was silence in the nymphaeum when the song had ended, and the last faint strains of the lyre faded away. And then, from the other end of the room, another musician began to beat a drum, and another joined in with cymbals, and another on the pipes. From the centre island, the boy slid back down into the water, offering his hands for the young woman to cross. Instead of stepping straight over, she stood with one foot in the boy's hands and then leaned down, extending her other leg for balance, and picked up an oyster in a shell from a floating tray that had butted up against the boy's thigh. Then she finished her crossing, and knelt down and held the shell out to the boy. He swallowed the oyster down before lifting himself out of the water, sleek as a dolphin. He left damp footprints across the marble floor as he padded away holding the young woman's hand.

"Aren't they captivating?" Nero asked proudly. "Such beauty can make a man weep."

"It can also make a man drink," Petronius announced, and a slave hurried forward to fill his cup.

"How do you put such sublime words on the page when you are such a boor?" Nero asked, his eyes bright with laughter.

Petronius raised his cup in a silent toast. "I like to think of myself as proof the gods have a sense of humour."

Even Lucan snorted out a laugh at that.

I reached out and nabbed a chunk of cheese as a wooden tray floated past.

Petronius regaled us with stories from the Satyricon, and it was impossible to tell if he'd imagined the wild events or if they had been built on truth. All of Rome loved to speculate, and Petronius knew it. He was far too clever to admit whether his characters were based on real people or not. If everyone was afraid they would be satirised, it kept them hungry for his next instalment of the adventures of Encolpius and Giton.

Lucan was still working on the Pharsalia, his epic retelling of Caesar, Pompey, and the civil war. His work was serious and majestic, while Petro's was bawdy and cutting, but they were both works of genius. Two very different sorts of genius, it was true. Petronius had once told me that Lucan wasn't the greatest poet in Rome—not *yet*, but he would be, and I saw no reason to doubt his assessment. He wasn't even envious of the fact that Lucan would one day surpass him. As far as I could tell, Petronius was so sure of himself that he was a complete stranger to jealousy. It was rare and refreshing to meet a man as honest as Petronius, and especially when one found him reclining at the side of an emperor. But Petronius cared for art, not politics. Lucan was perhaps more political—he was Seneca's nephew, after all, and Seneca at one time had lived and breathed the politics of the imperial court—but I had never seen any reason to doubt his friendship with Nero was anything but genuine.

"I had hoped Piso would come," I said, bringing the conversation back around. "He's asked me to see if I can find out what happened to Tertia, but I know very little about her."

Petronius hummed. "Last I saw her—apart from the other night, of course—she was just a little slip of a girl, and I didn't pay her much mind at all."

"You saw her a few times since she was a child," Lucan chided.

"Well, she didn't make an impression, then."

"Of course she didn't," Nero said, rolling his eyes. "A quiet girl like that. Even if she'd made a peep, who would have heard her in the same room as you?" He held his hand up and used it to mimic a talking mouth. "Who can get a word in edgeways?"

"It's true," Petronius said with a laugh. "I am the loudest man in a crowd!"

Nero rolled his eyes and looked at me. "She was young, and she was quiet, and Piso knew better than to invite her around this crowd. But I dined in private at his villa many times, just Rufio and I."

"Just the two of you?" I asked, intrigued. I had thought it strange enough at the boat party, when Nero had left all the Praetorians except Rufio on the shore, but at least they'd been with him for the short journey between the villas. Then I thought of how I'd first met Nero, on the Milvian bridge, trying his hardest to blend in with the crowd. Perhaps in Piso's villa, he didn't have to feel like the emperor for a few hours.

"Piso is one of my closest friends," Nero confirmed. "I've known him for much longer than all *this*." He plucked at his purple toga almost disdainfully. "Anyway, Tertia was sometimes there. She painted—" His brow creased. "What was it? Shells, yes. She painted shells."

"She showed you them?" I asked.

"No, but Piso did." Nero's smile was tinged with sadness. "He loved her very much."

"It's a tragedy," I murmured.

"Will you find who killed her?" he asked, his gaze suddenly intent.

"I aim to," I said. "I pray that I can."

I hadn't actually prayed for that yet, but perhaps a visit to a temple wouldn't be out of place. A couple of chickens or a pig might incline the gods to think favourably upon me.

Nero reached out and clasped my shoulder. "Piso deserves answers and, more than that, Tertia deserves justice." He smiled. "Now, drink more wine. Tonight is for joy. Sadness can wait for the dawn."

It was an imperial order. What else was I going to do?

The wine, of course, was the highest quality. Not just the immortal Falernian but also Surrentium, the grapes grown in nearby vineyards. The food was equally fine: seafood, of course, because one always ate seafood in Baiae, but also stuffed eggs, pork cooked in honey, and goat's cheese wrapped in pastry and fried. This was a commissatio, and every morsel of food was designed to be plucked easily from a floating wooden tray, although as the wine consumption increased, so did the chance of a clumsy touch scuppering a tray.

As the musicians played more cheerful music, tumblers and jugglers appeared, moving throughout the room to entertain the guests. A pair of them leaped to the middle island and began to grapple together, rolling and jumping. The conversation flowed as freely as the wine, and I even caught Atreus smiling and laughing when I knew that it was difficult for him to relax in company as esteemed as this. And yet here he was, a man who had to count his coins carefully in order to pay his rent, reclining on the same platform as the emperor himself. It should have been unthinkable, but Nero did not elevate men because of their rank or fortune. He measured value in other ways, and Rome was better for it.

The night grew old. Men who had drunk too much were removed by the slaves, to be taken outside and bundled into their litters for a jolting ride home. Those of us who had learned to pace ourselves were here for the long haul, and the commissatio eventually moved from the spectacular nymphaeum into a nearby sitting room, where the couches were more comfortable than marble, and the tone more intimate. We could call across the room here without having to shout, and our words weren't lost to echoes or to the tinkling of the water.

Rufio joined us this time, and we talked a little about my time in the east with Corbulo. Rufio had never served in the provinces, where the borders of the empire came to an end. As a Praetorian, he went wherever Nero did, and most of his duties were in Rome. I learned that he was an equite, and that his father was the procurator in Pannonia.

"He's buttering you up," Atreus said in an undertone when Rufio left us to join some other conversation.

"What are you talking about?"

"He's selling himself," Atreus said, raising his eyebrows. "He's hoping to become your next brother-in-law."

"Then he needs to sell himself to Octavia, not to me," I said.

"He'll figure that out," Atreus said. "He's smart. He's just testing the water for now, to see if you'd care that he's not patrician."

"His father's a procurator, and he's a Praetorian," I said. "Who would object to that? Besides, this is a new world. Patrician, equite, or plebeian, Nero doesn't care, and neither do I."

Atreus, living proof of that, gave me a wry smile and raised his glass.

As Octavia's paterfamilias, I could approve or disapprove of any marriage that she was offered. In theory, at least. In practice, that wasn't how things worked under my roof. Octavia was divorced, and she was independently wealthy, thanks to the fortune left to her by her ex, so unless I was willing to drag her kicking and screaming to the marriage altar—and I was not, to be clear—then there was no way I could force her to marry. Octavia also had a mind and opinions of her own, and she wasn't afraid to share either of them. Things might become complicated if she wished to marry a man who was entirely unsuitable, but Octavia was sensible enough that I trusted that wouldn't happen. She wasn't going to throw away her reputation for some oily gladiator. In that eventuality, she would, like all sensible women before her, marry some old senator who could no longer get it up, and entertain her oily gladiator in secret. It was the patrician way.

The slave boy who'd played the lyre slipped into the room, a cheeky grin on his face and a tray of honey cakes in his hands. I waved him away, too full to eat anything else, and he went and perched on the edge of Petronius's couch. Petronius gave him a suspicious look, and the boy's grin grew. Petro did love cheeky boys who flirted, but if it was turning into that sort of a party, it was probably time that Atreus and I left and headed home. Not because I was a prude, but because it was highly doubtful that I'd be interested in anything on offer. Like that patrician wife with a gladiator, my vices could only be indulged in secret.

I didn't think of Atreus as a vice, not in my heart, but I would be ruined just the same if the truth came out.

I caught his gaze and saw that he'd read the situation just as I had. Regretfully, it was time to leave.

Which was exactly when we heard the commotion: hobnailed sandals on marble and raised voices coming closer. The woman swept into the room before any of us could even rise.

"—to see my own *son!*"

She was imperious. Of course she was. She'd been born to the purple. Born to it, then married to it, then birthed it. It was dyed into the marrow her bones.

Agrippina.

She was not a beautiful woman; her features were perhaps a touch too severe for that, but she was striking. She carried herself proudly, her chin up and her shoulders back. Her dark curls framed her face. She wore a deep green stola and a blue palla, but she could have been dressed in a threadbare tunic with rags wrapped around her feet and looked just as commanding. She was the great-granddaughter of Augustus, and the tilt of her chin dared every man in the room not to forget it.

The Praetorian chasing after her—it was Celer, Rufio's scowling not-brother in arms—fell back as she stepped through the door, and who could blame him? What man would dare tell Agrippina she wasn't allowed in a room? What man would dare put his hands on the emperor's mother?

My blood ran cold as her gaze travelled over the room. I glanced over at Nero and couldn't read his expression as he rose from his couch.

"Mother," he said at last, holding out his hands. "What are you doing here?"

"Am I not permitted to see my own son?" She glided across the floor towards him.

Rufio rose too and went to stand at Nero's side.

Nobody said anything. Even Petro kept his mouth shut, which had to be some sort of event previously unwitnessed by nature and the gods. The slave boy shrank closer to his side.

"Of course you are." Nero took her hands and leaned in to kiss her on the cheek. "What nonsense. Of course you are."

If Agrippina heard the way his words rang hollow, her smile gave no indication of it.

She was a snake. When Nero had wanted to be free of her strangling coils, Atreus and I had given him the leverage he needed—a corrupt legion and a silver mine the imperial treasury didn't know about. And now here she was again, and only time would tell if she could wrap herself around him again, and if he would let it happen. Because she was a snake, but she was also his mother.

He led her towards his couch. She didn't recline. She sat, legs stretched out, her slender ankles crossed. A slave scurried forward with a glass of wine, and she drank.

"Ah, your poets are here," she said, her gaze falling on Petronius and Lucan before it travelled to me and Atreus. "And so is Aemilius Valerius and his vigile."

Of course she knew my name. That she knew my face as well was chilling, because we had never met.

Her gentle smile hardened as she looked me in the eye and said, "And how is your dear sister Octavia Junilla?"

Atreus's hand gripped my forearm tightly. Maybe he thought I was about to do something stupid like raise a hand to Agrippina. Maybe I was. But his fingers dug in, hidden under the fall of my toga, keeping me anchored to the spot while the roar of blood in my skull crashed like the ocean and threatened to sweep me away.

"She is well," I said, forcing an answering smile onto my numb face. "Thank you for your concern."

Nero cast a narrow look at Agrippina, more exasperated than anything. It was the typical expression of a young man annoyed at a parent overstepping again, as though she'd crashed his drinking party and was telling all his friends some embarrassing story of his childhood instead of making veiled threats against their family members. But then, perhaps she did it so often that exasperation was all he could muster. There was no way that Nero's experiences with his mother could be judged by any typical measuring stick.

Or maybe he just knew better than to show fear in front of a snake.

I wished Atreus and I had left when I'd first wanted. We might have avoided Agrippina if we had, but now we were stuck here, because to leave would draw even more of her attention. I sipped my wine and caught Rufio's gaze. His expression was strained, his mouth a thin, hard line.

Agrippina was charming. She asked Petronius about the theatre, and Lucan about his poems, and smiled and laughed at the responses they gave. She caught Nero's hand and squeezed it, the doting mother, and all I could think about was how much this woman hated me and Atreus and Octavia, and how she absolutely had the power to destroy my entire family. Anicetus had warned me not to underestimate her, and I didn't.

The audience with Agrippina—and it was theatre, make no mistake—was excruciating. It felt like hours before she rose, and Nero rose with her, and he excused himself to go and speak with her in private. Rufio made to follow after Nero, but the emperor lifted his hand and shook his head. Rufio didn't look happy about it, but nodded sharply and then hurried back to Atreus and me.

"You'd best go," he said. We were already moving.

"Are we in danger?" I dared to ask him.

His mouth twisted. "Don't ask me that, Valerius, please."

But he was ushering us towards the exit, the brilliant mosaics flashing beneath our feet as he hurried us, so I knew that his actions were worth more than his words. We were very clearly in danger, and Rufio was doing his best to get us safely home. He delivered us into the custody of a pair of armed Praetorians. One of them was Celer.

"See that you accompany Aemilius Valerius to his front door," he said.

"Is this on the emperor's orders?" Celer asked, jutting out his chin.

"Of course," Rufio said, although no such order had been given in my hearing. "And see that the Germans don't follow."

The Numerus Batavorum. The guard had been created in Augustus's day. If the Praetorians were the emperor's soldiers, then the Germans were his personal bodyguard. Given that Caligula, Nero's uncle and Agrippina's brother, had been assassinated by the Praetorians in order to install Claudius in his place, it was little wonder that they looked outside of Rome for bodyguards. The Germans, drawn from tribes such as the Batavi, the Frisii, and the Ubii, had no loyalty to the senate. Their only loyalty was to the emperor. I wondered how things stood with them now, given some of them guarded Agrippina and some of them guarded Nero, and what sort of interesting conversations they had over dinner in their barracks. Rufio didn't seem to doubt that Agrippina's Germans were loyal to her, though, since he'd ordered his Praetorians to watch out for them as they escorted Atreus and me home.

It was a chilling end to what had been an enjoyable commissatio.

It was a beautiful night, and had I not been anticipating the feeling of a blade between my ribs at any moment, I might have enjoyed the walk. The moon slipped behind playful wisps of clouds, and the light shone silver on the water. The cool, fresh air tasted of salt. The fate of all men was written in the glittering field of stars that spread across the sky.

The Praetorians walked with us past Piso's villa and to my own front door and watched with their hands on the pommels of their gladiuses as Vulso admitted us. Vulso's eyes bulged as he saw them lurking in the street, and he squeaked and took a step back.

I raised my hand to acknowledge the Praetorians, and they melted back into the darkness.

Vulso closed and bolted the door behind us, and I let out the breath it felt like I'd been holding since we'd left Nero's villa. From beyond the atrium, I could hear the rise and fall of voices. The family was still awake. I squared my shoulders, adjusted the fall of my toga, and prepared to go and meet them and tell them that I wanted them to go back to Rome. If I looked sombre and dignified, the picture of Roman nobility and authority, they'd have to listen, right?

And so I swept into the informal triclinium, grave and serious, and opened my mouth to greet them when the fucking dog launched at me and took me out at the knees.

* * *

"Ow," I said, blinking in the lamplight. Then I added, "Fuck."

"Give him some air," Atreus said, kneeling beside me and holding a cloth to my head. It took me a moment to realise it was because I was bleeding.

"Did the dog try to kill me?" I asked. I wasn't entirely sure how I'd ended up on the floor. My last memory had been a flash of yellow movement, and suddenly my legs weren't under me anymore, and I was treated to a close inspection of the informal triclinium's mosaics. Lovely work. Blurry though.

"Up," Atreus said, and the world shifted alarmingly as he and someone else lifted me so that I was sitting on a couch.

"You've got blood all over your toga," said the someone else helpfully. It was Maro.

"Yes, Maro. Thank you." I took over the stewardship of the cloth, nudging Atreus's hand away. My head throbbed gently along with my heartbeat, but the bleeding had stopped, so I set the cloth aside. "Well, if that doesn't sum up our evening, I don't know what does."

Atreus hummed his agreement.

I squinted past the cloth. "The dog is eating someone's dinner."

Julia shrieked, flapping her hands in the dog's direction, and the dog skedaddled.

With the dog gone, Julia pushed the remnants of her dinner away, her pretty face screwed up unhappily. Her expression shifted into one of concern when her gaze met mine. "Oh, at least the bleeding has stopped!"

"Hmm." I would have nodded except that would do my throbbing skull no favours.

Fulvia sat beside me on the couch, reaching for my hand and holding it between her own. "Are you alright, Quintus?"

Atreus rose to his feet and stepped away from the couch I was sitting on with Fulvia. It was something he did when we were with my family—putting deliberate space between us. I didn't like it, but I understood it.

I drew a breath and said to Fulvia, "I want you to go home." I looked around the room at each of them: Uncle Maro, Aunt Marcia, Octavia, and Julia. "All of you, and the children too. I want you to get out of Baiae and go back to Rome."

Instead of murmurs of agreement, nothing but silence greeted my announcement.

So much for being the respected paterfamilias.

I stared at my family, and my family stared back at me. Atreus folded his arms across his chest. The dog slipped inside the room again, its tail lashing hopefully.

Uncle Maro's bushy eyebrows did a complicated dance. "I'm sorry, Quintus. Can you say that again?" And he tugged at the hair growing out of his ears as though it had prevented him from hearing me. "Did you say you want us to return to Rome?"

"Yes," I said. "Because tonight I met Agrippina, and she asked how Octavia was."

Octavia raised her eyebrows, her gaze steady. "How polite."

Julia blinked a few times. "I don't understand."

Of course she didn't. Julia was still little more than a child. But everyone else in the triclinium knew a veiled threat when they heard one. And Agrippina could make a comment on the weather that would have hardened legionaries checking their wills were up to date.

Maro fluttered his hands, shifting in his seat like a wet bird trying to dry itself. "Well, I am arranging a dinner!"

"Maro," I said. There was no humour in my tone, when usually I had an abundance for the old man. He might have been thirty years older than I was, but I was still the head of this family, and we both knew it. I'd never pushed Maro before. I'd never had to. But his safety was at stake.

"The new silk napkins have already been ordered!" he fretted, and Aunt Marcia patted his arm sympathetically.

Fulvia and Octavia exchanged glances that said more than words, and I knew that the mutiny in the ranks would come from either one of them. It didn't surprise me that it was Octavia.

She leaned forward, the bangles on her wrist rattling as she adjusted the fall of her tunic. "And what about you and Atreus?"

"The emperor invited us," I said. I knew she was setting a trap, but I wasn't smart enough to see it yet. "We have to stay."

Octavia nodded. "And the rest of us would be safer in Rome, yes?"

"Of course."

She raised her eyebrows. "And what about the week it takes us to get home? On the road, or in an unfamiliar stabula every night? Do you really think that Juba could defend all of us, all of the time?"

I looked over to the doorway, to where the man himself was standing. Juba was massive, with muscles that could crack walnuts. He might have been comparable in size to the mythical Argus, but he didn't have the giant's hundred watchful eyes. And even those hadn't helped Argus in the end. He'd still got himself murdered, hadn't he?

I didn't doubt Juba's loyalty, not for a heartbeat, but he couldn't protect everyone.

Fulvia's voice was tempered with understanding, but it was still a voice of dissent. "I think Octavia is right, Quintus. If we are unsafe, the worst thing we could do is to travel. At least here, if the Praetorians come to break the doors down, our neighbours will know the truth of it."

"It won't be the Praetorians," I said, my voice rough. "It'll be the Numerus Batavorum."

Fulvia blanched slightly, as though the clarification made the scenario suddenly more real. Her hand shook in mine, but she lifted her chin as she said, "The Numerus Batavorum, then."

Juno's tits. Nothing was going to dissuade them. And the worst thing was, they were right. Well, not Maro, who could hold a dinner party anywhere, but Octavia and Fulvia. Baiae was dangerous as long as Agrippina was here, and her thoughts were turned towards me, but sending my family back to Rome would only give any attackers a better opportunity to strike, and I should have spotted that earlier. I blamed the shock of seeing Agripina for muddling my thoughts, and the dog knocking me down had only further rattled my brain in my skull. When it came to strategy, I had actual military experience learned at the right hand of the famed general Corbulo. I should not have been outthought by my sister and my wife, but then both of them had the uncanny ability to make me feel as thick as an elephant omelette. Which, in fairness, was sometimes deserved.

Tonight, though, it wasn't. If I'd panicked, it was only because I was scared for them. And I didn't appreciate their gentle condescension. Which may not have been condescension at all, but my pride was bruised, and I pulled my hand from Fulvia's and said, "I'm sure the distinction won't matter too much when we're all bleeding out on the floor of the atrium with knives in our guts."

And then, because I was a coward, I stood and stormed out of the room.

"Let him go," I heard Fulvia say, her voice still calm, and I hated her a little for it. If I was panicked and afraid, why weren't they? Didn't they know how serious this was?

My anger had worn off by the time I made it into the gardens. It had been a brief spark, nothing more. An abortive flame with no fuel. As it faded away, the night seemed cold, and I sat in the darkness under the spreading branches of a tree and felt foolish and ridiculous.

I tried blaming the dog again, or the wine I'd drunk at dinner, but it didn't work. I had nobody to blame but myself. The Stoics would have told me that I needed to keep a better control of my irrational emotions, but fuck those guys. Were their families being threatened?

A blur of movement beside me resolved into the yellow dog. He was kindly delivering me a scroll. I took it off him, squinting in the darkness to read the tag.

"I prefer my Cicero with fewer holes in it," I said, and patted him on the head.

He sat beside me, panting happily, then dropped down and rested his chin on my knee. I scratched him behind the ears.

"I wasn't wrong to react the way I did," I told the dog. "She is dangerous."

The dog drooled in what I took to be agreement.

Soft footsteps alerted me to Atreus's approach a moment before he sat down beside me. He curled his fingers around the back of my neck, the gentle pressure making me feel like a kitten held by the scruff. And maybe I should have spat and yowled, but I didn't. It felt good. Solid. Atreus had my back.

"You're upset," he said in a low voice. "And still a little drunk from dinner."

"But I'm not wrong."

"No, you're not wrong to be afraid for your family. But you were wrong to leave things the way you did."

I let out a long breath. "I'll apologise in the morning."

He rewarded me with a stroke of his thumb against my nape. "Good."

"I don't like being afraid. No. It's not that. Of course I don't like it, because nobody does, but it's not the fear. It's that the fear comes from being powerless, like a bug waiting to be squashed underfoot. She's the emperor's mother. She's killed more important men than me."

He hummed his agreement. "If you were truly a bug, you'd know the best thing to do is burrow down in the dirt and stay there, and pray to the gods that foot lands somewhere else."

I snorted. "That's your advice?"

"I was born in the Aventine, Valerius. I know a thing or two about keeping my head down."

"Do you?" I asked. "The same man who went after the gangster Bano and almost got us both killed for his trouble?"

"I mostly keep my head down," he clarified, and I could hear the smile in his voice.

I thought of walking through the Aventine when Atreus had been hunting

Bano, and vice versa. People had whispered at Atreus behind his back and pointed at him as he passed, telling themselves, and everyone else in the Aventine, that he was a dead man. He must have felt then how I did now. I'd admired his courage, but perhaps it hadn't been courage after all. Perhaps it had just been the knowledge that there had been nowhere to run.

The dog yawned, its head still resting on my knee, and then began to snore.

"So we're all staying in Baiae, then," I muttered.

"Hmm. At least Maro can keep planning his dinner party."

"Well, thank Jupiter for that. The real tragedy wouldn't be Agrippina murdering me and my entire family, it would be that Maro didn't get to hold his dinner party with gladiators and actors."

Atreus squeezed my neck again, his smile softening his tone. "Exactly."

"I'm sorry I brought you here," I said. "And Lucilla too."

"You didn't bring me," he replied. "You just reminded me that I'd be a fool to decline an invitation from the emperor himself."

"And do you still think I'm right about that?"

He was silent for a moment, and then he said, "I think that my life would be much simpler if Nero didn't know my name, but I'm not sorry for anything that has brought me here with you."

Warmth flared in my chest. "So now all we need to do is discover a way to survive Agrippina's wrath."

"It's almost as though we need someone who can see the future."

It took me a moment to realise what he meant, and I laughed for what felt like the first time in hours. "You mean the Cumaean Sibyl."

Atreus nodded.

I jabbed him in the ribs with the chewed scroll. "Yes. We'll keep doing what we always do. We've been charged to find out who killed Calpurnia Tertia. So what if we need to watch our backs? There's nothing new about that, is there?"

It was all false bravado ringing loudly from an empty vessel, but it was enough to lift my spirits for now and to convince myself to keep moving forwards. Because what else could we do? And at least I had Atreus by my side, and at my back when it counted, and we owed it to Nero, to Piso, to ourselves, and most of all to Calpurnia Tertia, to find her killer.

And as for Agrippina, all we could do was hope that she'd be distracted by another, shinier bug, and forget all about us for a while.

Chapter Six

Caecilia Didia was delighted to see Atreus and me again. She welcomed us into her home and took us through to the garden. Then she rang a little bell, and barefoot slaves came hurrying with fruit and nuts, cakes and cheese, and sweet watered-down wine. The food and wine were enough to kill the remnants of last night's hangover that breakfast hadn't managed to entirely vanquish. We sat on marble benches strewn with cushions, under the shade of a fabric awning that fluttered in the breeze, whipping and billowing like a sail. A fountain tinkled nearby, and the raucous calls of at least a dozen caged parrots interrupted the peace. A boy attended each of the cages as we ate, sweeping them out with a little brush and pan, and refilling the parrots' seeds and water.

"Aren't they lovely?" Caecilia asked, gazing at the shrieking birds adoringly. "They bring such brightness to the garden!"

They brought ear-splitting noise and the smell of bird shit, but I smiled and nodded anyway. "They are certainly very colourful."

Caecilia beamed and folded her hands on her lap. She was dressed in her customary peplos. Today's was yellow, not orange, but it still managed to clash with her dyed red hair.

"Caecilia Didia," Atreus said, ignoring the screech of a bird, "we were hoping that you could tell us more about the Cult of the Cumaean Sibyl."

She blinked at us. "Oh, well, I'm not sure!" She pressed a hand to her bosom and laughed so brightly that even the parrots shut up for a moment. "It's a cult for women, and all cults must have their mysteries!"

Probably to prevent their husbands from finding out they were being fleeced, I thought, although she wasn't wrong about the secrecy. I'd been in a cult before, and I was well acquainted with hidden rituals, clandestine meeting places, and the use of symbols and icons that could only be read by the initiated. That was half the attraction, to be honest—being part of an exclusive group of people that not everyone was allowed to join. Plus, in the military, almost every soldier had worshipped Mithras. You put him on like your helmet and greaves, and then packed him away again when you were safely back in Rome.

Atreus gave her an encouraging smile. "Well, maybe you could tell us where you meet with her, and we can see if she will speak to us. When we were here yesterday, you suggested we should ask her, after all."

"Oh, I *did* say that!" She blinked and nodded. "Well, I don't know, not really. I mean, of course, I know where to find her the times we meet—in her grotto! But…" Her brow creased. "Well, some months ago, I was in need of guidance, and when I went to the grotto, there was nobody there."

She sounded perplexed, as though it hadn't occurred to her why her mystical seer wasn't tucked up in a cave all the time. Which I supposed wasn't unreasonable for a prophetess with one foot in this world and one foot in the next. But what if your prophetess wasn't immortal after all, and just happened to be a very human woman who needed to eat, sleep, and piss like the rest of us? Of course she hadn't been in her grotto where Caecilia had expected to find her.

"We spoke to Galeria," I said. "She mentioned that it costs quite a lot of money to visit the Sibyl."

Caecilia clicked her tongue. "Well, yes, but what's mere money, Valerius, when she is offering you the *future?*"

I nodded, trying to keep my expression serious and understanding. I couldn't look at Atreus, afraid that if I saw my cynicism reflected in his gaze—and I knew that I would—that I wouldn't be able to keep the mask on. His cynicism would be tinged with disdain, I was sure, because Atreus kept track of every quadrans that he earned in order to pay his rent, and Caecilia's carelessness with money would annoy him no end. It almost annoyed me, and I was rich.

"Does the cult meet regularly?" I asked.

"Quite often," she said. "Once a month, at least. One of her acolytes visits to let us know. Charming young man. A little rough around the edges, I suppose, but he's very respectful."

"Do you know his name?" I asked.

"Oh, yes." She flashed me a brilliant smile and, thanks to the way she leaned forward again, half a breast. "His name is Mino, and he works at the Baths of Mercury."

This time, I couldn't help it—I exchanged a dubious look with Atreus.

Well, maybe the Cumaean Sibyl wasn't making as much money as we'd initially thought, if her acolytes had day jobs. What had happened to all the aurei the cult was getting every month from Caecilia and her friends? Maybe it was all siphoned straight into the cult's overheads. What *was* the going rate for the rent of a mystical grotto anyway?

A bird shrieked, and then the slave did, and Caecilia leapt up from her seat and hurried towards the ruckus. "What have I told you about poking your finger in his cage, you foolish boy?"

The boy blubbered.

Caecilia tsked. "Come and get a honey cake, then get back to work."

She led him over to the table, pointing out which of the snacks he could have. His tears dried as he loaded up on honey cakes, grapes, and cheese.

"Better?" Caecilia asked, her tone exasperated but fond.

The boy sniffled and nodded. "Thank you, domina."

"Go on, then." She flapped his hand at him as though he was a fly hovering over the table, then took her seat as she watched him scarper away. "I've told him a hundred times!"

I couldn't quite make up my mind about Caecilia. There were parts of her I liked—her crassness, and her kindness—and parts of her I didn't—her gaudy fashion sense and her parrots—and parts of her that I just didn't understand. She didn't seem like a stupid woman, so why in Tartarus did she believe this bullshit about the Cumaean Sibyl? She wasn't like Plautia Balbina, young enough to still be impressionable. She wasn't like Livilla Faustina, a woman whose own slave had described her as boring, and who was possibly looking for some excitement in her life. And she wasn't like Galeria Alba, excruciatingly shy and probably lonely. I didn't understand what a woman like Caecilia was searching for, or why she thought she'd found it in the Cult of the Cumaean Sibyl.

And I wouldn't have cared, usually, because she was entitled to believe whatever she wanted to believe, and it wasn't my money she was spending. But Calpurnia Tertia was dead, and the itch at the back of my skull told me that the Cumaean Sibyl, whoever she was, had something to do with it.

I could only hope that Caecilia wasn't right, and that the sibyl wouldn't see us coming.

* * *

The Baths of Mercury, like all the buildings in Baiae, had been constructed on land that was carved out of the hillside that sloped steeply into the glittering sea. The baths themselves were in the main building of the complex, but there were other buildings too. A caupona, a gymnasium, a wine shop, plus a series of small rotundas dotted along the terraces where patrons could gather in the shade and socialise. At the back of the complex, a sheer wall of rock rose up into the sky, and scraggly bushes clung perilously to whatever foothold they could find. The baths themselves were large and luxurious, and fed by one of the many hot springs that flowed underneath the town. The mosaics inside were colourful and rich, in bright shades of red and blue, and the domed concrete ceiling, with its round aperture that let in the light like a giant, unseeing eye, was the largest outside the Pantheon in Rome. It was exactly what one would expect from Baiae, a town built for the rich at play.

Atreus and I wandered down a wide colonnaded path towards the entrance of the bathhouse. It was still morning, so we weren't expecting to be allowed entry. Mornings in public bathhouses were reserved for women. But that didn't mean that we couldn't make enquiries about Mino, who apparently worked here when he wasn't acting as an acolyte for the Cumaean Sibyl. I doubted that he worked in the bathhouse itself—that was a slave's job, and most slaves didn't moonlight for fake soothsayers on the side. It seemed more likely that the mysterious Mino was engaged in one of the other commercial enterprises centred around the Baths of Mercury, and so Atreus and I veered off the main path and headed for the wineshop first.

There were only a few customers, and the girl behind the counter was bored and willing to chat. The sestertius I overpaid for two cups of wine pleased her, and a smile lit up her plain but friendly face. She had a smattering of freckles across her nose that shifted with her smile. They looked like a constellation.

"Mino?" she asked, her brow furrowing. "I don't know the name. What's he look like?"

"Couldn't tell you," I said. "A friend told us he's an acolyte, if that helps."

The girl raised her eyebrows. "There's no temple here, is there? It's baths. Closest temple is down the road." She pointed helpfully in the right direction.

"Not the sort of acolyte that belongs to a temple," I said. "An unofficial cult."

She raised an eyebrow. "Plenty of those around here. There's people living here that come from all over and have all sorts of gods," she said. "What cult?"

"The Cult of the Cumaean Sibyl."

The girl laughed, the smattering of stars on her nose crinkling. "Well, that'd be in Cumae, wouldn't it?"

She had a point. "You would think so, wouldn't you?"

"Sounds like someone's been telling you some bullshit," the girl said, which was the story of my life. She sounded sympathetic enough that it might have been the story of hers as well.

"Very possibly," I said, though I didn't doubt that Caecilia had told us the truth as she believed it.

The girl gave a thoughtful hum. "There are some more shops up on the next terrace. Costs a fortune to rent here. You should hear my boss complain! But it's where all the tourists come, isn't it? Anyway, they're always hiring and firing workers, so maybe he works up there?"

We thanked her for the information, finished our wine, and strolled back outside. The sunlight beat down on our shoulders, shone brightly on the marble colonnades, and glittered off the sea. The cloudless sky arched above us.

"It's such a beautiful day that I'd almost forgotten we're looking for a killer," I said, drawing in a lungful of salt air. "And that last night Agrippina threatened my entire family."

We both turned and looked down at the port, and at the little bridge of land that connected it to Baiae's natural shoreline. It looked quiet and peaceful from up here. My gaze shifted from Nero's villa to Piso's, and then to mine. The day was so lovely that it was almost impossible to think of any turmoil behind those silent walls. But there was clearly turmoil in Nero's villa, given the way both he and Rufio had reacted last night to Agrippina's presence, and I knew there was turmoil in mine since I'd been the one to dump it there by telling everyone we'd been threatened. And in Piso's… well, in Piso's villa, the body of a teenage girl lay garlanded in flowers in the atrium, waiting to be lifted on a pyre and set alight.

The thought of Tertia hardened my resolve. Fuck Agrippina. There was nothing I could do to prevent her from striking if she wanted to. But I could search for Tertia's killer, because I'd promised Piso and Nero that I would, and because Tertia deserved justice.

Atreus and I climbed a wide set of steps to the next terrace and found a row of marble-fronted shops. Tourists wandered in and out of them in a sun-soaked daze, happy to be relieved of their purses in exchange for glassware, jewellery, figurines, and fabrics. My gaze was caught by a glass vase inlaid with delicate pieces of mother-of-pearl. It shone gloriously in the sunlight, reflecting every colour of the rainbow. I knew, just from looking at it, that I couldn't afford it.

Well, I knew that I could afford it, but Atreus would give me such silent, disapproving looks that it wouldn't be worth the cost. I might mention to Uncle Maro that I'd seen it, though, and it would surely turn up at the villa sooner rather than later. It would look nice on the desk in my tablinum back in Rome.

Jupiter. I was turning into Maro, wasn't I? First it was vases, and then, before you knew it, I was hiring someone to knock down a few walls so that I could redecorate.

We browsed the shops and asked the shopkeepers if they knew Mino.

In the third shop, one filled with overpriced glassware, the man at the counter said, "Mino? He's not here today. What do you want him for?"

"I owe him some money," I lied, and the shopkeeper was a more honest man than I was if he fell for that old trick.

He sucked his cheeks in while he thought. "He's down at the port today, I think. Said he had to help his cousin with his nets."

"That's very generous of you to give him the day off," I said, wondering just how many jobs Mino had. And more to the point, *why*, given he was part of whatever shady group of people was fleecing the wealthy matrons of Baiae. If he hadn't been such an arsehole, I'd almost admire his work ethic.

The shopkeeper let out a breath and scratched his stubby fingers through his greying beard. "Well, it's hardly busy, and won't be until summer's properly here. And Mino's cousin gives me a good deal on fish, so it works out for everyone in the end."

"What's his cousin's name?" I asked.

"Also Mino," said the shopkeeper. "Not a lot of imagination running in that family."

Apparently not.

I bought an overpriced blue glass dish to thank him for being so helpful.

We strolled back down towards the port; walking downhill was a lot easier than walking uphill, and my calves thanked me for the respite.

"You were quiet back there," I commented to Atreus.

His smile was almost a smirk. "You're getting better at asking questions."

"Oh, really?" I elbowed him in the ribs. "Am I almost ready to be a vigile, do you think? I could probably give Manius a run for his money and everything."

Manius was fifteen, and the littlest vigile in the world.

"Well," he said, pretending to think about it. "I've seen you fight, so…"

If he hadn't briskly sidestepped out of my way, he would have got my elbow a second time. Still, I couldn't stop the flicker of pride that burned in my chest at his backhanded praise. He'd told me when we'd first met that I could be useful to him when it came to opening the doors of rich men. And women, I supposed, in the case of the ladies of Baiae. But the girl from the wine shop and the shopkeepers on the terrace hadn't been patrician, and Atreus had let me take the lead.

Also, I *was* a decent fighter. Just with a gladius and a cohort of legionaries, not my fists. Not that I was eager to prove it again. It would be nice, for once, if nobody tried to kill us while we tried to investigate a murder. I silently prayed that Fortuna heard that thought, and that she was in a generous mood, but on past experience alone, I didn't love our chances.

I would have felt better had Juba been with us, but despite Agrippina's veiled threat from last night, there had been no indication we were being followed. And we both kept checking to make sure of it.

The streets grew more crowded down near the waterfront, quiet villas and private gardens making way for insulae, thermopolia, bakeries, and food markets. The crowds were a mix of tourists, residents, and workers. The well-heeled rubbed shoulders with the barefoot, and nobody seemed to mind. Atreus and I found a wine shop that appeared to be filled mostly with port workers—who was currently working at the port was a mystery if all of them were here—and found space at the counter.

Atreus leaned in when the waiter approached, clearly ready to take the lead this time. "Looking for Mino," he said.

"Haven't seen him," the waiter said, the set of his mouth making it clear that our questions weren't welcome here.

"I meant Mino's cousin Mino."

"Told you. Haven't seen him," the waiter said, and all three of us paused for a moment as we considered whether or not it was worth calling him out on what sounded like a blatant lie, or even attempting to clarify which Mino we were talking about. Then the waiter said, "Boats are still out."

"Mino's boat?" I asked. "Was Mino on it?"

"It's his boat, isn't it?" the waiter asked.

We were getting nowhere fast.

"Tell you what," I said. "If you talk to Mino—either one of them—ask him, or them, to come by the house of Aemilius Valerius."

The waiter took in the cut of my tunic, the gold ring on my hand, and the haughty patrician expression that had been trained into me since birth, and said, "Is that you, then, sir?"

"That's me," I confirmed. "And if either of the Minos, or both of them, turn up at my house, I'll be sure to remember to drop back here and reward you for passing on the message."

There was nothing like a little bribery to grease the axle of an investigation.

The waiter gave me a narrow look. I was no fisherman, but I knew I had him on the hook. He'd pass the message on to Mino or his cousin. Whether or not one of them would turn up was another matter entirely. There couldn't be too many reasons for Mino (not cousin Mino) to come to the attention of a patrician, and he'd be an idiot if he thought it was for anything good. But sometimes you had to poke a stick into an ants' nest and stir it around just to see if any of them came pouring out, and whether they would sting you or not.

We left the wine shop and headed out along the street that ran past the port and eventually reached my villa. The sun-soaked street was wide, and the breeze was pleasant. We passed the shop fronts that made up the front wall of my villa. The girl who'd welcomed us to Cassia's shop was leaning in the shade under the awning and smiled at us shyly as we passed. The perfumer's shop was open. I wondered if her employees had opened it on her behalf.

Vulso, the door slave, was standing in the doorway of the villa as we approached, and bobbed his head respectfully.

"Any visitors?" I asked him.

"Yes, sir," he said, and my heart tumbled over a few anxious beats before he added, "Petronius Arbiter, sir. The mistress said he was welcome."

Faint laughter echoed down the passageway connecting the street to the atrium, and I couldn't help a wry smile. Yes, Petronius wasn't just welcome, he was making himself at home. He had that knack.

"No others?" I asked, and Vulso shook his head. "No messages?"

"No, sir." He nodded out at the street. "A couple of Praetorians have been past a few times, and I told the mistress, but she says that's fine."

"It's better than fine," I said, slapping him on the shoulder. "It's good."

On one hand, it was worrying that even in the cold, hard light of day that Rufio also thought Agrippina's threats were something to be taken seriously. On the other hand, he was keeping an eye on the place too, and I was glad of it. I didn't know Agrippina well enough to know how she operated, but maybe knowing that I had the Praetorians on my side—and, by extension, Nero himself—she'd keep her distance. I hoped that the last thing she wanted was another estrangement from her son. If she wanted that less than she wanted her revenge, then maybe we could ride out the next few weeks here in Baiae and head safely home to Rome, where we could get lost more easily in the crowd. What was that old joke? You didn't have to run faster than a lion to escape it; you only had to run faster than the people with you. And there were a lot of slow runners in Rome for Agrippina to choose from. Not a pleasant thought, but a pragmatic one.

Atreus and I swept down the corridor into the atrium.

We found Petronius entertaining Fulvia and Octavia in the informal triclinium, or perhaps being entertained by them. The slaves had set out a veritable feast of eggs and nuts and fruit and bread, and my stomach gave an appreciative growl.

Fulvia rose when we entered, and I gave her a kiss on the cheek and pressed the blue glass dish into her hands.

"Thank you, Quintus," she said. "How sweet."

"I saw it and thought of you," I said.

Fulvia's mouth quirked. She knew it was a lie. She also knew she'd get the full story later. "Come and sit. Petronius was just telling us all about the upcoming adventures of Encolpius and Giton."

I threw a look in Petronius's direction. "Ah, of course he is. How appropriate."

Petro grinned and shrugged. "They asked *me*, Valerius."

I actually didn't doubt that. Petronius's *Satyricon* was the talk of Rome. It was hilarious, incisive, and as filthy as a Transtiberina gutter. The old moralists hated it, but the rest of us—hypocrites of all ages—gasped in outrage at the rudest parts, then hurried to read the next instalment as soon as it was available.

"To what do we owe the pleasure, Petro?" I asked, sitting down on the couch opposite him.

He grimaced. "I awoke this morning, determined to be a good friend and neighbour and go and visit Piso. Then, when I remembered what a miserable task that would be, I walked straight past his house like a coward and came here instead. Fortunately, Fulvia Drusa and Octavia Junilla were sympathetic to my plight."

"They're used to dealing with cowards," I said. "They have me for practice."

"You've been avoiding him, too?" Petro asked.

"A little," I admitted. And while I didn't owe Piso more than the visit I'd already paid him after Tertia's death, where I'd promised to hunt down her killer, I could have done more. I *should* have. I doubted Piso would want me to intrude upon his grief, but as his neighbour, I was still obliged to make the offer of support so that he could rebuff it. And of course, he would want to know exactly what Atreus and I were up to. I should have been keeping him informed, even though so far we didn't know anything much at all.

Petro nodded, his expression grave. He was a man who made his fortune out of skewering Roman traditional values—and Roman patricians, especially—with his words, but even a satirist of his talent would be hard pressed to be able to wring any humour out of funereal rituals and grief. Especially because Tertia was only a girl, not some rich old man who'd lived a full life.

Atreus took a seat across from Octavia and Fulvia.

Petronius reached for an egg. "Though it wasn't entirely cowardice. I did want to see you after what happened at dinner last night. If I could bottle that moment, she descended on us like a god from the machine, I'd never have to worry about empty theatre seats ever again. It was as though the entire room was frozen in place, and none of us could look away."

"I'm fairly sure you don't have to worry about empty theatre seats."

He hummed, please. "True. Still, Rufio hustled you both out quickly, didn't he?"

"Was he overreacting?" I asked.

"I don't know." Petronius shrugged. "I wish I could tell you yes, but I'm afraid there are things going on behind the scenes when it comes to Nero and Agrippina that even I'm not privy to. She hates Lucan and I as well, if that's any consolation, but Rufio's never escorted us to our doors after dinner." He bit into his boiled egg. "She *really* hates Poppaea Sabina."

"Anicetus mentioned that."

Petronius nodded. "I passed him heading into Nero's villa as I was leaving this morning. Something's afoot. Then again, with Anicetus, something is always afoot."

Wasn't that the truth? The man was slipperier than a weasel dipped in grease.

"I don't think she'd try anything," Petronius continued, "since she's clearly here to worm her way back into Nero's favour, but what would I know about what she's plotting? Her mind is harder to unravel than the Gordian knot."

"If I remember that story correctly, Alexander came up with a succinct workaround."

Petronius snorted. "That he did."

I stood. "Come on."

"Where are we going?" Petronius asked me.

I glanced at Atreus, and he nodded. I said, "We're going to be good neighbours and friends and visit Piso."

* * *

Piso's slaves moved silently as they passed through the atrium, heads down and eyes averted so they didn't have to see Calpurnia Tertia as she lay on a couch with fresh flowers and herbs placed around her to drown out any smell of decomposition. Her makeup was pale and thick to hide the mottling skin underneath it. No sounds of conversation drifted through the magnificent house.

Petronius, for all that he usually played the fool, was solemn and respectful when Piso met us in his tablinum. He gripped Piso's arm and then drew him into an embrace. He patted him on the back while Piso stood there, unblinking, like a man afraid to even draw a breath in case it shattered him. That was the thing with grief. It wasn't a calm ocean. It was the tug and pull of the tide underneath, and every new moment another wave crashing on a rocky shore.

Atria Galla, Piso's wife, sat with him, and I stole a few glances. He had said she was plebeian. If he hadn't married her for her rank, then he also hadn't married her for her looks. She wasn't ugly by any means, but she was no striking beauty. She was plain and round-faced, with dark eyes and a snub nose. It made me warm to her even more, and to him, because if her face was as unremarkable as her family, I could only imagine she'd caught Piso's attention with something much more enduring than beauty: her personality. It was a little dulled today, I was sure, by the recent shocking events that had befallen them, but she held his hand the way that Fulvia held mine when I was feeling like shit, and offered her silent comfort unthinkingly.

"I'm sorry I didn't come sooner," Petronius said.

Piso's mouth quirked in a wry, self-aware smile that was tinged with bitterness. "I wouldn't have noticed if you had, my friend."

A slave brought wine. Piso's sat untouched. Atria sipped hers, not letting go of her husband's hand.

"I've spoken to some of Tertia's friends," I began, and Piso's gaze sharpened with hope. "I haven't learned much as yet, but what do you know of this cult of theirs? The Cult of the Cumaean Sibyl?"

"What of it?" Piso asked.

"Did she tell you much about it?"

His brow creased. "No. Not much. Why?"

"We spoke to Caecilia Didia, and she believes the cult members are given a personal audience with the sibyl."

Piso was slower to react than his wife. While his brow was still creased in confusion, her expression had already moved on to cynical disbelief.

"A personal audience?" she asked, a spark of fire in her gaze, and yes, I could see why Piso had married her. "With a prophetess who has been dead for five hundred years?"

"Or lost on the wind," Petronius added unhelpfully.

"Well, she wasn't lost on the wind when Caecilia Didia spoke to her," I said. "In fact, she charges four aurei per visit."

Atria's mouth pinched into an unhappy shape. "Oh, *Tertia*."

There was an edge of anger in her tone, but I didn't think it was directed at her dead sister-in-law. Atria gave the impression that if the imposter sibyl was in the room with us now, she would have gone for her lying throat, and I don't think any of us would have held her back.

Piso let out a long sigh and shook his head. "But I don't understand. You think the cult is involved, yes? But why would they kill Tertia if she was paying them that much money?"

He had us there. Had Tertia been coming to me that night to expose the cult? If so, what difference would it have made? Clearly, true believers like Caecilia Didia wouldn't be swayed with any evidence and would happily continue tossing gold coins at the fake sibyl. And in a town like Baiae, full of very wealthy people, I couldn't imagine the cult's pickings would be scarce even if they lost a few members. Plenty more rich fools where those came from.

"We're not sure of that part yet, sir," Atreus said. "But everyone we've talked to speaks so highly of Tertia. The cult is the only thing we've found that she was involved in that seems suspect."

Translation: there was never any boyfriend.

Piso nodded. "No, there was nothing else. She never gave us any trouble, did she, Atria?"

Atria shook her head. "Never."

"Could we speak with Tertia's maid, sir? Atreus asked.

Piso looked puzzled, as though we'd asked him if he could show us how to breathe underwater, or to complete one of the labours of Hercules. But then even the simplest tasks were impossible while grief held him so tightly.

"Petronius, have you tried our Caecuban wine? They say it is smoother than Falernian." Atria Galla waved to a slave, who darted away to fetch the promised wine.

"Ah, I do not believe it, but it is a theory I am more than willing to test," Petronius said. "We shall drink a little, yes, Piso?"

Piso blinked at him. "Oh, yes, I suppose."

Atria Galla released his hand and stood. "Valerius, Atreus. Follow me, please."

Leaving her husband in the care of Petronius, we followed Atria through the tablinum and into the peristyle beyond. The expansive holiday villas that dotted the beautiful coastline were not as formally delineated into public and private areas as were our houses in Rome, but as Atria led us along a colonnaded pathway and into a section of the villa that I had not seen before, it was clear that we were entering areas not usually seen by visitors. Not because they were any less luxurious, but because the few slaves we passed going about their daily business seemed slightly surprised to see us there.

"Lira!" Atria called, and a girl detached herself from a group carrying armfuls of blankets. She piled her blankets into the arms of another woman and came hurrying towards us. She was a a teenager, probably no older than her mistress had been, and she had frizzy dark hair that framed her head like a corona, and a gap in her front teeth. "This is Lira, Tertia's maid. Lira, you must answer their questions."

"Yes, domina," the girl said, bobbing her head and regarding us warily.

Atria looked at us and then looked at the slave and said, "I shall wait down the hall."

She was a clever woman. She knew there might be secrets that Tertia had confided in the slave girl that she had kept from her own family and friends. And she knew there was no chance Lira would spill them if the mistress of the house was listening in.

"My name is Junius Atreus," Atreus said. "I am a vigile, but I am not here in any official capacity."

Lira nodded, still wary, but not afraid. Perhaps she didn't grasp the significance of Atreus telling her he wasn't working as a vigile today. Usually, a slave's legal testimony could only be taken under torture. Atreus was assuring her she didn't need to fear that, but perhaps the slave was as sheltered and naïve as everyone had said her mistress was, because I didn't think she caught the implication at all.

"And I'm Aemilius Valerius," I said. "I am a friend of your master's."

She nodded again.

"Have you heard my name before?" I asked her.

"I think so," she said softly.

"From Tertia?" I asked. "Did you know she was coming to see me on the night she was killed?"

"No." Lira's eyes widened. "Why would she do that, sir?"

"That's what we're trying to find out," I said. "I think that Tertia wanted my help. I have a reputation for helping or for finding things out. Do you know if Tertia was worried about anything in particular?"

"No, sir." Her forehead creased. "I thought she was ill that evening because she didn't go to dinner. She asked me to leave her cloak out, but I thought it was for the morning. I left her to sleep, and then, later, I thought I'd take her some soup, but her bedroom—" Her eyes filled with tears. "It was empty. And nobody could find her anywhere."

It fitted with what we'd been told the night Tertia had been killed.

Atreus nodded. "Did you ever go with Tertia to the cult when she spoke with the sibyl?"

Lira shook her head. "No, sir."

"Who went with her?"

"The litter bearers, sir, and a boy with a lantern. But it's much safer here than in Rome. That's what everyone says, sir."

"Did she talk to you about what happened in the sibyl's cave?" Atreus asked.

Lira shook her head. "No, sir." She flushed. "I did once ask one of the litter bearers what happened, but he didn't know, because all the slaves had to wait outside. But she was always with her friends, and they are all respectable ladies."

"Of course they are," I said, although I had my suspicions about Caecilia Didia. "Is there anything else that you can tell us about Tertia? Any secrets that she was keeping from the family, that maybe she told you about?"

"No, sir," Lira said, her bottom lip wobbling. Her eyes filled with tears. "She was very kind.

There was nothing more she could tell us. Atreus pressed a coin into her hand for her trouble, and we met Atria at the end of the hall and followed her back to the tablinum. There was nothing Atria and Piso could tell us either, and so we drank our wine—the Caecuban truly might have been smoother than Falernian—and repeated condolences that landed hollowly on the sheer breadth of Piso's grief, and then said our farewells and left.

* * *

When we got back to my villa, Petronius was still with us, clinging like a stubborn grass seed. He insisted on a tour of the villa, and so I gave him one while Atreus slunk off to check on Lucilla. I felt a twinge of sympathy for both Lucilla and Mouse, who had been promised a holiday by the seaside and were now trapped behind the walls of the villa for their own safety. I needn't have bothered—Petro and I found both of them elbows-deep in the fish ponds, listening avidly as Zethos demonstrated how to allow new seawater into the ponds to keep the water temperature cool and the fish from being poached before they were even caught. Zethos was an old man with a thick Greek accent. The children weren't his only audience—Felix the terrible gladiator was watching too, eyes wide and jaw hanging, as though if he kept all his orifices fully open, he might actually soak up some Latin.

"And these are the fish ponds," I announced pointlessly to Petro. "Lucilla, your uncle is looking for you."

"Mmm," she said, still dangling her arms in the water.

Well, he'd find her eventually, I supposed. He was a vigile, and it was his job to be vigilant.

"Not a bad place you have here, Valerius," Petro said with a grin. "It's no imperial villa, but..."

"Well, it's lucky you're staying there instead of having to slum it here, where I don't have a single triclinium where dishes are floated to the diners."

"Agreed," he said, his grin widening. "Still, there's something to be said for not having to have a witticism or a poem on the tip of my tongue every time I'm with you. It can be exhausting."

"Is Nero very demanding?"

Petro pulled a face. "Not demanding. Just, well, you know how we artists are. Even among friends we get competitive, always trying to outdo one another."

I certainly remembered that from the murderous leadup to Nero's Juvenalia. A bunch of jealous, insecure poets and playwrights, all struggling to get to the top of the heap and bask in Nero's favour. I could easily believe it was still exhausting even if you made it to the top—there would always be some newcomer snapping at your heels. Nero was famously very generous with his artist friends. Their positions were enviable, and where envy lived, trouble usually followed.

"It's actually been good to get away from Rome for a few weeks," Petro continued. "Apart from all this business with Tertia and Agrippina, of course." He snorted. "One is a young girl without a single stain on her character, and one is, well, *Agrippina*. Sometimes the world makes no sense at all, does it?"

I hummed my agreement.

"Are we sure the sibyl is fake?" he asked. "Because I have a few questions I'd like to ask the gods right now."

I snorted. "Don't we all?"

We watched as Zethos showed Lucilla and Mouse how to catch fish in their bare hands while Felix, his arm in a sling, looked on jealously. He inched closer and closer to proceedings, almost nudging the children out of the way, when the sudden appearance of the yellow dog had him scrambling for safety behind Zethos.

"Tullius!" Mouse crowed, and the dog hit the ground like a sack of flour and presented its belly for a rub that both the children were happy to provide.

"Oh, it has a name now?" I called out.

"Aunt Octavia said he's called Tullius because he likes to eat Cicero most of all," Mouse affirmed, crouching down to better get to the wriggling dog.

Petro gasped, clutching his chest in mock horror. "What? But Cicero is so horribly dry! Your dog has no taste at all!"

Mouse grinned, and Lucilla giggled.

Well, of course the dog had no taste. Its idea of fun was licking its own balls, although that observation was best left unsaid in our current company.

I'd save it for later and a more appreciative audience. Fulvia would think it was funny, even though she'd roll her eyes. It was her job as my wife to pretend to be annoyed by my stupidity, while I secretly amused her. It was the reason our marriage had lasted. That, and the fact that marriage was always more of a gamble for a woman than a man. Fulvia's first marriage had ended with divorce. Her second, an improvement by her account of things, had ended with her husband's death, and then she'd been saddled with his awful relatives. She'd married me to escape them. Our genuine affection for each other had come as a surprise to us both.

As though summoned by a thought, Fulvia joined us at the ponds. She linked her arm through mine. "I thought you were taking Petronius on a tour of the villa, not showing him the dog."

"The dog that apparently only eats Cicero?" Petronius raised his eyebrows. "I'm delighted by it. How does it know? We ought to unleash it in a library and see what happens then. Would it know the difference between a Cicero and a Seneca? What would happen when it ran out of moralists? Would the lawyers be next, or the satirists? Would good Tullius here eat my *Satyricon*? And, if it violently disagreed with him, which end would it come out of?"

The children shrieked with delight at that image.

I laughed. "Jupiter, Petro!"

Petronius grinned, the sunlight dancing in his clever brown eyes. "All important questions, Valerius."

We moved away from the fish ponds, leaving the children playing with the dog, and Felix still sheltering behind a bemused Zethos. We moved through to the gardens, and Petronius made all the right sounds as Fulvia pointed out particular flowers and herbs. He was an entertaining guest and a diverting one. It allowed the puzzle of Calpurnia Tertia to bubble away in the back of my mind without consuming my thoughts and pulling me into despondency—and not just at her loss, but at the inevitable jump my thoughts took towards failure. I didn't care much about my reputation if Atreus and I couldn't discover her killer—I had Nero's friendship, which counted for more than any public duty I undertook—but I would hate to fail Piso. His grief deserved answers.

The Cult of the Cumaean Sibyl was at the heart of things, I was sure, but I doubted Mino or his cousin would deliver themselves to my front door. If I was helping to run a cult that existed only to rip off rich women from powerful families, I would certainly be circumspect about it. Sadly though, Mino was our only lead.

I wondered if we ought to travel to Cumae. Clearly, the sibyl operated from Baiae—legend had it that her grotto was on the shores of Lake Avernus—but perhaps the cult also had some members there. There was a chance someone would know something, or could at least point us in the right direction. A small chance, but Atreus and I had worked with less in the past.

Perhaps we'd go to Cumae tomorrow, via Lake Avernus. If the Cumaean Sibyl was seeing paying visitors in her grotto, then we ought to be able to find something apart from five hundred years' worth of dust, right?

"I take no credit, of course," Fulvia said. "This is the first time I've been to the villa."

"Valerius is a terrible husband," Petro said. "I can just tell."

I snorted.

Fulvia, her arm still linked through mine, patted my forearm. "He has his good points."

Petro's smile widened when he caught my gaze. "Well, let's just say I heard his name whispered on the Palatine some time before I met him."

"I knew you were testing me the night we met," I said.

"You didn't know you passed, though, did you?"

"I really didn't," I admitted.

"Well, I suppose all that is behind us now. You're in Nero's inner circle whether you like it or not."

"I like it," I said, "but Agrippina doesn't."

Petro hummed. "You're not wrong about that. But safety in numbers, I always say. You, me, and Lucan, we'll all stick together."

"Oh, yes. I fit in so well with a poet and a playwright."

"We are short an official cynic."

I laughed. "Well, in that case."

We went inside after our tour of the garden, and Petronius declined an offer to stay and eat with us. The villa seemed quieter after he'd left, which wasn't a surprise since he had the sheer force of personality of an entire legion of men. But it was only when Vulso had closed the door behind him and settled back into his little cubby that it occurred to me that the villa truly was emptier than before, and there was a reason for it.

"Where's Juba?" I asked.

Fulvia pursed her lips. "Shopping, I believe."

"Shopping?"

"Yes," she said, drawing me through the sunlit atrium. "Julia and Octavia were tired of staring at the walls, and you agreed we could go out as long as Juba was with us, remember?"

I rolled my eyes. "The emperor's mother has threatened my entire family, and they've gone *shopping*."

"Yes," Fulvia said, lifting her chin. "And you said that they could as long as Juba was with them."

"I know what I said!"

"Then why are you shouting at me?"

"I—I don't know!" I pinched the bridge of my nose. "Juno's tits."

Fulvia regarded me patiently. Far more patiently than I deserved.

"I'm angry," I said at last, since anger seemed to encompass the swirling mass of frustration in my chest. Then, wilting under Fulvia's gaze—she would give Medusa a run for her money—I settled for the truth instead. "Fulvia, I'm *terrified*."

She reached out and drew me into an embrace. "I know."

Her perfume smelled like orange blossoms and the ocean, and I took a deep breath of it. "When Atreus and I first came up against her, we didn't know. If we had, we probably would have walked away. *I* would have, anyway, because I'm not as pig-headed as Atreus. But by the time we knew it was her, we were in too deep. And so we made an enemy out of her, and she hasn't forgotten."

"Quintus, you took her silver mine off her. Of course she hasn't forgotten." Fulvia's faint laugh was a balm. She released me and gave me a frank stare. "But Octavia and Julia are both aware of your concerns, and Juba is with them, so I'm sure they're perfectly safe and haven't put themselves in harm's way."

Fulvia was right. Fulvia was *always* right, something I'd secretly always thought had led to her divorce from her first husband. Unlike Silanus, I wasn't stupid enough to resent the fact, though. I hadn't wanted to get married in the first place, but the decision had been my father's and not mine, and I could have done a lot worse than Fulvia. I hoped that she thought the same.

"You're right," I said, and gave her a kiss on the cheek. "As always."

"I know."

It turned out we were both wrong. An hour later, when Julia and Octavia returned from their shopping trip, I could tell by Juba's unhappy expression that something was wrong, even before Octavia opened her mouth and said, "We ran into Caecilia Didia when we were looking at stolas, and guess what?"

I exchanged a look with Fulvia, who no longer looked as sure of herself. "What?"

"She asked us to join her cult," Octavia said matter-of-factly.

My stomach plummeted. "And what did you say?"

"Well," Octavia said, twirling the ring on her thumb, "it would have been rude to say no, wouldn't it?"

"It would have been rude," Julia agreed, like one of Caecila's parrots.

If I hadn't immediately lost the ability to form words, I might have asked one of the slaves to mark today as a red letter day in the calendar, because, for the first time in recorded history, Fulvia Drusa was wrong about something.

Chapter Seven

The morning brought a cooler change to the weather and some grey clouds that hugged the horizon. To the surprise of absolutely nobody, neither Mino nor his cousin Mino had turned up last night after the fisherman came in for the day, or at dawn when they went out again.

At breakfast, Octavia remained as stubbornly unconcerned about having accepted Caecilia's invitation as she had been yesterday afternoon when she'd dropped the news on me. Julia was mirroring Octavia's careless attitude, but kept darting anxious glances my way when she thought I wasn't looking. It made me think almost fondly of the days when Julia hadn't given a shit about my opinions on anything.

"Caecilia was very friendly," Octavia said. "I don't think she has a single evil thought in her head." She tore off a piece of bread, popped it into her mouth, and chewed for a moment. "Not too many others either, honestly."

I wanted to laugh, because her appraisal of Caecilia was both accurate and cutting, but I was worried. "You should never have agreed."

"Why not?" Octavia asked. "She invited us, and we said yes. Caecilia isn't a bloodthirsty killer, Quintus. She's a bored rich woman whose husband pays her so little attention that she's convinced herself the gods have special messages for her."

There was probably a lot of truth in that. I'd wondered what Caecilia was looking for, and maybe Octavia had ferreted it out. Underneath Caecilia's brash, cheerful exterior, perhaps she was as lonely as Galeria Alba.

Octavia levelled me with a hard stare that reminded me she'd been meddling in dangerous matters long before I'd tripped over my first corpse. Unbeknownst to anyone, Octavia had fulfilled her ex-husband's wishes after his death, and spirited his slave—the secretary who knew everything about the legionary corruption Nasica had been digging into—to safety. It had put her in the path of some very dangerous people. It had caused Agrippina to know her name. But even knowing the risks, she'd done it, because she had loved her ex-husband and because it had been the right thing to do.

"I don't trust that she invited you, knowing that you're my sister," I said. "It might be a trap."

"I don't think so," Octavia said. "Fortunately, you did a decent enough job of not letting the fact you think it's all bullshit show on your face, so she has no reason to believe you're investigating the cult specifically. She just thinks you want to know who Tertia's closest friends were."

Which was how our investigation had started, before we'd realised all of them were being scammed.

I took a breath and let it out slowly. "I don't like it, Octavia."

In theory, I was in charge of Octavia because she was my sister, and because she had no husband or father. In practice, Octavia did what she wanted. I was not in charge of Julia, since she was now a married woman, but I couldn't imagine her husband would be happy with this turn of events. Then again, Florian was so earnest and soft-hearted that I bet Julia ran rings around him.

Octavia held my gaze. "I know, Quintus. But it could help, don't you think? If you haven't found Mino or the sibyl by the time the cult next meets, you could follow us there."

She had me there. I exchanged a look with Atreus, who was seated beside Lucilla as she spooned puls into her mouth. His breakfast looked almost untouched, and his expression was curious as he watched our exchange. There was judgement in it too—there always was with Atreus—and I didn't know if he was judging me or Octavia.

"I do think it could help," I forced myself to admit. "If we can find the sibyl, or even Mino the acolyte, then I believe we can find who killed Tertia. But I would rather let a hundred killers walk free than put you or Julia at risk of harm."

"I know that," Octavia said, her expression softening. "But please understand that neither Julia nor I have any intention of meeting with the sibyl."

Julia nodded eagerly, her earrings rattling. "We were going to come up with some reason we couldn't go in, like a fainting spell, or a sudden illness."

Jupiter! Really? My disbelief must have shown on my face, because Octavia said, "You know that if you and Atreus were women, you would have accepted Caecilia's invitation in a heartbeat."

"If Atreus and I were women, we wouldn't be hunting Tertia's killer to begin with," I pointed out.

Octavia threw me a challenging look. "Quintus, you are currently so concerned about a woman that you wanted to pack us up and send us straight back to Rome. Please don't let's pretend you think women are helpless, or worse, useless. You're better than that."

That was a trap, but I wasn't stupid enough to tell her that, actually, no, I *wasn't* better than that. But I also didn't want to get into a fight over breakfast, so I said, "I'm worried about you. Can we leave it at that?"

And, oh, she really, really didn't want to leave it at that, but I could see the moment she forcefully quelled the fire in her gaze and nodded. "Yes," she said. "Let's leave it at that."

A truce.

It was the best I was going to get, and the whole room knew it.

"Well, then," Uncle Maro said. "What do we think about trying to get some salpa fish for the dinner party? A fellow I've met says he can sell me some."

Even Aunt Marcia's jaw dropped.

"What?" Maro asked. "Are they not good? Has anyone tried them?"

"I think Baiae has broken you, Maro," I said, making a note to tell the cook *not* to serve anyone salpa fish should Maro turn up with a bucket full of them. "If you want to get everyone intoxicated at dinner, please stick with wine and not fish that makes you see things and hear voices."

Maro let out a sigh. "Well, I suppose you're right, Quintus."

He was mad. I'd always said it, yet he managed to find new ways to express that madness every day.

Vulso, the door slave, appeared at the entrance of the triclinium, his gaze seeking mine. I beckoned him over, and he bobbed his head and complied.

"Sorry to interrupt your meal, sir," he said, "but a message has come from the emperor, and the man is waiting for an answer." He waited for my nod before he continued. "Lucan is giving a reading of his *Pharsalia* tomorrow night, and the emperor is hoping that you and your family will attend."

"Do you see?" Maro asked. "How can we compete with that?"

"Jupiter, Maro! Not with salpa fish!" To Vulso, I said, "Tell the messenger that we would be honoured to attend."

Vulso bobbed his head again and scurried away.

"Are we really honoured?" Fulvia asked, cocking a brow.

"Honoured and also shitting ourselves a bit," I said, thinking of how my last evening at Nero's villa had ended. "But one doesn't say that to the emperor."

"One oughtn't say it over breakfast either," she said, frowning unhappily at her dish of puls.

I threw her an apologetic look, grabbed a boiled egg, and rose to my feet. "Let's go, Atreus. I think I need to ask Stilo about finding us a tour guide."

Atreus nodded and followed me out the door.

* * *

Since Mino and Mino had been an unsurprising no-show, I decided to go to Lake Avernus with Atreus to look for the grotto of the Cumaean Sibyl ourselves. Stilo, the villa's caretaker, knew a man who could take us there, so when he turned up, we loaded ourselves into his cart. Juba was with us— Fulvia had been the one to suggest it. She pointed out that since everyone else was staying home until the evening, we had a greater need for a bodyguard than they did, and I agreed. It helped that there were a couple of Praetorians lingering in the street outside my villa—Rufio was looking after the place.

It was good to have Juba with us again. He was clever and observant, and strong as an ox. I wasn't anticipating needing his strength, but I'd been surprised in the past, and I felt better with him with us. And Juba, I was sure, was pleased to be out for the day.

The wind whipped our hair as we jolted along the road out of Baiae, sweeping away the clouds as deftly as wielding a broom.

Lake Avernus lay a little inland from the coast, connected to Port Julius by Lake Lucrinus. They had once been separated, all three, by narrow bridges of land, but back in Augustus's day, Agrippa had dug the land out as part of his extensive works to build Port Julius. Joining the lakes to the sea had been momentous enough, but then he'd gone and outdone himself by digging a tunnel under a mountain to Cumae. Augustus might have ruled the empire, but Agrippa had built it.

Our driver and guide wasn't a talkative man, which didn't bother me. He repeated the old story when we arrived at the shore that any birds that flew across the lake would die, but since he said it as we watched a couple of sparrows alight safely on the shore after wheeling across the water, I wasn't sure that I believed him.

Juba whistled in the bright morning air.

Temples and villas dotted the edges of the lake. The breeze stirred up waves. We followed the road up a slight rise. From here, we could see nearby Lake Lucrinus—smaller and presumably more bird-friendly—glittering in the sunlight. Beyond that lay Port Julius and the massive sea wall that stretched across to Baiae.

The Tunnel of Cocceius was one of several built under Agrippa's command. It had been named after its architect. It led us underneath the mountain. It was wide enough for two chariots to travel abreast, and almost a mile long. To our north, the Aqua Augusta mirrored the path of the tunnel, and the close-flowing water a faint thrum that I could hear even through the rock walls. Shafts slanted down into the tunnel, providing light and air; the walls around the shafts were marbled with the stains from old rainfall. A colonnade hugged one side of the tunnel, its niches populated with statues.

Our tour guide's mules weren't intimidated by the tunnel at all. One was a morose beast with a hanging hand and a sad disposition. The other one was more interested in trying to bite anything it could reach.

We rattled down the tunnel towards Cumae.

Cumae had originally been a Greek settlement—the Temple of Apollo was said to have been built by Daedalus himself. It was also said that he'd hung his wings there as an offering to the gods. Probably as a partial apology, since the Temple of Jupiter had claimed the highest point on the acropolis, leaving Apollo on the less impressive lower ground.

The Tunnel of Cocceius deposited us just on the eastern side of the forum. Our tour guide promised to wait for us, and we left him eating his late breakfast in the sunlight. Cumae seemed like a pleasant enough town, and it was bustling. We stopped at a thermopolium for a stuffed vine leaf each, and then, fortified for the uphill part of our journey, stretched our calf muscles as we took the road up towards the forum. We asked a few shopkeepers about the Cult of the Cumaean Sibyl and only received directions to the grotto. We tried to ask about the sibyl and were told more than once, as though we were stupid tourists, that the sibyl had vanished five hundred years ago.

The entrance to the Grotto of the Cumaean Sibyl was older than the Roman tunnels that had been carved into the rock around it—in addition to the Tunnel of Cocceius, another tunnel led from near the forum down to the port of Cumae. Who knew how many more Agrippa might have built if it hadn't occurred to him to move the navy to Port Julius? Unlike the arched Roman tunnels, the entrance to the sibyl's grotto was made up of straight lines, like a diamond shape with its head and tail lopped off at the floor and the ceiling.

Tiny rocks crunched under my sandals as we approached. There was nobody present at the entrance, which meant the tunnel didn't have much value as either a sacred site or a tourist trap. There wasn't even a single local offering to give us a personal tour in the hopes he could overcharge us and then steal our purses in the dark.

"Doesn't look like much, does it?" Atreus said.

Juba hummed, and shrugged, and we went inside.

The entrance was wide, wide enough that it was easy to imagine a procession might have made their way through here once—priests, and attendants, and torchbearers, and slaves. It grew dark quickly. It grew warm as well, shockingly so, as we stumbled around inside for a while, following twisting passages off to the sides that led nowhere. Once, I heard water running, and thought of the Styx, but if there was a river running through the caves that we had to cross to reach the underworld, we didn't find it.

Even though there had been nobody at the entrance, someone must have been looking after the place because there were torches set into the walls here and there. Some of them were burned out, but a few still had some life in them. Enough that we could see a few steps in front of us, at least.

Sweat dripped out of me, plastering my tunic to my back. My feet slipped in my sandals.

It was disorienting. The flickering shadows cast by the torches and the echoes of our own voices coming from all directions made it almost possible to believe that we weren't alone in the darkness, and that we truly might have crossed over into the underworld.

And then we reached the cave. It was a vast empty space in the rock, whether carved out by nature or by design, I couldn't tell.

It was empty, and it felt as though it had been that way for a very long time. The air felt still and stale, not heavy and foreboding.

"There's nothing here, sir," Juba said, his voice echoing in the darkness, and all my vague thoughts of gods and spirits dropped away at the sound of his voice. I crushed them into the dust underfoot.

Just an empty cave.

And so we walked back out into the sunlight, leaving the spirits of the underworld behind us.

"It smelled stale," Atreus said, squatting down and tugging at some stringy grass. He squinted at a group of grubby children playing further along the road. "It should be a sacred temple, with offerings and incense, and whatever smoke made Galeria dizzy. That wasn't the place."

"She also said it was steep and narrow," I said, looking back at the entrance of the cave. The grotto had been neither.

"That might be the original sibyl's grotto," Atreus agreed, "but that's not where she is now."

I stretched, glad to escape the cave even though it hadn't been the entrance to the underworld after all. "Sons of Dis. We might actually have to follow Octavia and Julia to a cult meeting after all."

I didn't like the idea. There was too much that could go wrong. But it might be our only option since we'd had no luck finding the sibyl ourselves.

"We're not doing that," Atreus said. "I mean, it won't come to that. Just because Caecilia Didia won't give us information about where to find the sibyl, that doesn't mean the others won't. Galeria Alba's husband disapproved, which upset her. We could probably lean on her a little, and she'd tell us."

"You want to lean on a pregnant woman?" I raised my eyebrows.

"Figuratively."

"I know you meant figuratively!"

Atreus's mouth twitched. So did Juba's.

"And Plautia Balbina was Tertia's best friend," Atreus continued. "Neither she nor Galeria Alba seem to be fanatical true believers like Caecilia Didia. Maybe we can impress upon them the importance of speaking to the sibyl, and they'll tell us where to look for her."

"Maybe," I agreed. "It will certainly be better than twiddling our thumbs and waiting for Mino or Mino to seek us out."

If we cast enough nets, then with any luck we'd catch something sooner or later.

In the meantime, my stomach was calling out for another stuffed vine leaf, so we headed back to the thermopolium to shut it up.

* * *

Late in the afternoon, as the sun sank slowly towards the horizon, Calpurnia Tertia's funeral procession wound its way out of Baiae. As befitting her family's wealth and status, the procession was led by musicians, and mimes, and hired women who wailed and scratched their faces. Actors wearing ancestral masks followed the women, and then the litter bearers carried Tertia on her bier. Piso and Atria followed, along with members of their family and whichever freedmen clients they had here in Baiae. The rest of us walked at the end, following the noise, and crowds lined the streets to watch.

Not every funeral would have brought such a large number of spectators, even in Rome, but not every funeral was attended by Nero himself, who walked with the rest of the mourners. Rufio and a few of the other Praetorians walked with him, but they kept no formation. This was not a parade for the emperor—this was a funeral for a teenage girl.

When we reached the necropolis, I stood with Fulvia on one side of me and Octavia on the other. Julia stood between Maro and Marcia, with Atreus behind them. Atreus scanned the crowd, his expression appropriately solemn and his eyes as sharp as always.

A pig was sacrificed to Ceres, and prayers were said.

Piso looked the epitome of Stoicism as he lit the fire underneath Tertia's bier, and the flames caught. Smoke curled into the air and then billowed into clouds.

Seneca famously wrote that it does not matter what you bear, only how you bear it. Words to live by for all Roman patricians, and yet they must have been empty for Piso on a day like this. And wasn't that the crux of it? We were all Stoics when the wind was fair, but grief tested the best of us. I wasn't including myself in that number. If Seneca exhorted men to be among the best of us, then I was definitely relegated to the rest of us. When my father died, I had turned to drinking and partying, as though I might accidentally find some answers face down in a cratera of wine. To the surprise of nobody, I hadn't. And my father's death, although unexpected, at least hadn't been against the natural order of things. Fathers were supposed to die before sons, but little sisters weren't before their older brothers.

As though she could tell what I was thinking, Octavia showed me a shaky smile.

I watched the crowd with Atreus, although my motives weren't the same as his. I was sure Atreus was focused on the investigation—he was single-minded when it came to justice, and not just because the emperor himself had asked us to find out who killed Tertia, but because it was the right thing to do. Atreus didn't need eyes on him or the promise of praise to do the job he had been entrusted to do. It was one of the things I most admired about him. I was sure he was scanning the faces in the crowd, trying to read the faces of the people there and attempt to discern if they were hiding something. That wasn't why I was watching the crowd. I just didn't want to watch Tertia burn.

Petronius and Lucan were here, standing close to Nero and Rufio, and so, I realised with a jolt, was Anicetus the imperial spy. He kept his distance from the emperor, though. I didn't read anything into that. Anicetus made a point of never being noticed. He caught my gaze and nodded, and I returned the gesture.

The women from the cult were here as well.

Plautia Balbina, looking beautiful and fragile, was standing with Piso and his family. Her blonde hair was still messy, as per the custom for a woman in mourning, and tendrils were caught on the breeze and whipped back and forth. Her gaze was fixed on Piso instead of the burning bier, and her hands were clasped tightly in front of her. If I was any closer, I was sure I would see that her knuckles were white.

Caecilia Didia had not dressed down for the occasion. She shone and glittered like an insect in the sunlight. A silk cloth dangled from her fingers. She raised it occasionally to dab at her eyes.

Galeria Alba stood in the company of an older man. He was grim-faced, but appeared solicitous. When Galeria sobbed, he placed a gentle hand on her pregnant belly and leaned in to say something in her ear. She shook her head and squared her shoulders, her mouth trembling as she watched the flames.

My gaze caught mostly on strangers. I didn't know them, but I wondered if any of them knew me. Was Tertia's killer somewhere amongst the crowd, and did he know Atreus and I were hunting him? He must have, if he had eyes and ears. Half of Baiae had made its way to the necropolis to watch Tertia's last moments before her spirit was finally free to pass into the underworld, so it didn't seem unlikely that he might be here, either to gloat over his misdeeds or to get a measure of the men who were looking for him.

It was an unsettling thought either way.

I saw a group of men standing close together. They looked as though they might have been port workers. I saw another man who looked as though he'd come alone, and decided I didn't like the look of him. Then two men murmuring something, their faces set. Perhaps they were the killers? When I realised I'd painted at least half the crowd with a guilty brush, I bowed my head and stared at the ground for a long while, and forced myself to take breaths as deep as I could without tasting too much smoke.

When at last the fire had burned down, Piso sprinkled the ashes with wine, and Atria held the urn while he scooped the ashes into it.

It was a miserable ceremony to mark a miserable death.

We were quiet on the walk back to the town. It was dark now, but we were in the solemn company of other mourners, and we were carried along by a kind of subdued feeling of fellowship. We lost our companions in dribs and drabs along the way until we arrived at the villa alone.

Vulso opened the door to us.

There was a light meal waiting in the triclinium. Mouse and Lucilla were already digging in, and the rest of the family sank down onto the couches as though they were all carrying the weight of the world on their shoulders. I was tempted to join them, but I wanted to get rid of the smell of the smoke, so I helped myself to a piece of bread to tide me over and headed for the bathhouse.

One of the indoor slaves trailed along after me.

"It's fine," I told him. "I don't need an attendant. Just take my clothes and bring me a clean tunic."

I stripped off and eased myself into the steaming water. I sat on the step and leaned back against the tiles, letting the heat work at my sore muscles and, hopefully, my bleak mood. I wished I was back in Rome, where at least at my baths there I could pay for a massage that would rattle my brain hard enough in my skull that I'd be incapable of thought for at least a few hours afterwards. There was a woman there who could wrestle Hercules and win. I didn't stand a chance against her.

I heard the sound of footsteps.

"Just leave them over there," I said, my eyes still closed.

"You won't be able to reach them from there."

I opened my eyes to see Atreus setting down a plate within my reach.

Bread, olives, eggs, pork, and spears of blanched asparagus. Then he tugged his tunic off and joined me on the step.

"The attendant is bringing me fresh clothes," I murmured.

Atreus hummed his understanding and kept his distance. "The asparagus is good."

He was right, and I felt a little better once I'd eaten some. "I'm tired."

"From all the walking we did today?" His tone said he knew it wasn't.

"I promised you a holiday at the seaside, and instead we've got a murder."

He shrugged. "Well, I'm not blaming you for that."

"It's been days, and we can't even find the sibyl or Mino."

"Or Mino," he added, his mouth twitching in something too brief to be considered a smile. Then he let out a long breath. "We haven't found them yet, it's true, but there are no dead ends here. We just have to try harder."

"We have to lean on a pregnant woman," I reminded him and myself.

"Yes, I think that either Galeria Alba or Plautia Balbina will tell us where the cult meets," he said. "And I think that once we know that, we should be able to track them down, even if it means sitting and watching the place and seeing who comes and goes."

"As long as Agrippina doesn't strike in the meantime."

"There it is," he said, his voice as warm as the water. "That's your problem there."

"I think she's everyone's problem, Atreus."

He hummed again. "But what can we do?"

"Nothing!"

"So we do that," he said. "We continue to investigate Tertia's murder, and whatever will happen with Agrippina will happen. Our families are as safe as we can make them, so all we can do is to keep moving forward in whatever way we can. Everything else is in the hands of fate."

We fell into silence as the slave returned with my clean tunic. When he was gone again, Atreus climbed out of the bath and retrieved some oil and a strigil. Then he sat beside me again and nudged me with his knee to get me to slide into the deeper water.

I bowed my head as he rubbed the oil into my shoulders, his fingers digging into muscles that were tighter than they should have been. The pain was brief, and relieved some of the tension I had been carrying. My mind drifted. The bathhouse was quiet and filled with steam, and the water rippled with our movements, sending tiny little waves slapping against the edges of the bath.

"If you knew of an oracle that could truly tell the future, would you want to know?" I asked. The cloudy water swirled in my vision.

Atreus hummed, and a moment later, I felt the scrape of the strigil across my shoulder. "About some things, maybe."

"Like what?"

Atreus shifted behind me, the water rising and falling as he moved. "I'm not the emperor, or a senator, or a general in charge of armies. I don't need to know anything that will decide an heir or turn the tide of a war. I think that if I was given the chance to know the future, then I'd ask if Lucilla will be well. Will she be happy? Will she have a husband who is good to her, and children who are healthy? But then, maybe it would be better not to know, because what if the answer isn't something that I want to hear?"

Atreus wasn't often vulnerable like this, but it wasn't every day we watched a girl whose life had been cut short burn to ashes.

"You know that you will be there to see those things, don't you?"

He dragged the strigil across my skin again. "Can any of us be sure of that?"

Atreus's job was a dangerous one, even when he wasn't hunting killers.

"No, but we'd be driven madder than Maro if we dwelled on it. And you know that even if something happened to you, and to me, that my family wouldn't let Lucilla starve in the street."

He was silent. Of course he was. He hated it whenever I alluded to the idea that I could provide for Lucilla in ways he couldn't, even if it was the unassailable truth. Gods forbid, if anything did happen to him, he'd haunt my family for the rest of eternity just to remind us that he wasn't fucking happy about relying on our charity.

"Just think," I said, hoping to make him laugh, "she could be raised by Maro and Marcia. Her bedroom would be renovated so often that she wouldn't even recognise it if she came home after leaving the house for an hour."

He snorted, which was close enough.

The play of the lamplight on the shifting water created strange shapes. I watched them, my brain tired enough that they almost seemed to mean something, but as soon as my awareness sharpened enough to try to catch that meaning, it dissolved into the ripples and the steam. Atreus dragged the strigil across my skin, hard enough that I almost wanted to flinch away, but I knew my muscles would thank me later for enduring it now. If I couldn't get a good pummelling by that girl who could arm wrestle Hercules, I'd take this mild mistreatment by Atreus instead.

I leaned back into the press of the strigil. "Would you ask an oracle about us?"

Atreus was silent for a moment, and the strigil paused. Then he scraped it across my back again and said, softly, "No. I don't think so."

There was no admonishment in his answer, but there was still a sting in the words. I should have known better than to let the heat and the steam addle my brain and relax my tongue, because no good could ever come of asking him a question like that, just like no good would ever come of asking an oracle. Our relationship wasn't any long thread drawn out and woven by the fates. It could only exist in moments where the rest of the world did not; in stolen hours, behind closed doors, entirely isolated from the rest of the world and anyone in it. If our lives were leaves caught in the flow of the river of time, then the moments I shared with Atreus were the rocks too heavy to be carried along by the stream. They could not travel with us.

I was a Roman patrician. In a year or two, with the friendship and the favour of the emperor, I would be nominated to stand for election as a quaestor. Roman political life was public life. We were judged by our actions, and by our families and friends. Atreus could never be a part of the life I was born to lead.

Stolen hours and closed doors, and moments outside of time.

He was right not to want to ask an oracle about us. We didn't exist outside of this room.

"No," he said gently.

"What?"

"Wherever your thoughts are taking you, stop it." He tugged the hair at the nape of my neck. "We have what we have, and it is enough."

"I know." I reached over my shoulder, and he caught his fingers in mine. "I know it is."

His breath was warm on the back of my neck.

I leaned back against him and closed my eyes. "So. Tomorrow, we approach Galeria Alba or Plautia Balbina and see if either of them will tell us where we can find the sibyl's grotto. Ideally, before Octavia and Julia find it for us, and put themselves in unnecessary danger."

"Agreed," Atreus said.

"Because Mino and Mino, if they even got the message I wanted to see them, aren't going to help."

"At best, Mino the acolyte is swindling rich women. At worst, he's a killer." Atreus bumped his chin against my shoulder, and the faint rasp of stubble brought my skin out in goosebumps despite the heat of the bath. "If I was in his place, I would definitely be lying low right now."

I nodded. "And once we have the sibyl's grotto, we will have the sibyl."

"Hopefully," Atreus said. "At least, if the place isn't in the middle of the Phlegraean Fields, there might be neighbours who can tell us who comes and goes."

"Not that I'm being a cynic, but since when has our luck held when we've pinned our hopes on the helpfulness of neighbours?"

His silent laughter shook us both. "Well, the thing about luck is that it changes. And we are well overdue."

He was certainly right about that.

"Master!"

I jolted upright at the sound of the attendant's cry, and Atreus pushed me away.

The boy's bare feet slapped across the tiles, and he skidded to a stop at the edge of the bath, squinting through the steam. "Master! Rufio the Praetorian is here! He says they've pulled a dead woman out of the sea!"

Atreus might have been right, but fate, as it happened, didn't agree.

* * *

The girl hadn't been in the water long enough that the fish had started to nibble at her softer parts. She was as pale as a sea nymph where she lay on the jetty at Nero's villa. Her sightless eyes stared up at the stars. Slaves with lamps surrounded her as though they were performing some sort of silent vigil, but I thought it was because none of them wanted to get too close. On the same day the emperor had attended the funeral of a teenage girl, another one had washed up at his seaside villa. Let the omen be absent, as the saying went.

Rufio was less superstitious than the slaves, and he led Atreus and me through them without even slowing his steps. "One of the outdoor slaves saw her floating face down in the water, bumping up against the wall. The tide must have brought her. A couple of my men fished her out. What do you think?"

"I think it's a bad time to be a teenage girl in Baiae," I said, and Atreus shot me a wry look.

The girl was a stranger. She had dark hair, as lank and twisted as seaweed now, and a face that might have been pretty and lively when she'd had a heartbeat, but was now slack and stark and devoid of all expression.

"She's got a cord around her neck," Rufio said. "Like Calpurnia Tertia did."

Atreus knelt down beside the dead girl, his quick fingers finding the ligature around the girl's throat and the lines of swollen flesh that had almost swallowed the cord. He shivered as a cool breeze blew in from the water, and I tugged my cloak tighter around myself.

"Who here knows the tides?" Atreus asked the slaves. "Where did she go in the water?"

A few of them murmured amongst themselves, and one was nudged forward by his fellows. He was a middle-aged man, with skin tanned nut brown by a life working outdoors. He cleared his throat. "Most likely from between here and Port Julius, sir. If she'd been dumped in the Baian Harbour, she'd be caught there still."

It didn't tell us much, except that she'd been killed in a different location than Tertia. It wasn't so surprising. Tertia's killer had caught her close to home; perhaps he'd done the same with this girl.

"Does anyone know her?" Atreus asked, and this time there was no murmuring from the slaves, only shaking heads and blank stares.

I took a lamp from a slave and set it on the jetty beside the girl. The flame guttered for a moment, then came alive again. I knelt beside Atreus, and Rufio stood behind us, watching intently.

She was wearing a tunic. If she'd had a stola and sandals, the push and pull of the sea must have taken them. The tunic was plain orange and clung wetly to the soft planes of her body. She was wearing a bracelet—glass beads. I unclipped it from her wrist and slid it into my belt. If we found a family member, they might be able to identify it.

Atreus felt behind the girl's neck, and a moment later withdrew a chain. The amulet on it was long enough that it had been hidden under her tunic. He held it up to the light to inspect it.

It was Apollo.

A growing sense of disquiet—the sort that came from a dawning realisation, and not a happy one—crept up my spine, and I saw it reflected in Atreus's expression. Neither of us said it aloud because neither of us had to, but I had a creeping suspicion, and so did he, that we had found our elusive Cumaean Sibyl at last. And whatever had happened to her tonight, she'd proven herself a fraud by never seeing it coming.

Chapter Eight

Of all the cult members we had met in Baiae, Caecilia Didia had undoubtedly been the one who had gazed at the Cumaean Sibyl the most ardently. If any one of them could have described the sibyl in breathless, rapturous detail, it would have been her. And yet it was because of Caecilia's utter devotion to the sibyl that we didn't send for her now. We wanted straight answers, not an entire dramatic production that would rival anything Petronius had ever written.

Plautia Balbina, Tertia's best friend, was pale and nervous when the Celer the Praetorian delivered her to the boat shed that now housed the dead girl. I couldn't blame her. The Praetorians weren't known for making friendly house calls. Usually, if they knocked on your door, it was to let you know you were about to come to terms with your own mortality, whether you were sufficiently philosophically prepared or not. And Celer looked even more menacing than the rest of them. It was no wonder that Plautia was wide-eyed and trembling with nerves.

Still a better option than sending for the heavily pregnant Galeria, though.

"Plautia Balbina," I said. "Thank you for coming. I apologise for the inconvenience and for the unhappy task ahead."

She lifted her chin. "If it can help you find who killed Tertia, then I assure you it is no inconvenience, Valerius."

Despite her brave words, Plautia faltered as Rufio drew the blanket off the dead girl's body. What little colour she had in her face drained away in the space of a single heartbeat, and the old slave who had accompanied her for propriety's sake smothered a cry behind her gnarled hands.

"It's…" Plautia's bottom lip wobbled. "I don't understand. It's the sibyl!"

Belief was a funny thing. Plautia might not have been the fanatical follower of the Cumaean Sibyl that Caecilia was, but her clear confusion meant that she must have had some faith in the cult. Or maybe not. Maybe she wasn't shocked that the supposedly immortal sibyl was lying here dead. Maybe she just didn't understand how, on the same day she'd watched her best friend's body burn, yet another girl was dead.

"Are you sure it's her?" Atreus asked.

Plautia blinked at him, and then at the dead girl. "I… I think so. The grotto was dark and smoky, but yes, I'm certain that's her. It surprised me, the first time I went, that she was young."

It would surprise anyone who'd ever heard the legend of the Cumaean Sibyl, but the girl must have had a slick story and a convincing manner when she'd been alive. There must have shone an earnest light in her eyes at one time, bright and warm enough for people to seek out, for people to *trust* her. There was no light in her now. There was nothing left of her but the least of what made up a person—the flesh.

I wondered if her spirit was now walking through the underworld, following the paths she had once pretended to already know. Was she standing now on the shadowed banks of the Styx, afraid and alone?

I dug a coin out of my purse. It was only a sestertius. In life, the girl might have turned up her nose at such a scant offering, but it would be enough to pay the ferryman. I leaned down and slipped the coin into the girl's slack mouth and under her tongue. What happened to her soul after it crossed the Styx was out of my hands, but at least now she wouldn't spend eternity wandering the riverbank, condemned to haunt the world as a ghost as she waited for a ferry she couldn't board.

Rufio regarded the dead girl with a solemn, silent frown.

Atreus regarded Plautia with a matching expression. "Plautia Balbina, where did the cult meet?"

Plautia let herself be folded into the arms of her old slave. "I—" She shook her head as though to clear it. "There is a path from behind the Baths of Mercury. We always went at night; I don't know if I could find it in the day.

It was behind a gate and some bushes."

Shit. We'd been right on top of the sibyl's grotto the day we'd gone to the Baths of Mercury to seek out Mino. The hillside that Baiae had been stubbornly carved into was full of caves and fissures and crevices, like half of the coast of Campania. But who better to know every nook and cranny behind the Baths of Mercury than the mysterious Mino, who worked at one of the shops in the grounds of the baths? Our elusive acolyte was in this up to his neck.

I wondered if he knew the sibyl was dead. The next logical question was, if he did know, was he the reason for it? It didn't quite fit—not yet, and not with what little we knew. The sibyl was bringing in a fortune. Why kill her? But there may have been things at play we didn't understand yet, and even the pettiest dispute could escalate to murder in a sufficiently twisted mind. Mino could still be our man. We had the largest pieces laid out like the tesserae of a mosaic—Tertia, the sibyl, Mino, and the cult. We just needed to trickle enough lime and sand in the gaps to make sure it all stuck together. The difficulty was in making sure we had a bucket of sand and lime to finish the job, instead of one full of shit.

Well, there was a reason I wasn't in the business of making mosaics. And, given that analogy, there was probably also a reason I wasn't in the business of writing plays or poems. It was lucky I'd been born rich.

I exchanged a look with Atreus, throwing him a silent question that he answered with a nod.

"Where are you going?" Rufio asked, brows knitting together as Atreus and I headed for the door.

"The Baths of Mercury," I said. "Where else?"

Rufio looked at us, then at the trembling Plautia, then back at us again. "It might be dangerous."

He said it so hopefully that under any other circumstances, I might have laughed.

I nodded instead. "Are you coming with us?"

Rufio gave Plautia into the care of Celer, instructing him to make sure she and her slave got safely home again, and the three of us set off into the night.

Celer's glower warmed our backs as we left.

"He really doesn't like you, does he?" I asked Rufio.

"He's jealous," Rufio said.

"Because Nero likes you more?"

"Because I'm better at my job than he'll ever be," Rufio said with the easy self-assurance of a man speaking a plain truth.

The road that curved around the harbour was mostly quiet. We passed a couple of drunks and at least one amorous pair of lovebirds who thought they were hidden in the shadows—they weren't, and the moonlight danced brightly on their bouncing buttocks—but it wasn't until we reached the street that ran along the bottom of the town's terraces that we got a face full of famously licentious Baiae.

Whether the evening had officially been dedicated to Bacchus or not, this was clearly a Bacchanalia in spirit. Musicians and dancers paraded up and down the street, and people leaned out of the doors and windows of the wine shops and the cauponae and cheered them along drunkenly. Both men and women wore floral wreaths plastered to their sweaty skin. Some of them weren't wearing much more than that at all. Drums banged, cymbals crashed, and drunks screamed and yelled just for the fun of it.

I suddenly realised why my father hadn't brought me to Baiae once I'd reached my adolescence. While his attempts to steer me onto a straighter path hadn't been as successful as he'd probably hoped, at least he'd known to avoid the most obvious moral pitfalls. Like all of Baiae, apparently.

The streets grew a little quieter as we climbed the hill, the noise and wild revelry giving way to the closed faces of the walls and porticos of private houses. We relied on Rufio's lantern as we left the well-lit bacchanalia behind us.

The domed bathhouse looked like a temple at night. Torches burned on the main path leading through the gardens, but the bathhouse itself was in darkness. The moonlight shone on the dome, giving it an otherworldly glow, and making me think again of ghosts and the banks of the Styx. We made it halfway along the path before a watchman challenged us, and for once, I didn't need to use my name or a bribe to get us any further.

"I am Decimus Rufio," Rufio said. "I am a Praetorian. I am here on imperial business. Make way."

The gaping slave scuttled to the side and stared after us as we passed.

"That's a handy trick," Atreus said. "Is it really imperial business, though?"

"Why not?" Rufio asked with a shrug. "The emperor wants you to find whoever killed Calpurnia Tertia, so as far as I'm concerned, that makes it his business. Mine too, since I'm here."

I liked Rufio.

The thing I liked most about him was that he was clearly interested in my sister, but hadn't been crass enough to ask me what her dowry was worth. Men did. After Octavia's divorce, there had been a flood of them. I suspected that Rufio saw Octavia as a person, and not just a purse. It won him points with me, but whether or not it would with Octavia, I didn't know. That was her business, and not mine, which I know was an unusual position for a paterfamilias to take, but Octavia had already married once for duty. She'd loved Nasica, which wasn't as fortunate as it sounded since it had all ended so badly. It might have been better if her feelings had been cold towards him. But the next time she married, the choice of husband would be hers. Within reason, obviously, but Octavia was a reasonable woman.

We found another slave doing the rounds of the gardens behind the bathhouse and seconded him and his lantern. He was a tall, skinny adolescent who had clearly put all his energy into growing upwards instead of outwards. He looked like a woollen tunic that had been left hanging on a line to dry and had stretched beyond wear.

Stammering, he gave his name as Dio and proved to be immediately useful when we asked about Mino by saying, "Oh, yes, sir! Mino sometimes comes here at night with some other people. Nobody is supposed to, but I think he pays the overseer. I can show you where he goes."

The overseer should have cut Dio in on the deal. The boy was happier to sing than a nightingale.

The entrance to the grotto of the fake sibyl was in a fissure in a wall of rock behind the bathhouse, hidden away behind a small temple of what appeared to be of Greek persuasion, although in the darkness, I couldn't make out which god or goddess it was dedicated to. Dio pushed open a gate that led to a path between some unkempt bushes—this was clearly not an area the public was meant to access, and at first, I thought the entrance into the rock was part of the vent system from the baths. It wasn't until Rufio leaned in with his lantern and light expanded to fill the first few feet of the space that I saw it was the entrance to a narrow tunnel that cut down through the rock.

"They go down there," Dio said, wrinkling his nose.

"Have you been down there?" I asked.

He looked at me like I was mad. "No, sir. It's got *bats*."

Wonderful.

"If a bunch of matrons can do it, so can we," Rufio said, with the reckless sort of smile of a man about to launch an attack on a vastly superior force, knowing that he was about to die, but certain it would all be worth it as long as a coin would be struck to commemorate the battle. *Gloria exercitus*! He gripped the lantern and stepped into the entrance of the cave.

Atreus followed him, looking less enthusiastic.

I took Dio's lantern—he yelped in protest, but didn't resist—and went in after them. The walls of the tunnel immediately closed in, and I had no doubt that we were in the right place. Narrow and steep, we'd been told, and even before we'd ventured very far inside, there were points we had to turn our shoulders sideways to get through. I imagined I could feel the weight of the entire hill pressing down on us, and in my mind it was suddenly a mountain, and I was no Atlas.

Lamplight bounced off the narrow walls as we shuffled our way down the tunnel, shoulders turned. I heard the rasp of soles skidding on grit and pebbles, and Rufio swore.

"Are you alright?" I called out. I couldn't see past Atreus.

"Watch your step," Rufio said. "It gets steep here."

He wasn't exaggerating. The narrow path dropped sharply downwards. I scraped the lantern against stone as the walls narrowed even further, and then, trying to protect it, scraped my knuckles instead. I hissed at the sudden sting of pain, and then almost walked into Atreus when he stopped to check on me.

"I'm fine," I murmured. "Keep going."

Up ahead, the light from Rufio's lantern dipped and stretched, and then dimmed as he squeezed around a section of rock that jutted out into our path. I wondered if the cult had selected their members not just by wealth, but also by weight. The plumper matrons of Baiae would never have made it through.

There were points in the tunnel when the ceiling was so low we needed to stoop.

I heard the faint sound of running water, the noise distorted in the narrow passage. It was impossible to tell how far away it was. It grew hot as the tunnel continued downwards, the air growing thick and heavy. It carried the faint, sharp taste of sulphur, and tasted bitter in the back of my throat.

The tunnel veered right, and a breath of cooler air brushed against my face.

"Which way?" Rufio's voice echoed back to me.

I couldn't see a thing.

"Straight," Atreus suggested.

We moved forward, and I caught a glimpse of what might have been another narrow passageway that connected to this one, or might have been a shadowed fissure that led nowhere. Either Rufio had sharper eyes than I did to spot it was another tunnel, or his imagination was running even wilder than mine. And that was saying something, since every time a drip of sweat tickled my hair, I thought it was the forward scout of an entire legion of bats.

We had to be going in the right direction still—there were alcoves cut into the tunnel walls at regular intervals, with lamps resting in them. The lamps were unlit.

The heat was almost unbearable. It was as though we were trapped in a caldarium, without the benefit of the actual hot bath. It was almost impossible to remember that outside, the night was cool and pleasant. I was sweltering, my tunic plastered to my back, and my sweaty feet slipping in my sandals with every step.

We made a turn off the main tunnel, into an ever lower one. The sound of running water grew louder, and a moment later Rufio said, "Shit."

There, in the darkness below the earth, a stream cut through the tunnel, blocking our path.

Rufio crouched down and extended a palm. He held it over the water for a brief moment before pulling it back. "It's hot."

I held my lantern up and squinted into the darkness. I couldn't see the other side of the stream, and so I looked up and down instead. The stream came from blackness and vanished back into it. It wasn't the Styx—of course it wasn't—but my stomach clenched, and I felt a chill despite the oppressive heat as I imagined Charon appearing out of the darkness on his small boat.

We returned to the main tunnel, still following the path of unlit lamps in the assumption they would lead us where we needed to be. And then, just when the walls were closing in so much that I was ready to lose my nerve entirely, the tunnel opened up into what could only be the grotto of the sibyl.

It was a small room, but felt as large as an amphitheatre after the cramped tunnels leading into it. There were more lamps here, and braziers, and sprigs of mistletoe were discarded on the floor. Offerings to Persephone. There was a faint, smoky smell in here that I couldn't place. I stepped past Atreus and inspected one of the braziers.

Rufio joined me and took a sniff of the cold ashes. "Asterion?"

"Burn enough of it, and no wonder they were fuzzy-headed," I said. "Although, considering the journey down here, they wouldn't need more than a nudge to lose their senses entirely."

The entire place was disorienting and befuddling, and I knew it was a fraud. When even that certainty hadn't been enough to stop me picturing Charon appearing, I hated to think what the cult members had imagined. Especially once they emerged into this chamber, already eager to believe, and the sibyl delivered her cryptic prophecies.

"Mino has to be the brains behind it all," Atreus said. "He's the one with access to this place. But someone who knows him must know who the girl was."

I thought of the glass bracelet in my purse and nodded. Such a strangely modest piece of jewellery for a woman who was making more than enough to wear gold if she'd wished. A sentimental item? Then there was someone she had cared about who also cared for her. Someone would be missing her.

"We need to find Mino," I said.

"If he's not halfway across Campania by now," Atreus agreed, always the optimist.

I hummed my agreement, but I wasn't too disappointed that the grotto was empty and Mino was on the wind. We'd catch up with him eventually, if the gods willed it, and anywhere was better than here for a confrontation. And, not that I'd wanted the fake sibyl dead, but I was relieved the possibility of Octavia and Julia getting initiated into the cult had died with her. They might have insisted the plan had been a safe one, but I'd been involved in enough plans that had gone completely sideways that I knew there was no such thing.

Like Atreus, I was also always an optimist.

I took another long gaze around the gloomy chamber, eager to leave, but not at all looking forward to another journey through the cramped tunnels that led back outside. Then I remembered what Dio had said about bats, and suddenly the way out didn't seem so off-putting after all.

* * *

I didn't sleep that night. I dozed a little on the couch in my tablinum, but I didn't sleep. Juba prowled around the villa a few times, just like he did at home, pausing in the doorway of the tablinum to see if I needed anything. What I needed was to find out who had killed Tertia, and now the sibyl, but that wasn't anything Juba could help with. One of the villa's slaves, a skinny boy with messy hair as wild as Hursa's, tried to play my attendant for the evening. After he fell asleep on the floor some time after midnight, I nudged him awake and sent him off to bed with a face full of yawns. The villa might have been mine, along with the slaves inside it, but I didn't feel at home here the way I did in Rome. I even missed Hursa.

The boy was replaced by Tullius the dog, who seemed delighted to find there was someone still awake at such a strange hour. He lasted a little longer than the boy before he fell asleep with his head on my foot. I didn't nudge him awake. I liked him when he was asleep and not making a meal out of my scrolls.

Atreus was up early the next morning, before dawn. There was an unhappy cast to his expression as he joined me at my desk and helped himself to a wax tablet and a stylus. I'd hoped he would write down one of his lists—Atreus favoured lists—but instead he just scored a series of shallow lines through the wax.

"In the Aventine, I know people." He shook his head. "Here? I'm a fucking tourist."

In the Aventine, Atreus didn't just know people—he was known. There wasn't much that happened in his neighbourhood that didn't reach him in a day or two. Most often, thanks to reports from his vigiles, he had been caught up on all the night's happenings before breakfast. But here, in Baiae, we were both blind. Was Mino the acolyte a known criminal? Was his cousin the fisherman the same? Was the sibyl scam an open secret amongst the lowlifes of the resort town? Did somebody out there know who else was involved? We had no way of knowing, and didn't even know who to ask.

"The shopkeeper," Atreus said at last, drawing another line across the tablet. "Mino's boss. Maybe he can tell us where Mino lives, and what other family he has apart from the other Mino."

I nodded. "And anyone working at the port should be able to point out the other Mino." I glanced out into the atrium, where the darkness was just beginning to soften into dawn. "What time do you think the fishermen turn up to work?"

Moments later, we were strolling across the road to the port, with Juba in tow. After prowling all night like a caged animal, Juba was glad for the chance to actually get out of the villa. And, as he had pointed out when joining us, we were literally still in sight of the place, so it wasn't as though he was leaving it unguarded. He made an excellent point. He usually did. Also, it was amazing how talkative people could become once Juba loomed over them.

Luck and the tides were with us, because the boats belonging to the fishermen of Baiae seemed to still be in the port. I felt better than I had all night, though most of that was down to the fact I no longer had a mountain pressing on my shoulders. Instead, the sky was miles above me, the faint stars fading in the dawn, and a cool ocean breeze promised a fresh and bright new day.

Mino was not at his boat, and the men we spoke to hadn't seen him this morning. He lived outside of town, on the road to Puteoli, next to the brothel. It was as good a landmark as any, and I was confident we'd find our fisherman there and then, if our luck held, his erstwhile cousin.

Our luck did not hold.

The sun was up, and the port was in full swing by the time we'd spoken to enough workers there to confirm what we'd been told, and my stomach was complaining about neglect. I needed breakfast before we were looking for Mino. We headed back towards the villa, crossing the road to the row of shops that shared my front wall.

"Sir! Aemilius Valerius, sir!"

I turned to look behind us for the source of the tremulous voice. It was the girl from Aemilia Cassia's shop, and she was as pale as a wraith.

"Sir," she said. "Please, sir, there is someone here who wants to talk to you. He—he came in the middle of the night, and he won't leave. The men with him took Cassia away!"

Juba was the first one through the doorway into the shop, and by the time Atreus and I had reached him, he was holding a man up against the wall, with one hand wrapped around his scrawny throat. Disconcertingly, the man was smiling as though they were exchanging pleasantries about the weather.

"I think you ought to put him down, Juba," I said. "Let's at least make sure he's got enough breath in his lungs to explain himself before you break his neck."

Juba let the man slide down the wall so that his feet were touching the floor. He didn't release his grip by much.

"Thank you," the man said to me. "Much appreciated." He was thin and nondescript in almost every way, with mousy brown hair, eyes the colour of dun, and a couple of pockmarks in his cheeks. He looked like any man you'd meet in any street in any town or city in the empire, as ubiquitous as a brown dog or a rat. "My name is Lucius Agermus, sir. I am a freedman of Agrippina the Younger."

My blood ran hot with anger, then cold with dread. I'd kept my family locked away in the villa to keep them safe, and Rufio had put Praetorians in sight of the portico, and meanwhile this rat bastard had wandered into Cassia's shop like a customer, under all our noses.

"What the fuck have you done with Aemilia Cassia?" I asked.

Agermus showed us his palms. "Nothing, sir, I swear! She is safe and well, and at this moment stitching a stola or two for Agrippina." He gave another smarmy smile. "She will be well compensated for her time, Aemilius Valerius."

I tilted my head. "I've heard enough, Juba. Break his neck."

A flicker of genuine fear ran across Agermus's face. "Wait!"

I held up my hand, as though Juba had actually been about to kill him in the first place, and Agermus sagged slightly against the wall. The gullible fool. The killing would come after Cassia was safe, obviously.

"My mistress wishes to speak with you," Agermus said. "That is all. You are safe. You have my word."

"What makes you think your word is worth shit to me?" I asked him.

He blinked rapidly at that, as though he'd never considered things might go badly for him here. Yes, he had leverage, but that was worthless to him if we thought Cassia was already as good as dead. "I—it is *Agrippina's* word, sir."

"Same question," I said.

Agermus gave me a peevish look. Oh, he was an ex-imperial slave, alright. He was snooty, self-important, and so far up his own arse that he could taste last night's dinner. "It is *her word.*"

Well then. Clearly, neither of us was willing to budge. Not that it mattered. Agrippina was holding Cassia hostage, so there was no question I was going. We all knew it.

"Juba," I said, "go back to the villa and—"

"No," Juba said, without taking his eyes off Agermus.

I was so astonished, I looked away from Agermus to stare at him.

"No," he repeated, and then he added, belatedly, "Sir."

"You," Atreus said before I could even say anything. He motioned the girl forward and caught her by the arm. "Go to Valerius's villa. Tell Fulvia Drusa or Octavia Junilla where we have gone. Do you understand?"

The girl nodded, still trembling. When Atreus released her, she hurried through the door and out onto the street.

"That's not necessary," Agermus said, pursing his lips. "I told you that you will be safe."

Atreus folded his arms over his chest. "Then it doesn't matter who knows where we're going."

Juba finally released Agermus, and the freedman rubbed his throat reflexively as he stared at us haughtily. "Well, then," he said. "Shall we?"

And so, given we had no real choice in the matter, we did.

* * *

Agrippina had a villa on the edge of Lake Lucrinus. The gardens, which reached the shores of the lake, were dotted with pavilions, fountains, and shrines. Marble paths bordered by colonnades and trees cut through the gardens. A series of terraced pools glittered in the sunlight. Statues of gods and Julio-Claudians—and both, in some cases—flanked the entrance to the portico and ushered us into the first atrium of, presumably, many. Like any imperial residence, this one was expansive, made up of multiple buildings that formed a large complex. The walls of the atrium were painted in bright frescos, accented with gold. Mosaics depicted ocean creatures and nereids: porpoises, fish, and octopuses frolicked in the seafoam with Pherusa and Amatheia and their sisters.

Two Germans from the Numerus Batavorum joined us in the atrium and fell into step behind us. I was sure I wasn't the only one of us awaiting the sensation of a blade through my spine. Agermus led the way, in short but rapid steps, his shoulders pulled back, and his chin held high, like the proud little lap dog he was.

Slaves lowered their gazes and moved out of the way as we passed.

Agrippina received us in a colonnaded peristyle that was set on a slope that overlooked Lake Lucrinus. The couches were shaded by silk canopies that created a sea of rainbow colours as they rippled in the breeze. She was alone, except for the pretty young slave who waited on her, and four more Germans from the Numerus Batavorum who stood in pairs at either end of her couch. In a lesser woman, it might have read as paranoia, but I knew it for what it was: a warning. The bodyguards weren't because she was afraid of us—they were a reminder that we were dead men as soon as she gave the order.

"Aemilius Valerius," Agrippina said. She didn't rise. Her lips curled into a smile as her gaze travelled over Atreus and Juba. "How nice of you to join me."

"Agrippina," I said, and nodded my head. "Agermus gave the impression that the invitation was one I ought not decline."

Agrippina gestured to the couch across from hers. I sat. Atreus and Juba remained standing.

"Your seamstress is fine," Agrippina said. "She does good work."

"She does," I agreed, wondering how long she was going to keep up the pretence that this was a friendly conversation. Had Cassia's girl got the message through to Fulvia or Octavia? Had they known to send for Rufio? And, if they had, did it matter? Petronius hadn't seemed sure of where things stood with Nero and his mother. Was Rufio constrained by that? At least, I supposed, someone would know exactly where to point fingers when our bloodied corpses were found floating in the lake. Although, would that even make a difference? Agrippina had killed more important men than me, and everyone knew it.

"You think I am your enemy," she said, frankly.

"I think that I have caused you trouble in the past," I said. "And I think that you do not forget an injury."

She dipped her head in acknowledgement. "Do you play latrunculi, Valerius?"

"Very badly," I said, hoping nobody brought out a board.

Agrippina dipped her head, the light glinting on a jewelled comb tucked into a row of immaculate curls. "Then you know that sometimes you have to sacrifice your pieces to win the game."

She was being intentionally opaque, I was certain, but I forced a polite smile in what I hoped was a satisfying acknowledgement of whatever she thought her point was.

Octavia's husband, Nasica, had uncovered evidence of a legionary conspiracy: a hidden silver mine that funnelled money directly back to Agrippina, bypassing the imperial treasury. It was treason. More importantly, however, it had given Nero a reason to distance himself from his mother and to remove her from the machinery of government. The treason had never been made public, but Atreus and I had discovered it when we were looking into the deaths of some prominent senators, all of whom had been involved. We had unwittingly finished the job Nasica had started, even though we'd had no idea of Agrippina's involvement at the start of it.

I would never believe she didn't hold a grudge against us for that. She'd been scrambling to get back into Nero's good graces ever since, and she knew who to blame for her predicament. Apart from herself, naturally. Politics was a dirty game, and the people who played it best didn't care how much they soiled their hands. And Agrippina had been born to play politics.

She was the great-granddaughter of Augustus. She was Caligula's sister and had survived banishment after a failed plot against him. She was Claudius's niece and wife, and had positioned her son to inherit the purple even before Claudius's son conveniently died. And she was the mother of Nero. There was probably no other woman in the history of the empire who had been so close to the throne every time a new emperor sat in it. If she had been born a son instead of a daughter, I had no doubt she would have ruled the world.

"The individual battles do not matter, Valerius," she continued, "only who wins the war."

"As someone who has fought in several individual battles, Augusta, I respectfully disagree."

I didn't need to look at Atreus to feel his incredulous stare, but Agrippina, perhaps mollified by my use of her title, let out a short laugh that sounded as though it surprised her as much as it did me.

"And here I thought that using a military analogy would cause us to be on common ground," she said, and I caught a glimpse of not just her cleverness, but a wicked sense of humour behind it too.

Was it Virgil who said that fortune favours the brave? I hoped that was true, and that it extended to the blatantly reckless, because I was about to get braver. Or stupider. Or both.

I showed her my palms. "Alas, I was a mere junior tribune under Corbulo. The outcome of the war was less important to me than whether or not I ended the day with a Parthian spear in my gut. It's my belief that it must be difficult to give proper consideration to the political fate of Rome if your intestines are being tickled from the inside by iron."

One of the German bodyguards bit back a smile. Humour was the same throughout most of the ranks, despite ancestry. And if I hadn't quite made a new friend out of him with my relatability, then at least he might feel a twinge of regret when he was ordered to murder me. It was probably the best I could hope for.

"Well, then," Agrippina said. "To speak plainly, you are not my enemy."

"I am glad to hear that," I said. I didn't believe it for a second, but it was still nice to hear. The most pleasing lies always were.

She leaned forward, her gaze intent. "I approach you as a mother, Valerius. I have come to Baiae to seek a reconciliation with my son. I am asking you to not stand in my way."

I didn't trust myself to look at Atreus or Juba. I didn't ask Agrippina why she thought I had the power to sway Nero's mind. And then I realised that I didn't, and she knew it. This was another mask she was wearing—that of the unfairly maligned mother who only wanted her son's love, and it was just a coincidence that he happened to be the most powerful man in the world. She would fight for reconciliation just as strongly as if he'd been a slave employed to scrape the bird shit off the roof of a temple, and how dare anyone presume otherwise. And, in truth, nobody dared, especially not right to her face.

"I am not a fool, Valerius," she continued, and I had never thought she was. She'd outlived most of the rest of the Julio-Claudians, after all. "I know you have my son's ear. I am not asking you to whisper in it on my behalf. All I ask is that you don't drip poison in it."

Something had changed since the night I'd seen her at Nero's villa. She had been more certain of herself then, more audacious in her approach. But in the shifting sands of both political and familial alliances, perhaps the ground had sunk a little underneath her. If she'd truly taken a knock to her confidence, I had no way of knowing what had caused it, and she would never tell me.

Agermus pinched his mouth into an unhappy shape, and I knew that I was right. Agrippina was on the back foot somehow. It didn't stop her heartfelt maternal plea from sounding exactly like a threat—Agrippina could make a honey cake recipe sound like a threat—but if a threat was the worst that happened here today, I would consider myself the luckiest of men.

"I have never spoken to your son about you," I said, pleased that I didn't have to lie. The truth was that I didn't have to tell Nero what I thought: he knew how dangerous she was, and there were plenty of men willing to remind him even if I wasn't. Seneca, Burrus, Lucan, Petronius, Anicetus— and they were only the first names from a very long list.

Agrippina held my gaze for an uncomfortably long moment, and then she said, in an almost plaintive tone, as though she was willing me to believe her, "There is nobody else who can keep him at heel, Valerius."

I jolted, and my surprise spoke for me. "He is the emperor, not a dog."

"He is a wolf," she said, her lips curling into a faint smile that was almost proud, "and I am the woman holding him by the ears. Think on that, Valerius. Think on that."

* * *

In our little exclusive neighbourhood on the Baian waterfront, news travelled fast.

We met Rufio and a cluster of his Praetorians halfway back to Baiae, and he looked both relieved and astonished to see us, which was fitting, because I felt the same about surviving long enough to be seen by him. I couldn't answer the only question he asked me: What had happened?

"I don't know," I said, Cassia clutching my arm tightly as we hurried down the road. "She made a great show of telling me I wasn't her enemy. She says she's not looking for a sympathiser to get in Nero's ear on her behalf, but what else could it be? But then why approach *me*? Nero has closer friends."

Rufio shook his head "She is pulling so many threads at any given moment in time that even a spider couldn't untangle the web she weaves."

I had never felt more powerless. I was a Roman patrician, descended from senators. My ancestors had built Rome alongside the other great families. I'd been born to wealth and influence. I wasn't used to being nothing more than a struggling fly trying uselessly to escape an approaching spider. I didn't enjoy it.

Rufio accompanied us back to Baiae, all the way to the front of Cassia's shop. Nothing cleared the morning pedestrians quicker than an escort of Praetorians.

Cassia squeezed my hands. "I don't know what's going on, Quintus, but please be careful."

"I will," I said, warming to hear her call me by my praenomen just as she had when I was a child.

She gave me a worried look before going inside her shop.

I thanked Rufio for his help, and Atreus, Juba, and I went home to the villa.

"Master!" Vulso exclaimed when he saw us, and then turned and yelled down into the atrium, "It's the master!"

It wasn't a hero's welcome, exactly, but my family and the slaves all came running to check for themselves that we weren't dead. Tullius the dog seemed especially delighted, but then everything seemed equally delightful to him. Yesterday, he'd been in paroxysms of joy when he'd eaten a bug.

"You're not dead!" Maro exclaimed and slapped me on the back so soundly that it felt as though he was trying to remedy that. I was going to make a joke out of it before I saw that his eyes were shining with tears of relief. "Oh, my boy! My stupid, stupid boy!"

I hugged him. "I know. But she had Cassia, and I knew that you would send for Rufio."

"Stupid," he said, and thumped me between the shoulders hard enough to leave a bruise. "Morally correct, but *stupid*."

I couldn't argue with that assessment.

My womenfolk were also suspiciously wet-eyed.

"It's fine," I said, accepting hugs from all of them in turn, even Julia. "We're fine. I'll tell you everything, I promise. Can we get some breakfast, please? I'm starving."

It gave them something to do, and not just the slaves. Maro and my womenfolk rushed into the triclinium as though they needed to plump every cushion on every couch before it was fit for use.

Atreus, Lucilla on his hip, shot me a knowing look.

Juba stared at the impluvium.

"Juba."

He lifted his gaze and squared his shoulders. "Sir."

Agrippina wasn't the first person who'd made me feel as though I had no power today. Juba had done it first by refusing to obey me. I was his master, and he was my slave, and I had every right under the law to punish him for his disobedience. It was my legal and civic duty to do it. But I didn't have the stomach for it, because Juba had chosen to risk his own life to stand at my side.

Morally correct, but stupid.

Apparently, I wasn't the only one.

"I'll deal with you later when all this is over," I said, dragging a hand through my hair.

And then I turned on my heel and headed for breakfast, before I could see whether his reaction was one of relief or trepidation, and find myself caught in the familiar, unhappy trap of wondering why it mattered to me.

Chapter Nine

"Hey, handsome! You look tired!" The woman gave me a wink as she leaned on the wall, her tunic hitched up to expose her plump thigh. "Do you need a little pick-me-up?"

The Seashell Brothel on the Puteoli Road was the sort of establishment that believed in aggressive marketing. Not only did the girls tout the street for business, but the painted signs on the front wall depicted exactly what services were on offer inside.

"Not right now, thanks," I told her, and nodded at the two-storey insula behind the brothel. "Is that Mino's place?"

The woman squinted her kohl-rimmed eyes at me suspiciously and then, either deciding that I didn't look like a debt collector or a thug, or that I did and she just wasn't fond enough of Mino to give a shit, she said, "Second floor, third from the stairs."

I tossed her a coin for her trouble.

She caught it deftly. "Come see me on the way back, sweetheart. I'll bet I've got something you like."

I bet she didn't, but I returned her wink and Atreus and I continued along to the insula.

The entrance opened onto a dusty courtyard with a dribbling concrete fountain and cracked tilework. A couple of chickens strutted around the place, and a little boy was playing with some colourful pebbles at the bottom of the steps. It wasn't luxury, but I'd seen worse. Atreus and I headed for the stairs, skirting around a dog on a chain whose thin tail and hopeful expression said he was expecting treats instead of burglars.

We climbed the stairs and counted our way to Mino's door. Atreus banged on it with his fist, and, after a moment, it opened a crack. I caught a glimpse of a narrowed dark eye in the slit of a face.

"Mino?" Atreus asked.

"Yeah?" He made it sound like a question.

Atreus was a vigile. He didn't respect privacy, boundaries, closed doors, or any combination of them. He widened the crack in the door before Mino could close it, pushing his way into the room, and Mino had no choice but to move back and let us in or get flattened against the wall like a bug.

He was a young man. He was about my height, but scrawny, and he had the patchy beard and greasy hair of a man who had neglected to visit both his barber and the baths in the past few days. His brown tunic was rumpled, and his feet were bare. He looked as though he'd just crawled out of bed.

"You're the fisherman?" I asked, and his gaze—part belligerent and part baffled—flicked to me.

He nodded and scratched his chin. "Yeah. Who the fuck are you?"

"Aemilius Valerius," I said, and nodded at Atreus. "And Junius Atreus."

Mino sidled away from us along the wall.

His place wasn't much. There was a bed, a shelf, and a wicker chair with half the arse hanging out of it. Someone had bashed a couple of pegs into the wall, and Mino's clothes and sandals were hanging from them, all of them in various shades of brown. Sagging shutters hung in the window. The place smelled faintly of fish, which was an occupational hazard for a man in his line of work.

Atreus folded his arms. "We're looking for your cousin who works at the Baths of Mercury."

Mino's suspicious expression relaxed, and he even gave a little snort. "How much does he owe you?"

"Is he here?" Atreus asked.

Mino shrugged. "He comes and goes. Haven't seen him in a while."

"How long is a while?"

Mino shrugged again. "Three days? Four?"

"That's quite a while," I said. "Are you not close?"

Mino's mouth twisted. "Mino's always bringing trouble to my door. If he owes you money, I'm sorry, but that's none of my business."

"So if he's not here, where would he be?" I asked.

Mino shrugged and scratched his forearm. Perhaps his bed had fleas. "No idea. I'm his cousin, not his mother."

He might have been sick of his cousin bringing trouble to his door, but that still didn't mean he was willing to hand him over to strangers he thought were chasing up some debt.

"So where's his mother?" Atreus asked.

Mino made a sour face and scratched his shoulder. His fingernails left red marks on the pale skin of his shoulder where he pushed the neck of his tunic aside to reach the itch. "Dead. I'm his only family."

"Hmm." Atreus didn't sound very sympathetic. He nodded at Mino's shoulder, and then said, "I've never met a fisherman who wasn't tanned all over. And with such unblemished hands."

Shit.

Mino lunged for the door, but Atreus was already in his way. Mino had sheer determination on his side, though, and they both crashed into the door. I waded in and caught someone's elbow to the gut, almost knocking the breath out of me. I grabbed Mino by the back of the tunic and wrenched him off Atreus.

Atreus grinned at me, despite his bleeding lip.

I flung Mino backwards, not particularly caring where he landed, and he sprawled onto his flea-infested bed. Or rather, his cousin's flea-infested be, because this Mino was no fisherman. This Mino was the Mino we'd been looking for all along—the sibyl's acolyte who worked at a shop in the Baths of Mercury complex. He glared up at me, clearly unhappy we'd found him.

"You're the Mino who works at the baths," Atreus said. "Tell us about the sibyl."

Mino wrinkled his nose like a petulant child. "I don't even know who you are!"

"I already answered that. We're Aemilius Valerius and Junius Atreus, but that's not the important part," I told him. "The important part is that

Calpurnia Tertia is dead."

"That's got nothing to do with us!" Mino exclaimed. "We didn't have anything to do with it!"

"Really?" Atreus asked. He lifted his chin. "Then why is the sibyl dead too?"

Mino's expression froze, and then fell. He struggled to sit up. "What are you talking about? What do you mean she's dead?"

"She's dead," Atreus said. "Pulled out of the sea last night."

"What?" Mino blinked at him, his jaw slack. Then he blinked again, rapidly this time, his eyes filling with tears. "Are you *sure*?"

"We're sure," Atreus said. "Tell us about her."

"About—" Mino shook his head as though to clear it. "About Tita?"

It was the first time anyone had put a name to the sibyl. It reminded me that whatever she'd done in the tunnel and grotto that cut into the hillside underneath the Baths of Mercury, she had been more than her actions in that crowded, dark place, at least to the people who knew her. Caecilia Didia and her rich friends had thought, in varying degrees of faith, that young woman was a seer. Atreus and I thought she was a scammer. And presumably the people who knew her, like Mino, would remember things that the rest of us hadn't even imagined about her—her laugh, that song she hummed, that filthy joke she liked to tell.

"Tell us about Tita," Atreus said, the previously hard edges of his tone softened by sympathy.

Mino scrubbed at his face with the heels of his hands and gave us a mulish look. "Why should I?"

"Because you can either tell us, or you can tell the magistrate at Cumae," Atreus said.

Mino was silent for a moment, but he was smart enough to realise we were offering him the best choice he was going to get. And smart enough, too, to blame the dead woman.

"It was her idea," he said, his voice low. "All of it."

I caught Atreus's dubious look.

Mino scowled. "People like those women, they come here from Rome, and spend their money like it's nothing to them, and why shouldn't we get some of it if they're happy enough to throw it around?"

"It's not your entrepreneurial spirit we give a shit about," I said. "It's the fact that Calpurnia Tertia is dead. You know who her brother is, don't you?"

Mino's suddenly terrified expression confirmed that he did, but he tried to bluster his way through. "I already told you that wasn't anything to do with us!" His scowl deepened. "Why would we kill her when she was happy to pay?"

"Was she, though?" I asked. "Or had she finally figured out that the sibyl was fake?"

"She didn't have any idea!" he exclaimed. "None of them do! They probably wouldn't even believe it if you told them. They just like paying money for the gods to promise they're special and important!"

I suspected he was right about that. Willing ears were always open to honeyed lies.

"What happened to Tertia?" I asked.

"I don't *know*." Mino pushed his mouth into a crooked line. "Last I saw her was at the grotto. I went and collected the women from Caecilia's house, and we all went to the grotto. I showed them down there, collected the money, and Tita spun whatever bullshit she usually did."

"You didn't listen?" Atreus asked.

"No." Mino shook his head. "It's narrow down there—"

"Oh, we've been," I said.

He frowned. "Well, you'd know then. It's narrow, and dark, and my job was to keep them by the stream until it was their turn to go and visit the sibyl, because there wasn't enough room for all of them in there at once."

"So they went in singly?" Atreus asked.

"Yeah," Mino said. "Well, Caecilia Didia and Livilla Faustina did. The young ones, Tertia and Plautia Balbina, went together, but they did everything together. Joined at the hip, those two. Always chattering together like two little birds. Calling each other sisters. I thought they were, at first."

"And what did Tita tell you about what she said to Tertia that night?" Atreus asked.

Mino scoffed. "Tell me? She was in no condition to tell me a fucking thing."

"Come on," I said. "You're not going to pretend she was really in a trance or something, are you?"

"No," he said. "But she burned so much asterion I had to practically drag her out of there by the heels. She was so drunk from it she almost *was* talking to the gods." The anger drained out of his expression as suddenly as posca out of a punctured wineskin. "Is she—is she really dead?"

"Yes," said Atreus. "She was strangled, just like Tertia."

Mino looked as though he almost didn't believe us, because wouldn't life be a lot simpler if Atreus and I were lying to him? His eyes widened and he said, in a hopeful tone, "But we didn't hurt anyone."

I exchanged a disbelieving look with Atreus.

It was another honeyed lie, but this was one that Mino told only for himself, probably so he could sleep soundly in his cousin's flea-infested bed every night.

"Tell me about Tertia," Atreus said. "Was she the good little patrician girl her brother thinks she was, or did she like slumming it with men like you?"

Mino's face twisted. "No, she—I don't know anything about her, but like I said, her and Plautia were joined at the hip. She was quiet."

Atreus raised his eyebrows. "You said a moment ago she was always chattering like a bird."

"To Plautia, not to me! They were always talking about the brother, Piso, and his wife. Plautia wanted to invite the wife along too, but the other women didn't want her there. Thought she was above herself or some shit."

I remembered Piso saying that Atria Galla wasn't as accepted here in Baiae the way she was in Rome, for the audacity of having married so far above her rank. I wondered where the opposition to inviting her had come from. Was Caecilia Didia the snob, or was it the apparently dull as dishwater Livilla Faustina? Certainly not Galeria Alba who, even if she'd had an opinion on the matter, wouldn't have dared voice it to the others.

"Tell us about Tita," Atreus asked. "How well did you know her?"

"Grew up together, didn't we?" He turned it into a question, as though it was something we should have known, and then he gave us a mulish look. "She was my girlfriend, for a bit."

"What happened?" I asked.

Mino shrugged, and his shoulders sagged. "She left me for Mino. Then she dumped him too, and I didn't hear from here again until about a year ago. She turns up at the shop, takes me for a drink, and asks me if I remember showing her those tunnels behind the temple at the baths? Wants to know if I can still get my hands on the key to the gate." He shook his head. "She said it could make us both a lot of money."

It made sense that Tita had been the brains and Mino had just done what she'd told him to do, because he didn't give the impression that there was much of anything between his ears. I bet if I leaned closer as his mouth opened when he talked, I'd hear the sound of the ocean.

"But it didn't make you a lot of money, did it?" I asked, looking around the sparse little room. "Why is that?"

"She said she'd look after the money for us," Mino said, and scowled. "Then I found out she'd been gambling. She was up to her neck in debts to this arsehole money lender over in Cumae. So that's where all the money went. I got nothing."

Which was exactly what he deserved.

"I imagine you were very angry when you found that out," Atreus said. His tone of voice was so even that Mino mistook it for empathy.

"Yeah, I was! I was—" He caught himself. "I didn't kill her! I was angry, but I didn't kill her!"

"You have a very good motive," Atreus said.

It was a typical vigile tactic—frighten the suspect so much that in his eagerness to prove his innocence he might be inclined to share anything he was still holding back. I knew that Atreus didn't believe Mino was our killer any more than I did. Because it was true that he had a motive to kill Tita, but he didn't have one to kill Calpurnia Tertia.

But Mino didn't know how Atreus worked, and possibly all he saw were visions of the magistrate in Cumae, and then a sentence of death to be carried out in the nearest arena. Because before Atreus could soften his fear with an invitation to tell us any little thing he was holding back, however unimportant it seemed, Mino dived for the window, crashed through the sagging shutters, and had bolted halfway down the street outside before Atreus and I had even realised he was moving.

The little shit.

***

When we got back to the villa at Baiae, preparations for Maro's extravagant dinner party were well under way. The garden was full of dancers, musicians, acrobats and gladiators, mingling with bewildered men carrying shovels and trowels, planter boxes, pots and tiles. Maro presided over them like a king, sitting in a wicker throne and shaded by a massive sun hat.

"Yes!" he cried out. "Yes, you over there! That's where the fountain needs to go! Start digging!"

"Maro!" I sidestepped a woman wearing nothing but her undergarments. I presumed she was an acrobat, but at this point, it wouldn't have surprised me if she was just half-naked for no reason at all. It seemed like that sort of spectacle.

"Ah! Quintus!" Maro rose and embraced me. "Everything is under control."

Spoken like every person ever who had nothing under control. I knew the feeling.

"You're not replacing the fountain, are you?"

"No, don't be ridiculous," he said, his eyes gleaming. "We're putting in another one."

"What for?"

"Well," he said, "I'm not sure the original really works with the theme I'm going for."

The theme of utter fucking chaos, apparently.

"Maro, please don't bankrupt the family for the sake of one dinner party."

He laughed and clapped me on the back. "Don't be ridiculous! All of this is an investment in your future. Once you've been noticed by important men, you must do what you can to keep their eyes on you. You have Nero and his friends, my boy, but do you have the senate, hmm?"

"I can't imagine why I would *want* to have the senate, Maro."

He tapped the side of his nose. "Because one day when you're sitting in their ranks, even if it's twenty or thirty years from now, you'll need their votes for something."

I'd once foolishly thought Maro was less ambitious than my father, but I was beginning to realise I was wrong. My father had been serious and hard-working, and he'd been run ragged by the relentlessly shifting political landscape in Claudius's final days. Maro had impressed me by not seeming to care at all about who was aligning with whom in secret, and what factions divided the senate behind closed doors—it turned out he just played a longer game than my father. And no doubt he was right. I was never going to be the sort of man who won political friends on the strength of my oratory, but the strength of my Falernian? I could manage that.

"Just make sure you don't destroy the place entirely," I said, and escaped to the triclinium.

A strange atmosphere hung over the villa that had nothing to do with Maro's insanity, and everything to do with the fact that only this morning I'd faced Agrippina and somehow lived to tell the tale. I still wasn't sure if she'd been making an overture towards me, perhaps hoping for an uneasy alliance of some kind. Although why she would bother was a mystery, since I wasn't that important. Nero liked me, certainly, but he had a lot of friends. Or, if not an overture, perhaps a threat, although it had been so thoroughly wrapped up in words designed to obfuscate meaning that I couldn't even tell it had been there at all. Perhaps Agrippina was used to threatening smarter men, who didn't need it spelled out like a slack-jawed child struggling with Greek verbs. Or perhaps the threat had been entirely implied by her presence alone, and the reminder that she could reach me, or at least the people I cared about, even when I thought they were protected. In which case the threat had been a pointless one, because I had never once thought that I could protect anyone against her.

My mood hadn't been improved by Mino giving us the slip.

Atreus sat down on the couch across from mine, his expression customarily serious. "Do we believe Mino?"

I let out a breath. "I think we do. He wouldn't know honesty if it walked up and shook him by the hand, but he was right about one thing."

Atreus nodded. "Why would they kill Tertia when she was paying handsomely to be a part of their cult?"

"And he was right that even if she'd known it was a scam, it wouldn't necessarily stop the others from believing it. Jupiter, even if they lost Caecilia Didia, their most ardent devotee, they could just start over with the newest batch of rich tourists from Rome. It makes no sense at all for Mino to have killed Tertia, and even if he did—I can't see why he would, but if he *did*—then why kill Tita?" Mino's shock and grief hadn't been feigned. He wasn't a good enough liar for that. "The money isn't really a motive, and you're smart enough to know it. She might have gambled it away, but where the hell else is someone like Mino going to get the chance to even see money like that again without Tita to tell him what to do?"

Atreus shrugged. "I'm smart enough to know it, but is Mino? Maybe he got angry and didn't think ahead."

"Depends if you believe his shock at hearing she was dead was real," I said. "And even if you want to pin Tita's death on Mino, how does Calpurnia Tertia fit into that?"

Atreus leaned back. "Agreed. But the connection is the cult; it has to be, even if Mino's not our man. Both women were killed in the same way, and the cult was the only thing they had in common. What other reason would Tertia have to even know Tita?"

I grunted my agreement. "So where does this leave us?"

Atreus shrugged, the corner of his mouth lifting slightly in the ghost of a wry smile. "In dire need of a real prophetess, I think."

I snorted. "I don't care about the future. Right now, I'd settle for someone who could accurately tell us the past."

Fulvia sailed in, as was her wont. "I certainly care about the future, though, Quintus." She leaned down and brushed a kiss against my cheek. When she straightened up, she was wearing a judgemental look. "You need a shave."

I rubbed my barely stubbled cheek. "I'm fine."

She raised her eyebrows. "We are going to the imperial villa tonight. Lucan is reciting, remember? I've sent for a barber and a manicurist."

I relented. "Very well."

She gave me the sort of fondly amused look she always did when I was pretending I'd ever had a choice in the first place. "Thank you, Quintus."

I took the chance to bathe before the barber and manicurist arrived, and Atreus joined me. I sprawled on the steps of the bath as boneless as a jellyfish while a slave attacked me first with a sponge, and then with oil and a strigil. Atreus sat next to me, and I stole glimpses of his profile while he, apparently lost in thought, stared at nothing.

The steam rose like a ghost, curling around the frescoed ceiling.

"I wish we'd kept hold of him," Atreus said at last.

"Mino?"

"We didn't have any evidence," I said, as though that had even been the issue. Back in Rome we had an entire cohort of vigiles to call upon when we needed to track down a suspect, and we'd felt their loss today. Even if we'd had Juba with us, it might have made the difference, because Juba had an almost preternatural sense of which way a cornered little rat was going to run. "You're just stung that he got the drop on us. Besides, he's not our killer."

"No," Atreus agreed. "But he could use a few weeks staring at a brick wall in the dark."

I couldn't argue with that.

"Do we have a plan?" I asked him. "For tomorrow?"

He tilted his head back and looked up at the ceiling as though he was hoping to find the answer there. Then he closed his eyes, and said, "We talk to the women again, I suppose. Livilla Faustina wasn't home the first time we tried. Maybe she knows something."

"Her slaves said she was boring."

"Well, let's hope she's a boring woman who notices interesting things."

Hope. That was all we were running on at this point. The hope that the Fates would drop something useful in our laps. Because, for all Atreus's wishing, Mino wasn't the one staring at a blank brick wall after all, was he?

No, just like always, that was us.

And we were both getting pretty tired of the view.

* * *

The sun was a fat yellow yolk melting into the bay as our procession of litters arrived at Nero's villa, but that didn't prevent a veritable army of slaves from holding lanterns aloft on poles to hold back the gently encroaching night. We were ushered to the villa along a shifting, flickering river of light that would no doubt be spectacular once the sun slipped fully below the horizon and the first stars appeared. And ours was not the most spectacular entrance: out on the water, the ocean carried a flotilla of luxurious boats and barges that converged on the villa as unerringly as fish following a baited hook.

The boats appeared in a slow procession, each more lavishly adorned than the last. One had a prow carved into the shape of a gaping lion, its mouth stuffed with flowers. Another trailed silk streamers so long they coiled into the sea like tentacles. The boats brought music with them— pipes, lyres, cymbals and drums. The musicians on each boat were playing different tunes. The discordant sounds carried over the water, announcing the flotilla's arrival like the uneasy rumble of thunder before a storm.

All the important citizens of Baiae had been invited tonight. Those who didn't make the cut were gathered on the waterfront, watching the boats and cheering as though it was a festival parade. Not to be outdone by the guests arriving in boats, the crowd had its own lanterns, musicians, and party atmosphere. Baiae was just that sort of town. It swallowed decorum like a sponge swallowed wine.

Upon our arrival at the villa, we were met by slaves who washed our feet and then passed us over to others who carried wine and silver dishes of dates soaked in honey. Just in case, I supposed, we needed to fortify ourselves for the stroll down the terraces. Tonight's dinner party was outdoors—Nero did love his Arcadian pleasures—and the terraces that overlooked the ocean had been decorated with couches and colonnades, with shrines and shrubbery, and with slaves dressed as winsome shepherds and wanton nymphs. The shepherds wore short one-shouldered chitons that barely covered their backsides. The nymphs wore even less than that. And all of them shone as they moved, their skin oiled and dusted with crushed pearl.

"Oh!" Julia Drusilla exclaimed as a handsome nymph wearing nothing but a strategically placed garland of leaves approached us with a cheeky smile and more wine.

Fulvia took the wine and shooed the boy away. Julia's eyes widened as the boy's retreat put his shimmering arse on full display.

"Well," Octavia said wryly. "It's Baiae, after all."

Julia's wide gaze followed the boy.

The terraces looked very, very different from the last time I'd been here, when the slaves had pulled Tita's corpse out of the water.

For all the villa's decadence and delight this evening, I would have preferred to be elsewhere—Atreus and I had a killer to hunt down—so perhaps it was natural I was drawn to a guest I was also certain didn't want to be here: Calpurnius Piso.

Piso stood on the terrace, his gaze fixed on the approaching flotilla. Atria Galla stood with him, her arm linked through his, and Plautia Balbina, looking as fragile and overwhelmed as always, stood beside them. Her hair was neat today, as was Atria's—Tertia's funeral had passed, and so they were no longer in mourning. Outwardly, at least. They might have rediscovered their hairbrushes and razors and donned their party finery, but grief still clung to them all like a miasma.

I saw it in the way Piso smiled as he greeted me, as though it no longer came naturally to him and he had to remember which muscles to move. "Ah, Valerius. Walk with me?"

"Of course."

Atria and Plautia were subsumed into my family like straggling flowers overcome by a flood as Atreus and I strolled further along the terrace with Piso. Below us, on the jetty, there appeared to be something of a traffic jam as boats attempted to dock to allow their passengers to disembark in a flurry of greetings and bursts of laughter, others tried to leave, and still more approached. A few men in military uniforms—naval, I presumed—shouted back and forth, attempting to keep the confusion from spilling over into chaos.

"I wouldn't want their job tonight," I said.

Piso smiled faintly. "No."

"How have you been, Piso?"

He let out a weary breath that conveyed more than words could, and then said, "I wonder when it fades. I wake each morning with a weight on my chest, and every day it grows heavier. It's supposed to fade, isn't it, at some point?"

"It's supposed to," I agreed quietly.

Stoicism taught us that grief, like happiness, was fleeting. That men were masters of our own minds, and there was no emotion in the universe that couldn't be deflated like a wine skin with only the power of rational thought. And most of the time, we even believed it. But none of us were wise enough that death lost its sting. None of us could truly outthink grief. And if a Stoic out there existed who could, then I didn't want to meet him.

We stared at the harbour for a while, and then Atreus said, "How is Plautia Balbina holding up?"

Piso raised his eyebrows. "After you summoned her to look at a corpse last night?" He gave Atreus a moment to look shamefaced—Atreus didn't—and then continued. "She's as well as any of us, I suppose. She's staying with Atria and me. It gives her some comfort, and I suppose we are the closest thing she has to family now. It's better than her remaining alone in that empty house of hers."

Spoken like a true Roman patrician. Plautia's house wasn't empty—it would have taken a dozen slaves to keep it running at the very least—but I knew exactly what Piso meant. Plautia Balbina could hardly drop into the kitchen in the middle of the night if she was feeling lonely and chat with the slaves preparing the next day's bread. She couldn't engage the gardener in a discussion about Ovid's Metamorphoses and the transformation of grief, or confess to the boy who held her sunshade that she missed Tertia so much she couldn't sleep. Her house might have been full, but Plautia was still alone.

"And it gives some comfort to us, as well," Piso said, his expression grave. "It's what Tertia would have wanted, and to have someone else who understands, well…"

He didn't finish the thought. Perhaps he was going to, after mulling it over for a while, but at that moment the sound of trumpets rang out in the air, and from the pavilion on the topmost terrace, Nero made his entrance.

"My friends!" he exclaimed, as everyone on the terraces turned to gaze at him like flowers leaning toward the sunlight. "My most honoured and beloved friends! You are welcome! Let us drink and feast, and be glad of each other!"

He beamed then, basking in the applause and cheers of the crowd. Nero liked to be liked, and who could blame him for that? And what wasn't to like about a lavish party like this one?

Piso was drawn into conversation with another man who approached us, and Atria Galla and Plautia Balbina rejoined him, so Atreus and I went to look for the family. We found them settled on a series of couches on a wide terrace about midway up from the dock. Slaves hovered around with wine and food, and musicians danced past. Pungent smoke flowed out of a brazier, as thick as fog.

It was decadent. If the naked-arsed slaves hadn't given that away, the fact that the women were reclining as well as the men certainly did. Maro and Marcia were sharing a couch, holding hands like lovestruck teens. Fulvia and Octavia and Julia were sharing as well—there was no canoodling, but plenty of giggling—which left Atreus and I to share.

Rufio found us. He was wearing a toga instead of his uniform, and had a cup of wine in his hand. "It's good to see you again."

"And in much better circumstances than this morning." I lifted my wine in his direction in a toast. "What's the gossip around the villa about that?"

Rufio shook his head. "None, I'm afraid. Anicetus was here again, but it seems as though he's always here, and who can say what it's about? Nobody ever knows what Anicetus is up to."

"Well, perhaps I'm not that important after all," I said. "Gods willing."

Rufio smiled at that, and then turned his attention to Octavia. He cleared his throat. "The view of the bay is nicer just a little way along the terrace."

"Is it? It seems as though it would be exactly the same as from here." She raised her eyebrows and let him squirm for a long moment before she rose and put him out of his misery. She adjusted the fall of her stola and flashed Rufio a smile, and said, "Although I would like to judge for myself, if you'd be so kind as to escort me."

I tried not to laugh at his expression of both wonderment and abject relief.

"He's a good one," Uncle Maro said, wagging a finger in my direction as though I'd ever said otherwise.

"Handsome too," Marcia said approvingly.

"I wish our villa had terraces," Maro said a little glumly. "Just look at what you can do with terraces!"

I drank my wine and was quietly thankful that we weren't going to be here long enough for Maro to figure out what walls he had to knock down to extend the garden to the waterfront just so we could have terraces like these. My head was feeling muzzy already, and it was from more than just the wine. It took me a moment to realize it was from the smoke flowing out of the brazier.

Asterion.

I should have placed the smell sooner, given we'd caught a whiff of it in Tita's grotto deep in the hillside behind the Baths of Mercury.

"Shall we go and mingle?" I asked Fulvia, aware that if I sat for too long I'd fall asleep drunk on the smoke.

And so we went and mingled, Atreus walking with Julia a few paces behind us. We left Maro and Marcia to happily succumb to the warmth and intoxicating properties of the asterion and moved a little way down the terrace, stopping here and there to exchange pleasantries with other guests. Much was made of the weather, Fulvia's hair clips, and how marvellous the local oysters were—typical bullshit small talk, but Fulvia was so good at it, and all I was required to do was to smile and nod and maybe interject here and there with a word of agreement.

We strolled a little longer.

A particularly opulent boat eased towards the dock, its hull of inlaid mother-of-pearl shining brilliantly as the golden rays of the sunset caught it.

A woman stood at the prow, her arms raised in silent greeting like a votive statue. She was dressed in a white tunic. Her stola, which was Tyrian purple, was pinned in such a way that it flew in the breeze like a sail.

My gut clenched as a wave of recognition washed over me, and Fulvia tightened her grip on my arm.

Agrippina.

If I couldn't have guessed from her ostentatious boat, the stola gave it away. What other woman had the right, or the audacity, to wear the imperial purple?

The boat sliced through the water like a blade.

A blast of trumpets sounded, and a slave cried out, unnecessarily, "Agrippina arrives!"

The air snapped taut. Even the gulls fell silent.

"Do you suppose she expects to be greeted like a goddess?" someone murmured, and I glanced around to see that we'd been joined by Petronius and Lucan.

Lucan shrugged his slender shoulders. "She would say she already is one."

"Well, there's a lot of that going around," I said, thinking of Tita and her arrival at the jetty the night before in much less spectacular circumstances.

I looked again to the extravagant boat. There Agrippina was, standing at the prow, back rigid, face unreadable in that masklike way she'd must have been practicing her entire life, and had perfected since her son had ascended to the purple. The sea breeze tugged at her stola and sent strands of dark hair fluttering across her cheek. To the wildly cheering crowd watching from outside the villa's walls, she was a living relic of divine blood—daughter of Germanicus, sister of Caligula, mother of Nero. Those of us inside the walls knew exactly how dangerous she was.

"She threatened me," I said quietly.

Petronius raised his eyebrows. "So Rufio said. To us, at least. I don't know what he told Nero."

Was there a warning there? Was this a true reconciliation between mother and son, or just an empty gesture? Was Petronius making certain I knew that the tides had once again shifted in Agrippina's favour?

We watched as her boat neared the dock, joining the queue of boats already there despite the efforts of the men on the jetty to keep the traffic moving. But then—a jolt. A great cracking sound split the air. Wood buckled. Agrippina's boat rocked sharply to one side, and a scream rose. The attendants stumbled. One, a slender woman in a sea-green gown, toppled headfirst into the water.

Chaos erupted. Slaves shouted. Oars thrashed as sailors fought to stabilize the vessel. Agrippina disappeared from view for a moment—my heart tumbled over a few beats, though I could not have said why—and then she emerged again, gripping the railing tightly.

"A collision?" I asked, somehow still startled even though it was astonishing it hadn't happened before now, to be honest.

A collision, but not a dangerous one. Even the woman who had tumbled into the water was being safely fished out, and a smaller craft—one of the villa's—was already being launched from shore and sent rowing toward Agrippina's boat.

So much for her grand entrance. Instead of descending from her luxurious vessel like an empress, she'd now be arriving on something no bigger than a fisherman's boat.

"What caused that?" Atreus asked, always the investigator.

"Hard to say," Piso murmured. "The tides are capricious this time of year, and with so many boats arriving, well. And those pleasure boats are so top-heavy…"

"Accidents happen," said Lucan, but his tone was doubtful and his gaze never left the water.

Agrippina and her attendants arrived on the jetty in dribs and drabs, courtesy of the little boat that ferried them safely to shore. The crowds on the shoreline cheered for her safe arrival. Meanwhile, boats were now being turned back to prevent them from crashing into Agrippina's boat. They spun and swirled in the bay like leaves caught in a whirlpool, and I couldn't help but imagine a grinning god stirring the ocean with a stick, just so he could laugh at the resultant chaos.

I was very glad we'd arrived via road.

Nero hurried down the steps towards the jetty, the last glimmer of sunlight catching on his gold and purple toga. Attendants with torches scurried after him.

Nero and Agrippina embraced, and my stomach twisted. If we were witnessing the reconciliation of mother and son—and the cheering crowds on the shoreline certainly seemed to believe it—then my short-lived stint as one of Nero's friends was over. Then again, there were worse things than losing an emperor's friendship, and Agrippina had kindly reminded me of that when her freedman had taken Cassia from her shop. Still, I'd witnessed them embrace before, on the steps of the senate back in Rome. The crowd had been cheering that day too, as much for the happy family reunion as the coins Nero had flung into the air for the people to catch, and it had all been theatre.

I didn't know what to think, which was nothing new at all.

Ask anyone.

Nero was solicitous and gracious, offering up immediate thanks to the gods that Agrippina was safe, and insisting she take one of his boats home at the end of the night in case hers was damaged. He was the picture of a dutiful, doting son.

We watched the spectacle, and then, when it was over, returned to the couches we'd claimed. At least, we returned to the couches I thought we'd claimed, only to find the family had moved along the terrace.

"Ho! Petronius and Lucan!" Uncle Maro exclaimed, delighted, as we found him again. "You know, I didn't quite understand all your complaining about actors—yours, Petronius, not Lucan's, as I'm not certain Lucan complains."

"I know when to keep my mouth shut," Lucan said with a quick grin.

"Whereas I have never encountered any circumstances that aren't immensely improved by complaining about them," Petronius announced. "But what's all this about actors?"

Maro began to regale them both with the saga of planning his dinner party. I could see the moment they were both pulled in against their better judgement, and before too long, they were both reclining with Maro, rapt.

"But why gladiators?" Lucan asked, both confused and delighted. Maro had that effect on people.

I turned to Fulvia. "It's nicer here."

"Yes," she said. "One can actually breathe without getting drunk on asterion."

"It's a party," I said. "Isn't the point to get drunk?"

She snorted. "Oh, you say that, in the expectation that I'll get sleepy and mellow. What you don't know is that asterion turns me into a talker."

"Is that such a terrible thing?"

"It is when I don't shut up," she said, patting the couch beside her so that I sat. She leaned against me and caught my hand. "You might think you'd married one of Caecilia Didia's squawking parrots by mistake."

I laughed.

Atreus sat on an empty couch and watched our exchange, his expression customarily pensive.

She squeezed my hand. "What about you? I'll bet you talk nonsense too."

"Surprisingly, no," I said. "Straight to snoring, like Tullius after his dinner."

"Hmm." She gave me a wicked smile. "Perhaps I need to buy some asterion."

"Excuse you, I'm a delight," I said, then caught sight of Octavia and Rufio strolling back towards us. "Here comes Octavia. I wonder if she enjoyed the view."

When they rejoined us, Octavia was wearing an expression that would have given away nothing to a stranger, but I knew her well enough to know that she was tense. Less to do with the view and Rufio's company than with Agrippina's arrival, I suspected.

Rufio gave me a worried look and shook his head slightly. I read it as a silent admission he had no idea what the fuck was going on with Nero and Agrippina either.

In the meantime, rather than drowning in doubt and uncertainty, it seemed like the only thing we could do was enjoy the party. So I motioned to a slave for more wine, and resolved to do just that.

If I'd known what was going to happen next, I would have asked for an entire amphora.

Chapter Ten

Nero's party died like a protracted battle. Weariness came first, and then a lull. The fallen were removed from the field by their friends or left where they lay. Then the remaining legionaries rallied to the blast of trumpets and pushed forward once more, either to victory or to death. And at that point, it didn't matter, since they both felt the same.

Hours after midnight, a few musicians still trailed the terraces of Nero's villa, leaving notes of both music and perfume lingering in the cool air that faded slowly in their wake. The remaining dancers swayed like seaweed caught in the push and pull of the ocean, listless and limp. The slaves hid yawns behind their trays, and more than one guest was snoring on a couch.

Lucan's recital of his *Pharsalia* had been a triumph, of course, but now the night was dying, and sleep was calling me. Despite the beauty of the villa, of the terraces, and the view, it was time to go home.

The sea had turned to black glass beneath the moon, as if Neptune himself had toddled off to bed and left the waves to die down like an unattended brazier. It would make a smooth trip home for Agrippina. I leaned against a column in the colonnade that overlooked the terraces, and watched Agrippina's borrowed boat pull away from the private dock, its gold trim glinting faintly in the torchlight. A row of silent oarsmen bent in perfect rhythm.

"She's going at last," Fulvia said, wrapping her stola tighter around her shoulders, though the night wasn't too cool. She looked as dignified and precise as always, but I heard the note of relief in her voice, of tension held in for hours that she finally let out on a breath.

The party was in its last gasps. A few diehards still groped their way around, drunk and laughing too loudly. Someone was singing out of tune nearby—it sounded like Petronius. Slaves moved like shadows, mopping up oyster shells and spilled wine.

"At least I managed to avoid her all night," I said, "although I'm still half-expecting a knife in my ribs at any moment."

"That'll be from me, dear," she said. "For the way you sometimes eat with your mouth open."

"Well, at least I'll know I deserved it."

"Shall I gather up the family?" she asked me.

"Yes, I think so." I was looking forward to getting home. Maybe I'd go straight to bed, or maybe I'd set up the latrunculi board and see if anyone wanted a game. Sometimes, however tired I was, I needed to relax before bed. Especially after a party where I'd spent most of the evening on my best behaviour, forcing smiles as I guarded my tongue. I needed some time to feel as though I belonged in my skin again. Latrunculi helped. So would Atreus, if we were able to steal a few moments together.

We left the villa at the same time as Piso and Atria and their new houseguest, Plautia Balbina. Plautia was clinging tearfully to Piso, who looked quietly bewildered, and Atria hovered like a worried mother around the pair of them. I was sure Plautia wasn't the only one who'd had too much wine to drink tonight and lost control of her emotions. Still, they managed to get into their separate litters before we all did, because Maro, although he hadn't lost control of his emotions, *had* lost control of his toga, and had to be untangled by the litter bearers and Aunt Marcia before he could climb inside.

I stretched, glad we were leaving. I was so close to that latrunculi board that my fingers were already itching to hold the pieces. And then, from Nero's villa, came the blast of trumpets. These were not the kind of short, triumphant blasts that heralded the appearance of the emperor, or of a new performance to delight an audience. These were alarms—signalling calamity and calling for aid.

"What is it?" Fulvia asked, leaning out of her litter.

"Go," I told the bearers. "All of you, go. Whatever it is, go home!"

My family wouldn't listen to me, of course. They never did. But I wasn't going to wait around and argue with them either. With Atreus by my side, I ran back through the entrance of the villa, hoping that my sense of direction didn't fail me now as we passed galleries and colonnades and a seemingly endless series of moonlit atria that fed onto each other, and would hopefully deliver us eventually to the terraces.

Atreus and I were breathless by the time we found ourselves back at the scene of the party.

The sea was too calm for this kind of chaos.

Moonlight scattered across the bay like spilled silver, dancing off the oars of a dozen panicked boats. It should have been a quiet night. The gods had given us perfect weather—no wind, no storm, and no omen in the stars. And yet, somewhere out there in the dark, something had happened. The jetty was crowded with men, with boats, with chaos.

I caught a glimpse of Petronius, Lucan at his side, and dodged a knot of panicked dancers to get over to him.

He was blank-faced and pale with shock. "Her boat," he said. "Agrippina's boat—it's sinking. Or sunk. I-I—well, no one can say."

I'd never thought I'd hear Petro struggle to find words.

"She has survived worse," Lucan murmured.

He was right about that. Agrippina was a woman born of blood and ambition, too clever to die like this. But the sea didn't care about my opinions.

Boats were setting out now from the jetty, and I thought it wouldn't be long until another one sank—but that didn't stop me from hurrying down there to get on one. Atreus and Petro were with me. I'd lost sight of Lucan, who hadn't been quick enough on his feet to follow us. Perhaps he was being juggled onto another boat even now. We found ourselves on a smallish lembus, with six oars on each side. We didn't have twelve oarsmen, but we made do. We were an odd little group of sailors. A handful of patricians, slaves, a man I'd seen earlier playing a cithara, and two Praetorians. One of them took charge of the steering oar.

We struck out, as uneven as a one-legged duck, towards Port Julius.

The moon hung over the bay like a god's watchful eye—high, full, and cruel. It cast its silver over every ripple, every hull, every oar dipping into the dark waters. The sea was thick with vessels. Fishing boats, skiffs, and even wine barges had been pressed into sudden service. It was more crowded than the Subura on a market day. As we cut across the water, the night turned mad. Boats collided. Men shouted. A torch fell and caught on a sail; flame bloomed briefly before vanishing into the sea. Somewhere, a soldier barked orders—possibly from a naval boat out of Misenum, possibly not. Boats crisscrossed the bay like flies over rotting meat. Some bore torches. Others shouted names into the dark. Many were simply drifting, uncertain where to look. If Agrippina was anywhere, she was lost among them.

It was a fruitless search. By the time we circled back toward the mouth of the bay, the mood had curdled. The shouts were sharper, and the light brighter. One barge had caught fire—a torch knocked into its deck by a careless hand—and flames licked the sails before dying under a bucket brigade's frenzied attention.

We passed another boat, its passengers arguing. Their voices carried to us across the water.

"She's dead!"

"No, someone pulled her out! I heard it myself!"

"Fool. They fished out a servant."

I slumped against my oar. My limbs ached, and the sea no longer looked like silver—it looked like oil, slick and thick with secrets.

We passed a few more boats, but none had seen Agrippina or her attendants. One man claimed she'd been eaten by sharks. Another swore he saw her fly away on a winged horse. Drunk, most of them. Or mad. We reached land as the first light crept into the sky. Not full dawn—just the grey before it, when the shadows lengthened, and even gods seemed unsure of what sort of day was about to be born.

We landed at one of Piso's jetties to avoid the chaos at Nero's.

The musician and the slaves trailed back towards Nero's villa, followed by the Praetorians.

Petro and Atreus and I watched the water for a moment longer.

"She could have drowned," I said at last. "And there wouldn't even be a body."

"She's too proud to die like that," Petronius said.

I gave him a sideways look. "You admire her?"

"No," he said thoughtfully. "But I understand her brand of theatre."

I didn't reply. What was there to say? I didn't admire her, and I didn't know enough about her to even try understanding her. I wasn't ready to eulogise her yet, either. She was a survivor. And yet…

And yet I couldn't have been the only one of us thinking of the chain of events that had occurred earlier in the night that had led to Agrippina leaving the villa in a boat that wasn't hers. And perhaps that chain stretched back even further. I remembered Misenum, days ago, and tasted bile at the back of my throat.

"So," Petronius said, raising his eyebrows. "What now? Do we make sacrifices for her safe return, or prepare a pyre?"

"Neither," I said, staring at the surface of the water and thinking of the vast push and pull of the invisible tides underneath it, all moving in different ways, to different ends, for reasons beyond my understanding. "Not yet."

The small waves whispered against the stones below the jetty, and I could still hear the cries—real or imagined—from the water. My thoughts flew so wildly in all directions that even an augur wouldn't be able to track them, let alone divine any sense out of them.

If Agrippina was dead, what came next? A state funeral? Or silence?

And if she lived…

Well.

As the first tendrils of dawn ushered in a new day, Baiae was quiet.

And Baiae was never quiet.

Today, though, it felt as though the whole world was holding its breath.

* * *

We arrived back at Nero's villa in time to greet the dawn. It was morning, though the sea still wore its bruises from the night before. Baiae, for all its marble and perfume, could not quite hide the stink of salt and smoke when something unnatural had happened on the water. Atreus and I followed Petronius into a large atrium guarded by marble statues. Sunlight slanted across the tiled floor. Nero sat on a couch—sat, not reclined—his face drawn, his gaze fixed on nothing.

"Nero," said Petronius.

Nero looked up, an unasked question in his expression.

Petronius shook his head to indicate our search had been fruitless. We can't have been the first to report the same—the atrium was filled with men who'd spent the last few hours on the water, although there was space around Nero's couch as though none of them dared get too close. We Romans were a superstitious bunch at heart, and bad luck was contagious.

Only a single slave stood by, holding a cup of wine in case Nero's mouth grew dry.

When the crowd parted to allow another new arrival in, I recognized him immediately and my heart beat faster in the expectation of news at last. It was Agermus, Agrippina's freedman. He must have been on the boat with her last night. His tunic was stained and torn, and his hair lay flat on his head as though it had dried badly. His face was pale and taut, but determined. Not the look of a supplicant. The Praetorians didn't stop him. No one did

He dropped to one knee as soon as he reached Nero's couch

"Caesar," Agermus said, chest rising and falling like a bellows. "Agrippina lives."

There it was. Three words that shattered the air.

For a moment, no one moved, and then the crowd shifted as a wave, rising up on disbelieving murmurs. When Nero stood, not quickly, but with a slow, confused sort of dread, silence fell once more, but it was somehow a sharper silence than before. Nero's bare feet whispered across the mosaic as he stepped toward the messenger. His heavy brow creased as though he didn't comprehend Agermus's words. "What did you say?"

"I was sent," Agermus said, "to inform you that the Empress escaped harm. She swam to shore."

He said it plainly. No triumph, no accusation, though he must have already known what I'd slowly figured out sometime in the middle of the night as I'd splashed around with an oar in the bay. When I'd finally remembered what I'd seen at the bottom of the fountain at Anicetus's house in Misenum that day: a little sunken boat. Not a child's toy, like I'd thought at the time, but an engineer's model. A boat designed to sink.

The colour drained from Nero's face, all the confirmation that I needed. He did not blink. He suddenly looked very young. Not like an emperor. Not even a man. Just a child who had pushed a rock down a hill and now watched it, impossibly, rolling back up towards him.

A nondescript fellow unpeeled himself from the crowd. Anicetus, the man himself. He moved forward, not like a man startled, or concerned, but perhaps one taking a pleasant stroll around the neighbourhood after dinner. He looked as harmless as a flea.

"A blessing," he said, his mouth curving in a smile, holding his hand down to help Agermus rise. "The gods are truly merciful."

But his eyes weren't on Agermus. They were on Celer, the Praetorian tribune, who was pushing his way through the crowd towards Nero's couch.

It happened fast after that.

Anicetus bent down, casually, as if to adjust a sandal strap. Then he straightened, and he held in his hand, somehow, a knife. Not drawn, not wielded, simply found.

"Caesar," he said with breathless horror. "This was on the floor. Where the freedman stood."

He held it up like a prize in the arena. All eyes snapped to Agermus, who took a step back.

It was a common blade. Iron. Curved slightly. Small enough to hide in a cloak, large enough to open a throat. And it was enough.

A sickening realisation began to bloom in my gut as I understood the play we were all watching. The one we would applaud at its finale, because that was what an audience did. I glanced at Atreus, and at Petro, and then caught sight of another Praetorian across the room: Rufio. He was in his armour this morning, bright and burnished, and his gaze was locked on the unfolding scene. I couldn't read his expression from this distance.

Celer looked from the knife to Agermus, then to Nero. Nobody moved.

And then Anicetus said, "It must have fallen as the freedman knelt. A weapon meant for imperial blood. The gods have spared you, Caesar."

Nero didn't nod. He didn't speak. Just looked at Agermus, whose gaze had not wavered. There was no fear in the freedman. Only a kind of tired resolve. I wondered if he had known, way before I'd realised, that he had walked into an ambush.

"I brought no blade," he said plainly.

And that was when Celer stepped forward.

The Praetorian drew his gladius in one smooth motion, like it had been waiting in his scabbard for this exact moment. I opened my mouth to protest—not out of loyalty to Agermus, because I hated him as much as I hated his mistress—but because this was *blatant.*

Atreus elbowed me in the side, hard, jolting me back into my right mind and back into silence.

Celer thrust the blade cleanly into Agermus's gut. Not once, but twice. The freedman gasped, slumped to the floor, and did not move again. Blood spread out across the marble tiles beneath him.

Anicetus, still holding the knife, offered it to Celer.

"Take it," he said, loud enough for us all to hear. "Let it be shown that this plot reached all the way to Agrippina herself. She sends a weapon, not words. A blade, not a message."

Celer took it and looked to Nero.

"She will be at her villa," said Nero, voice rough with some emotion I couldn't name. "Go. Take some men. Do what must be done."

Celer saluted. He gave no protest, no question. Just turned and left.

I remained still. I could not look away from Nero, the emperor who was also my friend.

I had believed there was something in him that wanted to be better than the men who came before him. He had spoken of art, of peace, of a Rome made eternal not by conquest but by beauty. I had watched him listen to philosophers with the attentive hunger of a student. I'd watched him laugh and dance and play music with his friends.

I didn't see that man now.

Anicetus turned. His expression flickered as he saw me, and I wondered if it was regret or just recognition. And the worst past was, I understood. I understood all of this. I thought back to the dead perfumer and her son, who had whined over and over again in plaintive tones that she just didn't *listen*. I'd wager my entire fortune that Agrippina had never listened either.

But, more than that, she was a danger. Not just to her enemies, but to Nero as well. I knew exactly why this was necessary—I knew about her plotting, her politicking, and even her treason—but it didn't take away the bitterness I could taste at the back of my throat. Because this was matricide, and it was a crime against nature and the gods themselves.

I turned towards the exit of the atrium, Atreus at my side. Petronius didn't follow. The last glimpse I caught of him was of his shocked face, his eyes wide, his jaw as slack as that of a beast stunned by a butcher's hammer. Because even Petro hadn't dreamed up theatre like this.

Atreus and I stepped outside into the fresh air. The sun was fully up now, glinting off the sea like a knife's edge.

Agrippina hadn't drowned last night in that water as Anicetus had intended. The truth had drowned instead. And I wondered how many other men in the atrium had realised it yet, and if it even mattered in the end.

* * *

Atreus and I walked back to my villa. Any other day, I would have enjoyed the view, the salt air, and being alone with Atreus. Today, my muscles ached from rowing, and I was weighed down with thoughts of what we'd just witnessed, and what it meant—not just for Nero, but for Rome itself, and for the empire.

We reached the road that ran down to the port. The sails of moored boats drooped against their masts. Fishermen repaired nets, or stacked baskets, or did whatever it was fishermen did when they weren't fishing. A couple of men yelled at one another about who had first access to a mooring spot while a port worker studiously ignored them both. A dog took a piss on an old man's leg. The breeze picked up some dust from the street and shifted it a little further down.

"Juno's tits," Atreus said suddenly. "The little boat in Anicetus's fountain."

I couldn't even raise a smile because I'd figured it out before him. I nodded, and we continued down the street to the portico of my villa.

Vulso was watching the street, and he opened the door to allow us in.

"Did the family all come home last night?" I asked him, and let out a slow breath of relief when he confirmed they had. "Good."

They were waiting in the atrium.

Fulvia stood stiffly by the impluvium, her arms folded, and her dark hair drawn back in braids so tight they might have cracked. Octavia sat on the edge of a marble bench, worrying a bracelet with her fingers. Julia sat next to her. Uncle Maro and Aunt Marcia sat together on a bench across from Octavia. They were all wearing the same clothes they'd worn last night.

Juba paced back and forth like a lion testing the boundaries of its cage. Felix the gladiator watched him from close by, like an anxious understudy worried he might be called upon to perform.

"Quintus!" Fulvia exclaimed as Atreus and I strode into the atrium. She unfolded her arms, and her shoulders sagged. Then she hurried forward to embrace me and pressed a kiss to my cheek. "Thank Jupiter you're alright! Both of you!"

"We're fine," I said. "You haven't been sitting here all night, have you?"

"Where else would we be waiting for news?" Octavia asked. Her tone was as wry as always, but her voice wavered a little with relief. "Did they find her?"

"She survived the wreck of the boat," I said, "but she won't survive the day."

Octavia sucked in a breath. "What?"

"Speak plainly, my boy!" Maro exclaimed.

"Her freedman, Agermus, came to Nero to deliver the news that she was alive," I said. "He—a knife was found, dropped on the floor. It appeared to be an assassination plot."

I wasn't stupid enough to spell it out for them—any of the slaves could have been listening, and today's truth might so easily be tomorrow's treason—and my family was smart enough not to need it.

"Well, that's lucky, isn't it?" Julia asked. "That he dropped the knife right before he could use it?"

Well, apparently not all of them were smart enough. But that was an unfair assessment. Julia wasn't stupid, just naive. And naivety, when it came to something as incomprehensible as this, was a virtue and not a flaw.

She gasped. "Oh! But how awful for the poor emperor to be forced to act against his own mother!"

Octavia opened her mouth, and then closed it again, and folded her hands into her lap.

"Yes," I agreed hollowly. "How awful."

We were all silent for a long moment, and then Maro laughed. Just once. A short, sharp bark that echoed off the tiles of the atrium. "If the gods had given her a beard, she might have worn the purple for longer than any of her ancestors."

There was more than a grain of truth in that.

"Well, that doesn't matter now," I said. "Whatever she was, and whatever she could have been, she's dead, or soon will be, and the people who stood on the shore yesterday evening to cheer her are still waiting to learn which way the wind blows."

I felt irrationally angry at Agrippina, at the fact that this morning's dawn was the last one she would ever see, because I was supposed to be investigating the murder of an innocent girl, not wasting my energy going back and forth in my own mind about how I ought to feel about the murder of a dangerous woman. The world hadn't held its breath for Calpurnia Tertia, had it?

"I need a bath," I said. "Then Atreus and I are going to speak with Livilla Faustina to see what she can tell us about Tertia and the cult."

"Sir." Atreus's tone was dubious.

"What?"

"Do you think that's a good idea? We've been up all night. We need to rest."

"Atreus is right," Fulvia said, before I could point out Atreus's hypocrisy. He'd hardly slept at all around the time we'd first met, and would arrive on my doorstep at dawn to work with me, after having already patrolled the Aventine all night. "And I know we would all feel better if you stayed inside today. At least until, as you say, the people have seen which way the wind blows."

In times of civil and political crisis, the Roman populace was notoriously restless. Just ask Mark Antony, who had leveraged their discontent into violent unrest at Julius Caesar's funeral. More to the point, ask Brutus and Cassius how that worked out for them. The people had loved Agrippina once. They had feared her too, and love and fear were the two sides of a coin that was soon worn thin. Who knew how that coin would land if it was tossed up into the air today? Would the people rise in support of Agripina, or of Nero? And were the residents of Baiae as fond of rioting as their counterparts in Rome?

Fulvia was right. It would be smarter to stay inside until the mood of the people, whatever it was, settled.

And so, at the very same moment as the emperor's mother was being assassinated by Celer the Praetorian, I was sitting in the bath yelling at Tullius to get out of it, and Atreus and Uncle Maro were laughing at me. And after that, I ate, and then I slept, and after I slept, I still felt tired, so I dragged myself as far as the garden and dozed in the sunlight while Mouse and Lucilla played tag around the fountain. And once or twice I even smiled, as though, outside, the world was turning just like every day, and no act had been committed that might prompt the gods towards retribution, or shake an empire down to its very foundations.

It was late afternoon, and the shadows had settled in long stretches over the garden when Vulso trotted out to tell me that Rufio was here. I told him to send him through to the informal triclinium and have one of the kitchen slaves bring wine. I had a feeling Rufio would need it more than I did.

When I arrived at the triclinium, Rufio wasn't there yet. He'd been waylaid in the atrium, and my heart clenched when I saw him speaking in a low voice with Octavia. My little sister was as composed as always, but Rufio looked like a man almost at his breaking point. I wondered if that was because of everything that had happened since last night, or if it was something happening right now, in their whispered conversation.

I slipped back towards the triclinium before they saw me.

Atreus joined me. So did Juba, who stood silently by the entrance, looking imposing enough that even a Praetorian might quail a little. Felix was still shadowing Juba. They were of an approximate size, but Felix, with his arm in a sling and a constantly bewildered expression on his face, didn't come close to Juba in the intimidation stakes. I could only presume that was because he didn't speak Latin and literally had no idea what was going on. Ever.

"Sit, Rufio," I said, when he finally stepped into the triclinium. "You look as though you need to."

"Rough fucking night," he said, and sat down heavily on a couch. I watched him warily for a moment, still unsure of where he fitted into everything that had happened, and then he said, "I wasn't there."

"But you know what happened?" I asked.

He nodded, opening his mouth and then closing it again as the kitchen slave came in with wine and cheese and olives. He waited until she'd left before he spoke. "I spoke to one of the men who went with Celer. An auxiliary, not a Praetorian. I know—I know what she was, or at least I have some sense of it, but she was also Germanicus's daughter. For a Praetorian to stand against Germanicus's daughter…well."

Had there ever been such an example of the ideal Roman as Germanicus? Patrician, soldier, and hero. Germanicus had restored to Rome the eagles lost in the Teutoburg. He had been virtuous, dashing, and brave. One silently wondered if the fact he had fathered both Caligula and Agrippina was an attempt by the gods to balance those virtues in some great cosmic ledger. If so, they had outdone themselves.

"Celer is a Praetorian too," I pointed out.

"Not the Praetorian he thinks he is," Rufio said, and then shook his head. "Well, perhaps he is the loyal one after all. I don't know after today. I know what she was, but his own *mother*."

And wasn't that the crux of it?

"What happened?" I asked.

Rufio let out a breath. "They went to her villa. She made no attempt to hide. She was too clever not to expect it, I suppose, and too proud to flee. She said, 'Strike the womb that bore him.' And Celer did."

A chill ran through me at her fearlessness. Whatever else, she'd had a core of iron. Her father's daughter to the end, no doubt. She had been my enemy. She had been responsible for more deaths than anyone would ever know, including the death of Octavia's ex-husband. I had hated her and feared her in equal measure, and yet I could at least admire her strength.

I raised my cup. "To Agrippina Minor, daughter of Germanicus, sister of Caligula, wife of Claudius, mother of Nero. And, perhaps, the last true empress of Rome."

We drank, because not drinking would have been an insult to something too ancient to name. I swallowed, and thought of what she had said to me that day at her villa, and hoped that it wasn't true, hoped that it wasn't needed.

There is nobody else who can keep him at heel, Valerius.

But what did any of us know, on a day like this one?

Outside, the sun dipped low over the bay, and the water turned the same red-gold colour of old coins, or blood under torchlight."

* * *

The worst part about all of this," Maro said glumly over dinner, "is that we shall have to cancel the party."

I blinked at him. "I don't think that's the worst part, Maro."

My mad uncle waved a dismissive hand in my direction. "Oh, you know what I mean, Quintus."

I didn't, but I was used to the feeling, so I just nodded and reached for another piece of bread. We were on the first course so far: bread, fish, eggs dressed with garum, and lettuce drizzled with oil and sharp vinegar. I wasn't sure I'd see the next course. Both my body and my mind were weary, and the thought of my bed was more appealing than any food the slaves might bring in next.

"I still don't believe it," Octavia said, setting down her cup.

"Me either." Uncle Maro let out a grunt, pushing aside the dish of eggs in front of him. "I won't get my money back! I've spent days organising it. Musicians from Neapolis. Some Greek fellow who does shadow plays. Do you know how hard it is to get the best oysters when you're competing with the imperial villa *and* Piso?"

"Uncle Maro," Octaiva said with a sigh.

"What?" he asked. "I don't have it in me to mourn Agrippina, but I'll mourn those oysters, or at least the cost of them."

Fulvia brushed a few stray crumbs from her stola. "Had you already sent out the invitations. Maro?"

"No," he said with a sign. "Not yet. That's some consolation, I suppose."

"For the slaves, at least," Fulvia said, "who now won't have to run around town taking them back."

"I suppose we must return to Rome," Maro said.

"You suppose?" Octavia asked.

"What else is there to do?" Maro asked glumly. "This was a holiday. A celebration. But it's over now."

I almost envied his single-mindedness, like a small child upset that his toy had been taken away. Agrippina was dead, Nero had ordered it done, and possibly what happened here could shake the empire itself. It would certainly shake the senate. And Maro was most upset at cancelling his dinner party.

He shot me a wry look, as though he knew exactly what I was thinking. He held his cup up in my direction and said, "Ambition has a way of ending in knives."

"And yet you are always reminding me to think of my career," I muttered.

Maro clicked his tongue. "My boy, just because being a patrician means you must navigate a sewer, it doesn't mean you ought to gleefully swim in shit. Mark the difference."

Ah, there it was. Maro had once famously been the only senator not to vote in support of some new accolade for Claudius because he'd been distracted by his home renovation plans. Claudius, who had known Maro's reputation, had reportedly laughed when he'd been told. Maro was a fool, but he was a canny old fool who knew exactly how to ride the rising wave of success and popularity without being dashed onto the rocks of ambition. Because he only cared for frivolous pursuits and not politics. Or at least that was how he appeared to those who didn't look too closely. Maro didn't involve himself in senatorial infighting or political plots against others, and his eccentricities dissuaded other men from drawing him into whatever schemes they were hatching. If Maro was a fool, he was the smartest fool in the world, and he had a lot to teach me.

I raised my cup at him in acknowledgement.

Outside, the night was cool. From the atrium, a lyre was playing, gentle and wavering, like a memory unravelling. I wondered if one of the slaves played, or if this was a musician Maro had hired. Painted scenes adorned the triclinium, frescoes in vibrant shades of blue and red and green. On the wall opposite me, Anchises and Aeneas—parent and child, and symbols of loyalty and piety—walked through the underworld.

I couldn't tell if that was ironic or not.

Probably not.

A girl came in with a dish of veal dressed in a honey, onion, date, and allec sauce, and garnished with celery leaves. It smelled divine, and I rethought my initial plan of going to bed early.

"Did any of the oysters arrive yet?" Maro asked the girl. "Bring them out too, why don't you? We might as well get started on them since we'll be eating them until Parilia." He sighed. "Send the lute player in too, hmm?"

The girl nodded and slipped away. A moment later, a young man with a lute appeared. I didn't recognise him, so he must have been one of Maro's outside hires. He set his stool down in a corner of the room and continued to play softly.

Big dinner parties be damned, honestly. This was much more pleasant. Just family, food, and gentle music in the background. Although I had to admit I was a little regretful that I'd never see what Maro had planned for the gladiators and, apparently, the shadow puppets. But some mysteries were best left unsolved.

With that thought, naturally, my mind turned towards Calpurnia Tertia, and to the strange, dark tunnels in the hill behind the Baths of Mercury, and what Tertia and the other women had been searching for down there. Caecilia Didia was a true believer, and Galeria Alba was a shy, awkward girl too afraid of her new friends turning on her to voice any real dissent, but where did the others fall? Had Tertia believed the fake sibyl's bullshit? We would probably never know.

Maro was still fretting about the money he'd wasted on the dinner party. "And I ordered asterion! Well, I suppose we can burn it before we head home."

"We will not, thank you, Maro," Fulvia said dryly, taking a sip of her wine. "I told Quintus last night that it might make most people sleepy and warm, but it loosens my tongue more than the strongest wine, and I have too many secrets to keep to risk it!"

Maro beamed, delighted. "Oh, well, in that case, we *must* burn some!"

Everyone laughed, except Atreus, who suddenly sat up straight, as alert as a hunting dog who'd just caught a scent.

"Areus?" I asked.

"You said that last night," he said.

Fulvia tilted her head to give him a puzzled look. "Yes."

"I didn't—" Atreus shook his head. "With everything else that happened, it didn't stick." He rose to his feet, and then turned to me and said, "I know who killed Calpurnia Tertia."

Well then.

So much for our quiet family dinner.

Chapter Eleven

Piso's door slave was surprised to see Atreus and me—and even more surprised to see Juba and Felix lurking behind us—but he opened the door and led us into the atrium. My gaze went immediately to the place where Calpurnia Tertia's body had lain in repose, awaiting the funeral pyre, but that space was empty now. Even the couch had been removed; probably nobody could bear to use it again.

The smooth mosaic floor, depicting Neptune and his nymphs, gleamed with evening light. I could hear the clatter of cutlery and the low sounds of conversation coming from somewhere close nearby.

"Please wait here, sirs," the door slave said, bobbing his head, and then he scurried off in that direction.

Juba watched his retreating back. Felix blinked around, looking as baffled as always.

The door slave was back in moments. "My master asks if you would like to join him in the triclinium, or if you would prefer his tablinum?"

It was a subtle way of asking if our business with Piso was public or private. The last thing a man wanted while trying to enjoy his patina of pears was his wife and family discovering exactly how much money he owed in gambling debts. There was a reason the tablinum had doors that could be pulled closed, unlike the triclinium.

I exchanged a look with Atreus and said, "I think we'd prefer to join him in the triclinium, actually."

The slave bobbed his head again and led us through.

It was a smaller family dinner than the one Atreus and I had left. It was just Piso, and Atria Galla, and their fragile houseguest Plautia Balbina.

Piso rose from a couch as we entered the triclinium. "Valerius! And you, Atreus. The entire town is in uproar—the entire empire, probably. What happened?"

"Agrippina is dead," I said, "on Nero's orders."

Piso shook his head. "Jupiter. That's what all the gossip has said, but I didn't know if it could be believed."

"For once the truth is as outrageous as any exaggeration."

Piso's expression was grave. "I never imagined it would come to this. It is—well, it is unthinkable, despite her nature being what it was."

She had been a snake, but even snakes weren't killed by their own young, were they? I could tell that Piso wanted to think the best of Nero, and that he was struggling even though he didn't have the added difficulty of having seen Agermus framed for an assassination attempt. And perhaps Agrippina had driven Nero to act—of course she had, she was Agrippina—but to kill one's own parent was a crime that the Roman mind instinctively recoiled from. It could barely even imagine it, let alone come anywhere near reconciling it. It was unthinkable, except that Nero hadn't just thought it—he'd gone through with it too. If he hadn't been the emperor, he would have been sewn into a leather sack with a rooster, a dog, a monkey, and a viper, and tossed into the nearest body of water to drown. Well, to drown eventually. The frantically struggling animals would do a lot of damage with their claws and fangs first, so presumably the actual drowning came as something of a relief by that point. It was swift and brutal retribution for an unthinkably vile crime, but the laws hadn't been written with women like Agrippina in mind. She, too, had been in so many ways unthinkable.

Well, we were all being forced to think of her tonight in Baiae, weren't we? And in the days and weeks to come, her name would be whispered throughout an entire empire. She would probably consider that the least of what she deserved.

"I don't know what to even say," Piso said.

Probably smart, given that everything was still up in the air and none of us knew how they would settle. Piso and I were friends, but that didn't mean

I'd ever tell him exactly what I thought of Agrippina. In the coming days, she might be damned in memory, or made a goddess, or anything in between. And my public opinion of her, and of what had happened here in Baiae, would happily align with whatever everyone else said. That was politics.

"We're not here because of Agrippina," I said. "We're here because of Tertia."

His expression faltered and then lit up with a curious mix of hope and dread.

I looked over to where Atria Galla and Plautia Balbina sat, their chairs pulled close together, like friends, or sisters. Atria reached out and took Plautia's hand, and Plautia squeezed it, her bottom lip trembling in anticipation of startling news.

Well, startling to some, at least.

"Atria Galla," I said, "could you stand, please?"

Atria's forehead creased, and she exchanged a look with Piso, but she stood. "What is this about?"

"Please, step over towards me," I said, and held out my hand.

"Valerius," Piso said, and Atreus stepped between us to prevent him from interfering. The slaves were watching avidly. So was Plautia Balbina. I felt like a man facing off with a beast in the arena. Some big cat, who was just waiting for its chance. Except—

Atria took a tentative step towards me, and I caught her hand and pulled her close. She gasped as I pushed her behind me.

Except the cat wasn't Atria.

"Thank you, Atria," I said without looking back at her. "I needed you to move away from Plautia, given there's a very good chance she intends to murder you."

It was very dramatic. Petro would be sorry he missed it.

Sweet, fragile Plautia Balbina blinked at me like a long-lashed newborn calf, and said, tremulously, "I don't know what you mean, Aemilius Valerius."

"You know exactly what I mean," I said. Atreus and I had run through everything we knew on the walk to Piso's villa. We didn't know much, but it was only a short walk. And, importantly, we knew enough. Mino, when he had spoken to us before bolting, had unwittingly given us all the information we needed. And earlier, Fulvia's comment about asterion had suddenly made everything very clear. To Atreus, at least. He'd had to explain it to me.

"I do not," Plautia said, her voice still shaky, and sent a beseeching look in Piso's direction.

I stared at her. "There were three of you in the sibyl's grotto the last time you went there, and now two of you are dead. Something happened in there, didn't it? Atreus and I went down there. It still stank of asterion. Tita the sibyl was drunk on the stuff, Mino told us. And so were you and Tertia."

Atreus said, "It doesn't make you sleepy like it does most people, does it? It makes you talkative. You spilled secrets to the sibyl. Secrets that you should have kept to yourself. Secrets that Tertia heard as well."

I raised my eyebrows. "I'll bet when you always told Tertia how you two were as close as sisters, she never guessed that you intended to make it happen."

Plautia's fingers flexed, and she clenched her jaw tightly for a moment. She tucked her hands in her lap. "I don't know what you mean."

"Except you do," I said. "This wasn't even about Tertia, not really. This was always about Piso."

"What?" Piso exclaimed.

"He's one of the most influential men in Rome," I said. "He makes every other rich man in Baiae look like a beggar in a gutter. This villa is nicer than Nero's. He's rich, he's politically powerful, he's good-looking, and, most importantly for you, he already married a plebeian once. Why not twice then, hmm? Isn't that what you thought?"

Plautia's little crush on Piso had been evident from the first time she'd mentioned him. But it turned out it ran a lot deeper than we'd guessed, and, tainted by ambition, had twisted into something dark. It was the only thing that fitted. This had never been about anything Tertia had done. This had only been because she'd been standing in the way of what Plautia wanted.

"You had it all planned out," Atreus said, something like grudging respect in his tone. "Was it you or Tertia who called you sisters first? I think it was you. Did you ever truly love her, or was she only ever a means to get closer to Piso?"

"I-I *loved* her! I did!" Tears brimmed in her eyes.

"Maybe so," Atreus said. "But you couldn't let her live once she knew."

Plautia just stared at us with wide, watery eyes, her posture as demure as a Vestal's. I might have believed her expression of wounded innocence if I didn't catch the tic in her jaw that told me she was clenching her teeth.

"Where it all fell apart was in the sibyl's grotto," I said. "You got drunk on the smoke and spilled your secret. Both Tertia and Tita heard it. When you sobered up the next day, you must have realised you had to kill them before they told anyone." I raised my eyebrows. "You were lucky Tertia didn't have the courage to approach me when she had the chance at the party. If she'd made up her mind on the spot to do it, she'd still be alive."

Poor Tertia. She must have been horribly conflicted, torn between her loyalty to her best friend and her brother. Atria Galla was an obstacle that Plautia had needed removed—and so was poor Tertia herself. Had she even realised? Had she even guessed she might be in danger before she'd heard footsteps behind her in the rain?

"No!" Plautia exclaimed, and this time she let a few tears slide down her pretty face. "But I saw her the day she was killed! She came to my house! Why would I let her leave again, if I was planning on hurting her?"

"Even you're not reckless enough to kill a Calpurnii in your own house," Atreus said. "I'll bet you thought about it though, didn't you?"

Plautia's bottom lip wobbled. "Piso, how can you let them say such things?"

Piso blinked at me. "Valerius, surely you don't think…"

He couldn't finish the thought, as though it was too ridiculous to speak aloud. Plautia was a woman who knew how to trade on her pretty face and her tears. Even Atreus and I had fallen for it, and she hadn't has as long to play us as she had Piso and everyone else under his roof.

"I don't know what was said between you when Tertia visited," I said to Plautia. "And frankly, I wouldn't believe you if you told me. But I imagine it was something along the lines of how you'd been speaking nonsense in the grotto. There may be truth in wine, but I bet you tried your hardest to convince Tertia the same isn't true of asterion. But it wasn't quite enough, was it? She wasn't sure enough of your guilt to tell Piso, but she wasn't certain you were innocent either. Then that night, the perfect solution fell into her lap when she met my family at Piso's boat party and discovered that I have a reputation in Rome for ferreting out answers to knotty problems."

Jupiter, but I wished Tertia had sent for me instead of going outside into the storm on her own. But she'd loved Plautia and hadn't wanted to believe the worst of her friend. Not even enough to risk sending a slave with a message, in case anyone found out and asked what business she had with me.

"We'll find out who you paid to follow her and kill her," Atreus said. "It wasn't you, was it? Would a small woman like yourself even have the strength to do it? Maybe you even relied on that assumption, but it doesn't matter, because it's easy enough for a woman of your means to pay someone else to do your killing for you. We'll find them, and we'll see that they tell the magistrate in Cumae exactly what you ordered them to do."

Plautia pressed her mouth into a thin line that spoke more of annoyance than fear. It was that tiny gesture that convinced me beyond a doubt that our accusations had hit the right target. Despite all appearances, Plautia Balbina had ice in her veins.

"I don't understand," Piso said, and Atria moved to his side and grasped his hand. His eyes were wide with confusion and disbelief. "I don't... *Plautia?* You mean nothing to me."

It was the wrong thing to say.

The gold bracelet on Plautia's wrist, set with green stones, flashed in the lamplight as she uncoiled as rapidly as a viper. She didn't scream. She didn't shout. She simply lunged, and my brain—reliably slow on the uptake—took a moment to register the other glint of light as a blade clasped in her hand.

I'd thought she'd go for Piso, or even Atria, because what soured faster than love spurned? It never even occurred to me that Plautia would attack me. Clearly, nobody had ever told her not to kill the messenger.

"You have ruined it!" she screamed at me, a maenad now instead of a Vestel. "You have ruined *everything!*"

I stumbled back, cursing and knocking into Atreus, and then Juba stepped between us as suddenly as a door slamming shut. The knife sank into his side with a sound like tearing canvas. Juba didn't cry out. He just grunted, twisted, and grabbed her wrist, but she was wiry and fast. She yanked free and raised the blade again.

Which was when Felix, who probably had no idea what the fuck was going on, stepped forward and punched her in the face with his good hand.

Plautia crumpled backwards, blood running from her nose. The knife clattered to the mosaic floor, bouncing across a dolphin's eye. Plautia lay slumped in her chair, moaning, like a matron who'd stuffed herself silly at a banquet.

"What—" Piso stared at her, and then at me, and started again. "Valerius, what is *happening?*"

I turned to look at the doorway, where a crowd of open-mouthed slaves had been drawn by the ruckus. I pointed at a few larger ones. "You three. Over here. Lock Plautia Balbina in a room." I exchanged a look with Atreus. "Make sure it has no windows."

Atreus had grabbed a cloth napkin off the table and was attending Juba's wound.

"Is it bad?" I asked.

"I think it was a fruit knife," Atreus said. "It's not too deep."

Blood dripped from the hem of Juba's tunic onto the tiles, and he looked paler than a man from Aethiopia ought to.

The slaves half pulled, half carried Plautia away. She was weeping, but it did her no good. None of us who'd seen her lunge with that knife would mistake her for anyone frail and delicate again.

Atria rose. "Stichus! Send for a physician at once. Verna, fetch bandages and vinegar. Atreus, please help him to the couch."

Juba grunted as Atreus and I got him situated, and then he stared, unimpressed, at the remains of the dinner Plautia Balbina had been eating only moments before, and bled gently all over the expensive couch.

"Are you alright?" I asked him.

He held the napkin against his wound. "Yes, sir."

He looked more annoyed than anything, which seemed like a good sign.

Nevertheless, I peeled back the torn flap of fabric on his tunic to inspect his wound. It didn't appear too deep. There was probably nothing a physician could do for him that the household slaves couldn't, but I felt better knowing one was on the way, just in case.

"The bleeding is already slowing."

"She had good aim," Juba said, "but about as much strength as a kitten."

"Luckily," I said, and he grunted his agreement.

Atria pressed a cup of wine into Juba's free hand, and I helped him sit up a little so that he could drink.

"Felix?" I straightened up and turned. Felix stood in the middle of the chaos, his forehead creased and his nose wrinkled. When I caught his gaze, he babbled something in his incomprehensible language. I held up a hand to staunch the flow of his words. "You did very well. Good job."

He stared warily at my hand.

"Good job," I said again, abandoning my scant patrician dignity to give him a smile and a thumbs up. Then I slumped down on the couch opposite Juba. "Atreus, make a note on that tablet of yours to find out what language Felix speaks, and to track down someone who can speak both it and Latin."

"Yes, sir," Atreus said, but didn't make a note at all.

I poured myself a wine and downed it one long swallow.

"Valerius," Piso said, his voice shaky. He reached out for Atria, and she sat beside him and curled her fingers through his. "Are you saying that Plautia killed Tertia?" He shook his head. "Because of *me*?"

"She's in love with you," I said. "You're a catch, Piso, and Plautia was trying her hardest to hook you."

Piso looked bewildered, but Atria let out a long breath. She must have had an inkling, I thought. Not about where all of this had led, but she must have noticed a longing glance or a flirty laugh from Plautia here and there. She must have noticed and then ignored the signs completely, because it was clear even to me that Piso was wildly devoted to his wife and wouldn't dream of leaving her. Not for a pretty young thing like Plautia, and not for anything in the world. Where any normal crush would have perished on the shores of the realisation that Piso adored his wife, Plautia's had not.

Because if Piso wouldn't ever consider making himself divorcee, Plautia could certainly make him a widower.

"But the grotto," Atria said. "You said that Plautia must have told a secret that Tertia overheard. It couldn't be just that she was in love with Piso."

And if the logical jump from crush on a married man to murder seemed like too wide a leap, perhaps it wasn't. At least not the second time around.

"No," I agreed, and exchanged a look with Atreus. "Well, in the end, it's the only thing that fits, isn't it? Plautia was keeping a secret so dark it only came out under the influence of asterion. A secret worth killing even her best friend over." I held Atria's gaze. "Poor Plautia, the young widow that everyone pities, killed her husband, Atria Galla, so that she could move onto yours."

* * *

The physician came and went while Calpurnius Piso got very, very drunk. Piso blamed himself for Tertia's death. He blamed the cult. Then, finally, he blamed Plautia Balbina. Throughout it all, Atria sat by his side and refilled his wine with the calm understanding of a woman who knew the storm had to build before it broke.

Atria reminded me of my womenfolk. In a crisis, she took charge, and the world was a better place for it.

"I never met her husband," she said, holding out a dish of olives towards me. I waved them away, and she set them on the table. "I remember hearing that he'd died, and that it was very sudden. I didn't even think for a moment that—" She let out a huff of breath. "Jupiter. I thought her such a little wet blanket, and she *killed* him! And she killed poor Tertia too."

"She wore a very good mask," I said. I thought back to what Mino had said about Plautia and Tertia always talking about Piso and Atria. About Plautia wanting to include Atria in the cult. Poor Tertia must have thought it was a measure of her friend's goodness. She couldn't have known then that Plautia only wanted to get closer to Atria in order to kill her.

We overlook our womenfolk, us Roman men. Stupidly, and to our detriment. Because they have ambitions too, and not all of them are as obvious about them as Agrippina. But Agrippina was a woman who had long ago outgrown the need to pretend she was weak and fragile and naïve. Plautia had still found it a useful costume to wear. And she'd worn it incredibly well.

"Tertia invited her to stay with us in Rome, did you know?" Atria asked. "And I thought that Rome would eat her alive, this sheltered little girl from Baiae. I thought she was a child, and this whole time…" She shook her head. "We opened our *home* to her."

Beside her, Piso shuddered into his wine.

A final indignity visited upon them by Plautia Balbina. Not her worst, by far, but certainly adding insult to injury. It would take Atria and Piso a long time to come to terms with what had happened to Tertia, and especially the why. Perhaps they never would.

Atreus and I left them to their bewildered shock and grief and set out for home. Felix and Juba followed, Juba in a borrowed litter.

Our path took us past the walls of Piso's villa, sun-bleached in the day, but ghostly at night. Vines twisted like lazy serpents, and the sea murmured beside us. The lights of Baiae glimmered over on the mainland. We stopped at the tree where we had found Tertia's corpse and waved Felix and the litter bearers on.

I didn't speak for a long while, because anything I said would have felt small. But then the words came unbidden, and I didn't care that they were petty—they needed to be spoken.

"She'll already be forgotten," I said. "Any other week, and the murder of a Calpurnii daughter would be shouted from the rooftops for months. The scandal of it. The horror. But nobody but Piso and Atria will remember what happened here, because even in death Agrippina had to take centre stage, didn't she?"

"You won't forget her," Atreus said. "And neither will I."

He was a liar, because my thoughts were already turning away from Tertia to Agrippina. "She ruled half the empire from her son's shadow."

Atreus inclined his head, the moonlight catching his gaze.

"She played consuls against generals, made emperors, unmade them. Claudius. Britannicus. Anyone in her way. She could whisper, and cities would burn. She survived exile, poison, scandal. And then…"

"And then the sea took her," Atreus said. It was a poetic euphemism for murder, and Atreus wasn't usually a man who favoured either poetry or euphemisms. But even a man as plain-speaking as him knew how dangerous it was to call Agrippina's death matricide.

"She'll be remembered for centuries," I said. "Statues, scrolls, histories carved by men who hated her and still couldn't look away. Every schoolboy will know her name. But Tertia? A girl with sand on her feet and a mark around her neck, who only tried to do the right thing. She'll be barely a whisper in Rome, then a rumour, then nothing."

Atreus held my gaze, as patient he always was whenever I spewed nonsense at him.

One death bent the empire. The other didn't even stir the dust.

Sourness rose in my throat. Not grief, exactly. Not yet. Just the bitter taste of things being wrong. Of people wearing masks, of lying. Always fucking lying. I thought of Agrippina again, and of how she'd come here to reconcile with her son. Had that been the truth? It didn't matter, in the end, because she'd been playing so many different games, wearing so many different masks, that she could have stepped into a room wearing nothing but the naked, unvarnished truth and nobody would have recognised it. Not on her. Not on any of us, probably, because we all laughed and smiled and flattered our friends and our betters. We all hid the truth, to varying degrees. We all wore masks as garish and bright as those Petro's actors wore on stage, so that the audience would remember which role we had been assigned. We were all careful to keep them on so that nobody could glimpse what was underneath.

I was a Roman patrician, and Atreus was a plebeian vigile. Nobody was allowed to see anything different. There were no witnesses to the way his hand slid down my spine in the moonlight, in a gesture of comfort, and perhaps of something more, that filled me with both warmth and sorrow.

"Tertia deserved better," Atreus said again, quietly.

I swallowed around the ache in my throat. "She did."

"And Agrippina?"

I exhaled and thought of Rome, of the senate and the empire, and especially of Nero's inscrutable expression as Anicetus had held up the knife that damned both his mother and her freedman.

"She deserved justice," I said. "But not mercy."

We walked the rest of the way home in silence.

After being interrogated by my family, I escaped into the garden, where I sat with a jug of wine, a cup that I kept full, and the stars. It didn't take long before I was disturbed.

"Maro is still upset that he doesn't get to put on a dinner with a gladiatorial display," Fulvia said, wrapping her stola around her as she sat next to me on the marble bench. "So am I, if I'm honest. I was curious as to how it would work."

"It was never going to work."

"Well, exactly. I was curious as to what form the disaster would have taken."

That wrung a smile from me.

She sipped some of my wine and then passed me the cup. "This seems a lonely sort of celebration, Quintus."

"I'm not sure it is one."

"It should be." Her tone left no room for argument. It never did. "There is a time to mourn the dead, and a time to celebrate your victories. You and Atreus have brought a killer to justice, and that's no small thing. You have kept the promise you made to Piso. You have done well, and you should remember that, even if the rest of the world has gone mad today."

"Has it gone mad?" I asked.

She shrugged. "I don't know. Not all ripples cause waves, I suppose. All we can do is wait and see."

"We have to go back to Rome," I said.

She laid her hand on my arm. "The slaves are already packing. We can leave as soon as you like."

"I think I want to be back in Rome before we know if it's a ripple that will tickle our feet, or a wave that will crash over the entire empire."

Baiae was too far away from Rome to catch any news as it was fresh. I wanted to be home as soon as possible, to see which way the Senate leaned when it came to Agrippina's death. There was nobody tugging at the hem of Nero's Tyrian purple toga, was there? Agrippina had made sure of that, dispatching stepbrothers, cousins, and in-laws wherever necessary as Nero grew up, but who was to say there wasn't some popular general with a couple of legions up his sleeve who, when he heard of Agrippina's death, would take his chance at ruling the empire? I wanted to hear the rumours straight from the Forum, because forewarned was forearmed.

"At first light, then," I said, and she gave me one of her looks. "What?"

"Not at first light," she said. "Perhaps an hour or two after."

"Why?"

She leaned towards me and kissed my cheek. "Because the children deserve one more moment to enjoy the beach. We'll take them down before breakfast, and give you the chance to sleep in, or take a bath, or a walk, or whatever it is you and Atreus would like to do undisturbed."

Her words hung there, an unasked question lurking behind them. Or perhaps it was a declaration hiding in that slight uptilt of her voice, not a question. Whether her tone was inviting a challenge or an answer, I felt the shift in the air. It froze me.

Fulvia caught my hand and said, "Do you remember when we were first married, and you asked me, given the benefit of my age and experience—"

"I'm sure I wasn't stupid enough to say it like that." My voice rasped as I aimed for levity and failed to find it.

"No, you weren't," she allowed. "But you asked me, in my opinion, what I thought was the most important trait for a young man on the threshold of a political career. Do you remember what I said?"

I nodded, wooden. In my skull, I heard the roar of the ocean, as though tilting my ear to a seashell. "You said he ought to pick his friends well."

Fulvia squeezed my hand. "And Atreus is a good choice of friend, Quintus."

She knew. Any doubt that we might have been talking at cross purposes was extinguished in that moment, because Atreus was *not* a good choice of friend. He was a plebeian vigile from the Aventine, with no pedigree, no money, and no political prospects. But he was honourable and, most importantly, he was discreet. He was a terrible choice of friend for a young patrician man who hoped to carve out a political career, but for something more than a friend?

Yes, Fulvia absolutely knew.

"My first two marriages were unhappy, both for very different reasons," she said. Her mouth curved in a smile. "I like this one, Quintus. I want to stay in it."

"Yes," I said. "I do too."

She lifted my hand to her mouth and kissed my knuckles. "Good. Then I suppose that's what we'll do."

I'd always known Fulvia was smarter than me.

* * *

The morning light glittered on the bay, and Atreus regarded me dubiously outside the awning of the dingy thermopolium by the port. "It's our last morning in Baiae, and this is where you've brought me?"

He had a point. There were plenty of dingy thermopolia at home in the Aventine for Atreus to frequent.

"Yes," I said. "Stilo says they do an excellent oyster broth."

The sun crested the green hills behind Baiae, illuminating the bay with a warmth that turned the water to molten gold. Morning in this place had a kind of music to it—soft oar strokes from the fishing boats, distant gull calls echoing above the tiled roofs, and the melodic hum of voices drifting from the piers. There was something lazy and luxurious about Baiae at dawn, despite the early morning industry at the port, with the town as slow to wake as a cat in the sunlight.

Atreus and I found seats beneath the faded red awning of the thermopolium. The place was little more than a counter with a few benches under cover, but Stilo had promised the owner made an oyster stew worth crossing seas for, and from the number of fishermen eating here before they took their boats out for the day, I had no reason to doubt that assessment.

I glanced around, wondering if any of the men were Mino—the fisherman, not the fake acolyte and Olympic runner—but I wouldn't have known him it I did spot him.

The sea breeze ruffled my hair and tickled my legs.

"I'll miss the view," Atreus said when the man behind the counter had taken our order, his tone wry enough to suggest that was the only thing he'd miss.

I couldn't fault him for his opinion.

We turned around on our stools as we waited for our food and gazed at the port and the bay. The tide must have been right for the boats to depart; sails bobbed on the water like feathers, and the fishermen in the thermopolium were finishing up their breakfasts in dribs and drabs before meandering across to the water. Over at the port, a line of men unloaded amphorae of wine from a merchant vessel, and a little fishing boat darted happily around it as it headed for the open sea. The scent of salt and fish mingled with the smoky tang from the thermopolium's ovens.

It was only moments until our breakfast arrived, and I turned my back on the scene to better pay attention to my oyster broth. I wrapped my hands about the wooden bowl, letting the warmth seep into my palms as I inhaled the delicious aroma. My stomach growled in anticipation, and I dug in.

The broth was rich and briny, and it put both Nero's and Piso's cooks to shame. The burst of flavour on my tongue was so exquisite that I closed my eyes to savour it. The oysters themselves were fresh and salty, and the sharpness of pepper, garum, and vinegar added a welcome, invigorating kick to the taste. When I at last swallowed and opened my eyes, there was a nondescript man seated beside me. He was wearing a large sun hat and a faint smile.

Despite the warm broth in my stomach, I felt a chill. "Anicetus."

On my other side, Atreus froze.

Anicetus inclined his head. "Good morning. I hear it is your last in Baiae."

"It seemed prudent to return to Rome as soon as possible," I said.

"Quite so. The emperor himself will be leaving in the next few days."

And he would beat us back, of course, because he had travelled here by boat. So much for his holiday plans in Baiae, but then if I was stirred by an urgent need to be back in Rome, of course Nero was. Whatever reception he would receive there would decide the fate of an empire.

"Safe travels to you both then," I said.

"I am not returning to Rome," Anicetus said, still wearing his faint smile. "I am retiring to Sardinia."

I didn't dare ask him if it was a punishment or a reward. Perhaps it was both. Anicetus had fabricated a reason to have Agrippina murdered, but only after he'd failed to kill her with the boat he had engineered to sink at sea. Either way, he was a braver man than I was if he was facing a journey across the ocean with a smile on his face. Then again, with the games of intrigue that a man like Anicetus played, perhaps the fact he wasn't already dead on the end of a Praetorian's gladius was reason enough to smile.

I wasn't naïve enough to think of Anicetus as a friend, but he had been an ally in the short time I'd known him. He had been as impenetrable as fog, but I'd never doubted his loyalty to the emperor. I still didn't—but I wondered if I was starting to doubt mine.

No. It wasn't my loyalty to Nero I questioned. It was our friendship.

I understood exactly why the emperor had done what he'd done. Agrippina was a dangerous woman, and I knew how politics worked. I could—and *would*—honestly and gladly swear my loyalty to Nero, the emperor of Rome, but Nero my friend? Perhaps I'd never known that man at all.

"Good luck to you then," I said, because what else was there to say?

He inclined his head. "And you, Valerius."

He rose from his seat and wandered away, his hands clasped behind his back. He looked like a harmless tourist out for a morning stroll.

"Well, shit," Atreus said in a low voice.

I hummed my agreement, because, yes, that seemed to sum things up. Agrippina, Anicetus, Nero, and the possibly precarious state of the empire. Not the oyster broth, though. The oyster broth was ambrosia, and I was determined to enjoy it on this, my last morning in Baiae.

Across the street, a group of port workers argued over a load of sea sponges. A man in a blue tunic haggled with a fruit seller over a basket of figs. A group of well-dressed women were out and about early, ready to hit the shops. They were bright as parrots, and I thought of Caecilia Didia and wondered how long it would take for her to find some new prophetess to worship. Not long, probably.

The scent of pressed olives, brine, and sweet honeyed wine drifted on the breeze. Even the sea seemed to sigh.

A man taking the stool Anicetus had vacated bumped against me and didn't apologise. I didn't mind. That was the main reason we'd come here, despite the allure of the oyster broth. I was already dressed for travel. Nobody here knew that I was a patrician, let alone Aemilius Valerius who owned the fancy villa behind the wall of shops on the waterfront. Nobody knew that Atreus, a lowly plebeian vigile, should not have been my friend. And nobody cared if we sat close enough that our shoulders knocked together as we ate.

The stuff ocean breeze stirred the hem of my tunic. Over at the port, a sailor lifted a net heavy with writhing silver fish. Gulls screamed. Somewhere, someone was singing a deep, low song that seemed somehow familiar, as though I half-remembered it from childhood.

I almost snorted. I hadn't even had any wine, and yet here I was entertaining nostalgia. Jupiter knew I'd have plenty of time to think fondly of Baiae over the next week, when my spine ached and my arse was bruised from riding in a carruca that bounced over every pothole and wheel rut between here and Rome. For now, I wanted to enjoy the view, the oyster broth, and Atreus's company, because by tonight we'd be miles and miles away from Baiae.

And so, I did.

Chapter Twelve

Eight days later

The Forum smelled of smoke, cooking meat, stale piss, and the stench of hundreds, possibly thousands, of people packed in between the grand marble facades of the buildings. It was crowded and chaotic, and my ears picked up a handful of different languages and dozens of accents. Nero was due to appear in the senate today, and the crowd had grown in anticipation, people flowing in from the streets that fed onto the Forum to catch a glimpse of the emperor, or, like me, to see which way the wind was going to blow for the empire. Atreus and I stood beneath a slice of flawless blue sky, braced as best we could against the push and pull of the crowd, and I was struck by the splendour of the buildings that surrounded us. This was the heart of Rome—grand marble edifices built to last centuries, and restless crowds that could turn in the space of a single breath.

The Forum had been filling since dawn. Senators in stiff white togas had gathered in clumps like flocks of uneasy storks, whispering under porticoes, glancing up and down the Via Sacra. They had been admitted into the Curia some time ago, leaving the rest of us, plebeians, patricians, and slaves alike, massed wherever we could find space. Street vendors squeezed through the crowd, peddling oily olives and suspicious meat pies to those with more hunger than sense.

As one of them, I ate my pie while Atreus gave me a judgemental look.

Petronius and Lucan found us at last. How they managed it in the crowd, I had no idea. Lucan looked grave and serious, but then he usually did. Today, though, even Petronius looked solemn. The loss of his sharp, knowing smile didn't suit him. It made him look like an entirely different man.

"So, you're back," he said, gripping my forearm in greeting. "How was the trip?"

"Long," I said around a mouthful of pie. "How was yours?"

"Fast," he said. "Though it seemed interminable when I spent half of it throwing up."

Petronius and Lucan had travelled back to Rome with Nero. Petronius had been lucky to be seasick. He had the perfect excuse to avoid what must have been some very awkward conversations over meals. Nero loved to surround himself with friends, but what was a friend supposed to say after he'd ordered his mother murdered? Or perhaps Nero hadn't wanted them with him this past week as he grieved, or celebrated, or veered wildly back and forth between the two; I hoped so, for their sake.

Rome was buzzing with the news of Agrippina's death, naturally, and today the Senate would hear it straight from Nero's mouth. I thought of Maro, inside the Curia now, perched like a chicken on a roost with his fellow senators on their tiered benches. I had no doubt which course the senators would decide—they would choose the stability of the empire over the truth. They would believe Nero, or pretend to, because what other option was there? But whether the crowd would follow, I had no idea. Agrippina had been popular enough to sway the people while she lived. Did that power hold even after her death? Today would tell us.

The murmur and the movement of the crowd stilled like a bird startled mid-song. Atreus straightened. I turned, squinting up the slope of the Clivus Capitolinus, where the imperial retinue began its descent.

The Praetorians in polished breastplates, their eagle-crested helms catching the sunlight like shards of some forgotten god. From this distance, they all looked alike. I couldn't pick either Rufio or Celer from the rest. Behind the Praetorians came the lictors, fasces held high.

Then, Nero.

He rode in a litter draped in Tyrian purple, borne on the shoulders of six muscular slaves. The curtains had been drawn back so we might admire him in full: a vision of both guileless youth and imperial grandeur. His face was boyishly plump, and his expression was both noble and humble, as though he was a schoolboy called to give account of some accidental misdemeanour to his tutors and did so with all possible respect and deference.

It was theatre. Everything was theatre.

The crowd murmured, restless again as Nero's litter was set down before the Curia. He stepped out, graceful in his shining purple toga, and raised one arm.

The crowd erupted into applause.

Nero did not bask in their praise. He acknowledged it with another wave and then, solemnly, he ascended the steps into the senate. His Praetorians flanked him. The bronze doors boomed shut behind him.

Lucan exhaled, slowly. "Well," he said. "It begins."

"It already began in Baiae," I said, "the moment she died.

I went and bought another pie.

The Forum grew hotter as the sun climbed. Vendors gave up their cries and found shade under awnings. A pair of urchins chased each other around a statue of Mars until someone barked them away. Pigeons fluttered from the temple roofs, indifferent to the tension in the crowd below them.

Time stretched out.

Then, at last, the doors to the Curia opened again, and the crowd surged forward to hear the news. A praeco stepped forward and began to announce the decrees passed within: praise for Nero's wisdom, prayers of thanks for his delivery from Agrippina's plot against him, and a vote of confidence in his divine mandate.

It was exactly what I'd expected. Atreus and Petro and Lucan too, going by their wary expressions that all asked the same silent question: What next?

But the crowd cheered and roared Nero's name.

I didn't wait around to witness the emperor's triumphant exit from the Curia. Something sat heavily in my gut, and it wasn't just that second pie. I began to elbow my way out of the crowd, with Atreus by my side.

I had seen enough.

* * *

The magistrate Septus Severus visited in the afternoon, and Hursa came to my tablinum to tell me.

"Sir," he said, and then followed it up immediately with, "Argh!"

Tullius leapt at him excitedly, hit him squarely in the balls, and both of them collapsed onto the ground in a tangle of skinny limbs.

My declaration that Tullius would stay in Baiae had been vetoed by every other member of my family, obviously.

Hursa and the dog wrestled and wriggled on the ground. The dog seemed to think it was some sort of game. I wasn't sure what Hursa thought. I wasn't sure *if* Hursa thought. Certainly, he'd never shown any evidence of it in the past.

Tullius grew bored of the game first, darting away to harass the other slaves, or chase the cat, or eat my library, or something, and Hursa climbed to his feet. His face was shiny with dog slobber, and his hair was wilder than usual. He looked like a bedraggled yellow hedgehog.

"Sir," he attempted again. "Septus Severus is here."

"Show him through," I said, although Severus, having had experience with Hursa, had obviously not trusted his message would be delivered, and had wandered into the tablinum himself. I rose to meet him. "Severus."

Severus was a proud, portly man. He was wrapped in a toga and the scent of saffron. He had a slave with him, one of his many clerks.

"Valerius." Severus clasped my arm. "I hear you've been hunting down killers even in Baiae."

"News travels fast."

"Especially scandalous news."

"Was it scandalous?" I asked, waving my hand at Hursa to fetch wine.

"Any gossip attached to a Calpurnii has the whiff of scandal about it," Severus said, "whether it is deserved or not. But Piso wrote to me of your help in the matter. He wanted to be certain that I knew."

Severus was, I supposed, my unofficial patron. He was a magistrate, and I acted as his intermediary with the vigiles, because he hated dealing with them. Case in point: he glanced around and saw Atreus standing there, and he said, with an unimpressed grunt, "You're here too."

"Sir," Atreus said, and ducked his head respectfully.

I didn't bother to tell Severus that I couldn't have found Tertia's killer without Atreus's help, or that it was Atreus who'd put it all together in the end—I'd tried to give credit where it was due in the past, and Severus refused to hear it. I generally liked Severus. He wasn't the smartest man, but neither was I, and he was friendly and sociable, and I had hitched my political wagon to his. My successes were his, and vice versa. But he viewed dealing with the vigiles and, I suspect, anyone who hadn't been born patrician and wealthy, with the same instinctive revulsion as though he'd been told to clean the Cloaca Maxima with his tongue.

Our business was brief. We talked for a little while about Baiae, both of us conspicuously avoiding the subject of Agrippina's demise, and I asked after the health of his wife and children. His wife and children were some of Severus's favourite subjects, and he happily related that everyone was well. I smiled and nodded while he went through the catalogue of his children's most recent achievements, from the son who was outpacing all the other boys he practiced athletics with on the Campus Martius, to the daughter who had lost her final baby tooth.

"Excuse me a moment," I said as Calliope, one of the indoor slaves, brought wine and a selection of olives, nuts, and cheese. It would keep Severus busy for a little while.

Atreus came with me.

I found Juba in the peristyle, supervising the outdoor slaves as they tugged weeds. It wasn't usually the sort of job he would have to supervise, but since Felix was involved, one-handed and all, Juba probably wanted to make sure he didn't destroy the flowers instead of the weeds.

"Juba," I said. "With me."

He joined us in the shade of the colonnade, his expression unreadable.

I moved a little way along the colonnade to afford us some privacy. Atreus and Juba followed.

"In Baiae, you disobeyed me," I said. "I gave you an order, and you refused it. I told you I'd deal with you when we were back in Rome."

Juba didn't bother argue. He dipped his chin in a nod and lowered his gaze. "Yes, sir."

"And it wasn't the first time."

His head snapped up. The muscles in his jaw worked, but he kept his mouth clamped shut.

"I've always allowed you more latitude than perhaps I should have," I said. "So the failure is mine as much as yours. I mean to remedy that today."

He nodded again, his brows drawing together. "Yes, sir."

"Come with me."

It was a short trip back to the tablinum, but we gathered a small audience of startled slaves who whispered amongst themselves but were too nervous to follow. I had never been a harsh master, preferring laziness to actually managing my slaves. For the most part, it worked. They knew their duties (except Hursa) and did them diligently (except Hursa). It must have been shocking for my slaves to see one of their fellows taken away for punishment. And unthinkable that it was Juba.

"Ah!" said Severus, and rose to his feet. He held out his hand to his clerk and clicked his fingers as the youth fumbled in his leather bag.

Juba's eyes widened as the clerk held out a rod.

Atreus took it, nodded at me, and then lifted the rod and touched Juba on the head. Then he said, as *adsertor libertatis*, "I want this man to be free from this moment."

Severus looked to me, eyebrows raised as he silently asked if I objected.

I didn't.

Atreus took Juba by the hand, turned him around, and released him.

And, just like that, he was free.

* * *

I gifted Severus a jar of Falernian for his trouble, then returned to my tablinum. The late afternoon shadows in the atrium were long. I had to fight through a gaggle of chattering slaves to get inside to find a bemused Juba seated in front of my desk, turning his pileus over and over in his hands.

"You don't have to wear it," I told him, nodding at the soft felt cap. "But I think it suits you."

An oil lamp flickered on my desk, the flame trying uselessly to hold off the gathering darkness of dusk.

"I don't think it suits anyone, sir," Juba said, regarding the hat in surprise, as though seeing it for the first time.

He might have been right about that.

Atreus, perched on my desk with his arms folded across his chest, snorted.

"Sir." Juba's throat bobbed as he swallowed, and I'd never seen him look so unsure of himself. "Why did you do this?"

"Believe me, I didn't want to," I said. "How many times have you saved my life? No, don't answer that. I want to retain at least some of my pride." Juba didn't smile. "I did this for you, Juba, because you are smart, and loyal, and you have proved that too many times to count."

"Thank you," he said, his voice hollow.

Atreus threw me an exasperated look. "Valerius hasn't left you high and dry, Juba. He's paid the rent for an apartment in my building, if you'd like to be my neighbour. There's also a job going at the barracks if you want it."

"As a vigile?" Juba asked cautiously.

Atreus shook his head. "As Leander's apprentice."

Leander was the physician of the first century of the Fifth Cohort of Vigiles, and Juba had always been interested in watching him work. Even the gruesome parts didn't seem to bother him, and I imagined the most important qualification for becoming a physician was a strong stomach.

Juba folded the hat over in his lap, and I noticed for the first time that his hands were shaking. "Thank you," he said again, and cleared his throat. "Thank you, sir. But who's going to teach Felix how to not be scared of the dog?"

"Felix may be unteachable," I said.

Atreus stood and clapped Juba on the shoulder. "Go and say your goodbyes, and I'll show you to your new place. You can have dinner with Lucilla and me tonight, and tomorrow I'll take you around the neighbourhood and show you the best places to eat where they won't overcharge you."

Juba nodded, dazed, and rose unsteadily to his feet. Still clutching his pileus, he stepped outside the triclinium and into the group of excited, chattering slaves.

"You'll keep an eye on him, won't you?" I asked Atreus.

"Of course," he said.

I let out a breath. "Jupiter, what's wrong with me? He's the best slave I've ever had, and I'm giving him his freedom and keeping *Felix*."

"And Hursa," Atreus agreed with a grin. "Yes, Maro pulled a fast one on you there, didn't he? You ended up with Felix *and* Tullius."

"That's Maro for you."

He laughed.

"Don't laugh at me, or I'll free Hursa and make him your neighbour as well."

"You wouldn't dare."

I glanced at the doorway to make sure the slaves had left with Juba to help him collect his things, and then closed the space between Atreus and me. I pushed him back so that he was perched on my desk again. "There are a lot of things I dare."

I kissed him.

He allowed it for a moment, then pushed me gently, regretfully, away.

I leaned on the desk beside him and knocked our shoulders together. He brushed his knuckles against mine.

"You still owe me that holiday," he said softly.

"I took you to Baiae."

"Not a holiday."

I hummed. "That's fair. Where would you like to go?"

"Nowhere," he said.

The oil lamp burned low beside him, its light flickering like breath on the verge of failing. Outside, the garden shimmered in the fading golden sunlight of the afternoon. The dying rays caught in the basin of the fountain and created deep shadows beneath the laurels. I barely heard the trickling water. All my senses bent towards the man beside me.

Atreus gazed at the opposite wall. He said nothing, and neither did I.

The silence between us had never been empty. It breathed. It watched.

"I fear for the future," I said at last, my voice too soft, too formal. Like I was speaking through gauze.

Atreus didn't look at me. "For the empire, or for yourself?"

He always spoke plainly. There was no artifice in him. Not like the senators, who celebrated Nero's escape from a plot that never was, or Nero's circle of friends with their wit and their poetry, or the pomp and ceremony of Rome itself, which was nothing but *theatre*. No, Atreus said what he meant.

"Both," I said honestly.

He nodded. "You say you fear for the future, but just now, with Juba, you showed that you still believe in a hopeful one."

I decided not to point out that men often freed their slaves before they died, because Atreus was right. I hadn't freed Juba because I thought the future was bleak and uncertain. I'd freed him because I thought it could still be bright. Whether I would still believe that tomorrow or the next day, I didn't know. No man did.

The side of Atreus's hand pressed against mine, and that was enough. The world was an uncertain place, today more than ever, but Atreus? I was certain of him. I was certain of us. In this quiet moment, in that sacred hush between heartbeats, I believed wholeheartedly that this, this thing between us, that it mattered and that it would endure, whatever else was coming.

Even in Nero's Rome.

Acknowledgments

Thank you to L.C. Chase for drawing the map.

About the Author

Jennifer Burke lives in tropical North Queensland, Australia, with three cats, two dogs, and more geckos than she wants. She spends half her time as a government minion, and half her time writing. She studied History and English at university, though she likes playing with them more than she ever did studying them. Jennifer also writes mm romance under the pen name Lisa Henry.

AUTHOR WEBSITE:
  https://www.jenniferburkebooks.com

Also by Jennifer Burke

Writing as Jennifer Burke:
Sub Rosa: A Valerius Mystery
Juvenalia: A Valerius Mystery

Writing as Lisa Henry:
Love Notes: A Harmony Lake Small Town Romance
All I Want for Christmas is Stu
Full Throttle (Lights Out)
Not Until Noah (Star Crossed #1)
Because of Ben (Star Crossed #2)
Only for Ollie (Star Crossed #3)
The Parable of the Mustard Seed
Naked Ambition
Anhaga
Two Man Station (Emergency Services #1)
Lights and Sirens (Emergency Services #2)
The California Dashwoods
Adulting 101
Sweetwater
The Island
Tribute
One Perfect Night
Fallout, with M. Caspian
Dark Space (Dark Space #1)
Darker Space (Dark Space #2)
Starlight (Dark Space #3)
Hellion

With Sarah Honey:
The Amazing Alpha Tau Boyfriend Project (Alpha Tau 1)

The Amazing Alpha Tau Self-Improvement Project (Alpha Tau 2)
The Amazing Alpha Tau Pledge Project (Alpha Tau 3)
The Amazing Alpha Tau Romeo and Juliet Project (Alpha Tau 4)
The Amazing Alpha Tau Reunion Project (Alpha Tau 5)
Awfully Ambrose (Bad Boyfriends Inc, Book 1)
Horribly Harry (Bad Boyfriends Inc, Book 2)
Terribly Tristan (Bad Boyfriends Inc, Book 3)
Red Heir (Adventures in Aguillon, Book 1)
Elf Defence (Adventures in Aguillon, Book 2)
Socially Orcward (Adventures in Aguillon, Book 3)
Cool Story, Bro
Road Trip

With J.A. Rock:
Washed Up Former Child Star Ryan Lee
Fran Cuthbert Ruins Christmas
When All the World Sleeps
Another Man's Treasure
Fall on Your Knees
The Preacher's Son
Mark Cooper versus America (Prescott College #1)
Brandon Mills versus the V-Card (Prescott College #2)
The Good Boy (The Boy #1)
The Boy Who Belonged (The Boy #2)

The Playing the Fool Series:
The Two Gentlemen of Altona
The Merchant of Death
Tempest

The Lords of Bucknall Club Series:
A Husband for Hartwell
A Case for Christmas

A Rival for Rivingdon
A Sanctuary for Soulden
An Affair for Aumont
A Scandal for Stratford

www.ingramcontent.com/pod-product-compliance
Lightning Source LLC
Chambersburg PA
CBHW020758310726
48969CB00002B/599